The Protectors Series

Sid

BY

Teresa Gabelman

THE PROTECTORS

SID

Gabelman, Teresa (2014-1-5).

SID (THE PROTECTORS SERIES) Book #4.

First Kindle Edition.

Editor: Hot Tree Editing

Photo: www.bigstockphoto.com

Cover Art: Indie Digital Publishing

www.teresagabelman.com

www.facebook.com/pages/Teresa-Gabelman/191553587598342

Acknowledgements

I would like to thank all the readers who have followed this series. Your support keeps me going when it gets hard. The messages and love you give are so special to me. I appreciate every single one of you. I do what I do not only for the love of writing, but to connect with new friends. You guys are my Rock Stars and I thank you for everything!

Chapter 1

Frigid air burned her lungs as she raced back and forth through the woods, trying to throw them off her trail. Small clouds of steamy fog puffed from her lips. Terror threatened to seize every muscle in her body, but she fought it back, willing her legs to pump faster. She hated being chased.

Slipping in the mud to a full stop, she tilted her head to the side, holding her breath. The woods were silent except for her own heart beating a frantic rhythm in her ears. Slowly, she moved only her eyes, afraid of what might be behind her. Her breath eased out in a smooth exhale as she willed her brain to work. She had to go back, had to circle around before she went too far into the woods.

Hearing rustling from her left, she held her breath again, pushing herself behind a thick tree. Whatever was out there was coming closer. Leaning her head back, she closed her eyes, praying whatever was there wasn't one of them. A loud snorting noise from behind her hiding place echoed through the trees. Jumping, she squeezed her eyes tighter, and then cursed at herself for being a coward while her friend was still back there enduring God only knew what. Lana Fitzpatrick was no coward, nor was she stupid. When she had the chance to run, she ran, but it looked like running was no longer an option.

Wanting to be the one with surprise on her side, she fisted her hands and jumped out from her hiding place, determined to face whatever had found her. Her scream of outrage turned into a hysterical yelp as a deer jerked back, staring at her wide–eyed, before turning to escape deeper into the woods. Slapping one hand to her chest and the other across her mouth, she stared in shock where the deer had disappeared. "Son of a…" Her words were muffled by her own hand.

Hearing more movement, followed by voices, snapped her out of her shocked state. They were too close to out run. Glancing around frantically, she stumbled toward another tree, and without hesitation, she climbed, even as a warning of dread sent her heart skipping. Climbing as high as she dared, she

attempted to make herself invisible, if that was at all possible. Pressing her cheek against the tree, thc cold bark bit into her skin; her eyes searched out the voices that became more audible the closer they got.

There were two vampires and her friend, who seemed to be currently unharmed. Breathing a sigh of relief, she momentarily froze as golden eyes shot to her hiding place. She quickly slid herself out of view.

"Where, oh where has our little Lana gone?" The voice of the leader had a sharp edge that commanded attention. He had told them his name was Vincent; he seemed stupid enough to give his real name. "Oh where, oh where can she be?"

Trying to control her breathing, Lana wished more than anything that she had a weapon. She had nothing but her wits, and at the moment, she was screwed in that department. She was defenseless and tired. She knew that at any moment she would be spotted. Lana considered her options, but came up blank. She had no idea how she was going to get herself and her friend out of this nightmare. A movement out of the corner of her eye drew her attention. Okay, her wits were definitely gone because she could have sworn she saw the flash of a man dart between the trees.

"Lana, I know you're up there. Not only did I hear you, but I can smell your fear." Vincent calmly walked under the tree. "Now, come on down here." His voice held steel with a hint of amusement.

"Go to Hell!" Lana peeked around the tree making eye contact with the golden-eyed vampire. His eyes were filled with an evil glint that promised Hell on earth.

"Been there and back," he chuckled without humor. "We could have done this the easy way, but since you're being a stupid bitch…"

The tree shook causing Lana to grip tightly. "Oh, shit!" Lana whispered as she scrambled around to the front of the tree. With one kick of his foot, the tree uprooted and began to fall as if in slow motion to the ground. The only thing she could do was hold on for the ride. Before the tree hit the ground, she pushed off, not wanting to get caught underneath the large trunk. She hit the ground hard. Air whooshed out of her lungs as she rolled to her back. Looking up, Vincent stood above her, a cruel grin on his face.

"…we will do it my way," he finished his sentence. Reaching down, he grabbed her by the hair, dragging her through the limbs of the downed tree. Effortlessly, he tossed her in front of the other vampire and Amy. "Get up," he ordered nudging her with his foot.

Standing was the hardest thing Lana had ever done at that very moment, but she refused to cower in front of the bastard. If she was going to die, she was going to die in defiance. Slowly, she rose, locking her knees in place, her eyes making contact with a terrified Amy, which wasn't good; she needed Amy on her toes. Lana's eyes then met those of the other vampire, who was supposed to be her date. His golden eyes looked angry, but not cruel. There was something in his gaze that surprised her, but before she could think more about it, Vincent stepped into her vision.

"Now, are you finished being a pain in my ass?" Vincent reached out, grasped a strand of her hair and pulled hard.

"Probably not," she replied, knocking his hand away, knowing she was playing with fire. Lana had already convinced herself that she was dead anyway, so she refused to hold back and figured she would go down being her typical smart-ass self.

He pinched her face in a cruel grip, bringing it close to his. "Is it true? Can you speak to the dead?"

Lana didn't say anything; didn't flinch. She focused a steady gaze on Vincent, refusing to submit and give anything away.

"I could crush your skull, Lana Banana." A smile was placed firmly on his face, but his eyes promised he could and would do exactly that.

"Then you'll never know the answer to your question, will you?" She was able to reply with her lips scrunched together.

His laugh was even and cruel. "You're a brave one, aren't you?" He let go of her face with a push. "I don't like that trait in women. What about you, VC? You like that trait in women?"

"Not usually looking at traits when I'm with a woman," the vampire called VC replied, his voice deep, as his eyes drilled into hers.

"True," Vincent chuckled. "I am a man who loves big tits, but that's about all she has going for her."

"I would have to disagree," VC grinned, his eyes roaming her body with a very confident gaze. "I think me and Lana would get along quite well."

Lana tried to slump her shoulders so her breasts weren't so prominent, but that was like trying to hide a bus behind a Volkswagen; it just wasn't happening. Her actions made the handsome vampire, VC's, grin spread, which made him even more breathtaking, and that pissed her off. He was the enemy for shit's sake.

"As a matter of fact…" one-step and he was directly in front of her, looking down into her eyes, "if we're not in a hurry, I'd like to finish our date."

Lana's eyes widened. Was he crazy? "Like I'd give you the time of day, moron."

VC actually laughed. "Moron?" He cocked an eyebrow at her and gripped her chin in his hand, bringing her face closer to his. She noticed that his grip was gentler than Vincent's. "I'd have you screaming within seconds, my lovely Lana."

"Yes, you would," she hissed, pulling her face away, her skin tingling from his gentle grip. "In disgust." When she looked into his eyes, she saw the confident gleam that he could and would probably have her screaming as he boasted. He had a body to make any woman…Lana shook her head looking away from him and his smug grin. *Dammit, focus, Lana,* she mentally screamed at herself.

"Oh, we will see, lovely Lana." He gave her a slow wink.

Lana shot him her most evil glare. She hated when people gave her nicknames, and her name was prime for stupid rhymes.

"We don't have time for this," Vincent interrupted with a growl. "And they need to be handed over untouched."

"Handed over?" Amy took a step back, making eye contact with Lana. "Handed over to who?"

"How much are women going for these days?" Lana ignored Amy's glance. The guy, VC, was watching her too closely. She needed time to think, to stall.

"Enough to make me turn over my momma, if I had one," Vincent replied; his eyes narrowed at her with a greedy gleam. "And you, my pain in the ass, will bring triple with your talents."

"I'll kill myself first, you bastard." Fear gripped Lana. The women who had been found were damaged beyond repair, both mentally and physically. If she left this spot, she and Amy would be lost along with all of those other women.

"And I'll just bring you back." His laugh was wicked. "I can do that, you know. Honey, you're my ticket to more money than I've ever seen."

"You sure this guy is legit?" VC spoke up. He had taken a step away from Lana. "I'm not risking my ass for a few dollars, man."

"Oh, he's legit. He's calling the shots now. Killed the last big guy who ran the operation, and no one fucks with him. If I pull this off, I may be his second in command," he boasted, his chest inflating with pride.

'Not if I have anything to do with it', Lana thought to herself. This stupid man with his puffed-up ego needed to be taken down. Dammit, she needed a plan. She looked to the other one called VC who was staring at her, his eyebrow cocked as if he could read her mind, but Lana knew that wasn't possible. She was an expert at keeping her thoughts closed off behind a steel door of 'get the fuck out of my business, asshole'.

"Yeah, well to me, he's nobody," VC grunted, turning his focus back to Vincent. "I'm making the drop with you."

"No," Vincent shook his head. "I'm making the drop while you wait here. I'll make good on my promise."

"I don't think so." VC took an aggressive step forward. "I don't trust anyone with that amount of money, and I'm ass-deep in this shit now. Who are you making the drop to?"

As they argued, Lana sent a message with her eyes and a small nod of her head to Amy, who, thank God, was paying attention. Taking a step back, she edged herself toward the woods. Amy tried to do the same thing, but she wasn't as careful. Walking backward, she tripped over a log.

"Get the fuck over here!" Vincent grabbed Amy's arm. Reaching behind him, he pulled out a gun, holding it to Amy's temple as his eyes landed on Lana. "Everybody just calm the fuck down. I'm in charge here, and what I say goes."

Lana stopped, staring at the gun pointed toward Amy's head. "You're crazy," Lana hissed, knowing she had to react and fast. Taking a quick look at VC, Lana noticed something that didn't make sense. He looked to be assessing the situation like she was. She didn't know what the hell was going on, but something was definitely not right.

"Think of a number," Vincent interrupted, pushing the gun harder against Amy's head. "Hey! You bastard." Lana took a step toward Amy, but stopped when Amy cried out in pain as the gun was shoved harder into her temple. "Why don't you put the gun down and play like a real vampire." Lana frowned wondering what the hell she meant by that, but seeing him with a gun had thrown her.

"What?" Amy cried, her eyes wide with panic, glaring at Lana.

"Think of a number!" He jerked Amy's arm hard, ignoring Lana. "You have one?"

Amy nodded, sucking her bottom lip between her teeth. Her eyes were wide with fright; her chin quivered slightly, but her eyes never left Lana's.

"Now, *Lana*, in the bar your little friend here told me you had a talent for talking to the dead." Vincent looked hard at Lana. "Is that true?"

Lana remained silent. She stared him in the eyes, praying his threat was a bluff. When he pulled back the trigger, she realized he was far from bluffing. Lana cursed under her breath, and then noticed VC taking a step closer to Vincent and Amy.

"In three seconds, I'm going to blow her brains out." He nudged the gun into Amy's head again, making her cry out. "And it is going to be *your fault,* Lana Banana. After I blow her brains out, you are going to tell me the number she has been thinking."

"If she's dead, how will you know if I'm lying or not?" Lana was desperate for more time. This couldn't happen. Not to Amy. Not to her. She knew that if she admitted that she had the talent—she almost scoffed at the choice of word, more like curse at this moment—then they were as good as dead anyway, both of them. She was not going to be sold to anyone. This was not going as planned, and she hated when her plans didn't go her way.

Vincent's raised voice pulled her out of her thoughts. "Because she's weak!" he yelled, spittle spraying from his mouth. "I can read her like a fucking book."

"Then you should know if I have the talent or not without me saying a word," Lana replied, trying to keep the shaking out of her voice. She was scared shitless, and that wouldn't do. She had to get control over of herself. Watching someone die in front of her very eyes was not going to happen, especially when the person was her responsibility.

"Unblock your mind, and I will," Vincent countered, his eyes glowing black with anger.

"I'm wide open," Lana lied. She was closed off with her 'special' steel door. She had to keep his focus off Amy. She had to get the gun away from Amy's head, and if pissing him off would do the trick, then she was pretty good at pissing people off. It should work like a charm. A small grin tilted one side of her mouth. "You can't read me, can you? What kind of vampire are you? You can't read me, and you have to use a gun. Your vampire daddy must be so proud." Lana knew her mouth was just spouting shit that didn't make sense, but she had to get him to point that gun way from Amy's head.

"Your three seconds have started, you bitch!" He turned the gun sideways like a gang banger, the barrel digging into her friend's temple. "Now, answer me!"

"I'd rather us both die than become mindless whores and playthings for bastards like you!" Lana screamed fuelled with an outrage she had never felt before. "You are pathetic!" she spat out. Lana's eyes met Amy's in a moment of warning. *Shit, I hope this works,* she thought to herself just before Amy reacted.

"Lana, how could you? Tell him, please!" Amy screamed, a scream that echoed around the trees. Then her legs collapsed out from under her.

As Vincent lost his grip on Amy, Lana saw her chance, her only chance. With no other thought but to get the gun away from the lunatic, she pushed her way past VC. As if in slow motion, she watched the barrel of the gun aim her way. Now that her plan was working, it didn't seem like such a good idea. She wasn't going to make it. When people say it's 'a good day to die', well screw that. She wasn't ready to die. At least Amy had a chance to get away; she hoped. She gained a small amount of satisfaction at the surprised look on Vincent's face. She wasn't going down without a fight; she never had in the past and today was no different.

To her surprise, VC darted in front of her, his muscled body ready to take the bullet meant for her. Taking Vincent down to the ground, he ripped the gun out of his hand tossing it into the woods with speed so fast it was hard for the human eye to track. He suddenly went from bad guy to avenging angel in the blink of an eye, and Lana was trying to figure out what the hell was going on.

"What the fuck are you doing, you stupid son of a bitch?" Vincent struggled beneath VC, who was much larger and stronger than the vampire underneath him.

Glancing over at Amy, Lana quickly made her way to her side, helping her up. "Come on, dammit!" Lana whispered, trying to pull her along, but stopped when she ran into something large. She looked up and then around; golden-eyed vampires surrounded them. She looked toward Amy, who was being helped up by one of them. Turning around, she watched as VC held Vincent to the ground.

“Stay still, or I’m going to knock you the fuck out!” VC gripped his throat, pushing him into the ground.

“What the hell are you doing?” Vincent spat up at him. “I swear if you screw this up for me, I’ll kill you.”

“Who are you making the drop to?”

“You think I’m stupid?”

“Yes, I do,” VC replied. “Answer the question.”

“I’m not answering shit!” Vincent ground out, and then turned his head looking around. Seeing others surrounding him, he looked back up at VC. “Who the hell are you?”

A grin split his face. “You never asked my last name?”

“What?” Vincent spat, before his eyes widened knowingly.

“Ah, so you’re not as stupid as I thought.” He stood, pulling Vincent up with him.

Vincent looked from him to the other four vampires who had appeared. “You’re a Warrior.” It suddenly dawned on him the trouble he was now in. “You’re a fucking Warrior.”

“Yeah, VC Warrior at your service, you stupid fuck.” Sid held him tighter when he started to struggle. When it became clear that Vincent wouldn’t be calming down anytime soon, Sid knocked him out cold with one punch.

"I can't believe you used VC as your name," Jared laughed, shaking his head as he watched Vincent fall face first into the wooded muck. "You got balls, Sinclair, and Sloan is going to have them nailed to his wall when he finds out you used that name."

"Yeah, well, hopefully, I can keep it, but it seems my cover's been blown." He glanced over at Lana, who was staring at him. "But the ladies seem to like it." Sid winked at her.

Lana couldn't quite grasp what had just happened. She was frozen in place trying to put the last few minutes' events into some semblance of order. They were safe. *We're okay,* she thought in relief. Just as the relief hit her, a new emotion brimmed to the surface. Rage. She was fucking furious in an instant. Her legs moved forward of their own volition and then stopped in front of Sid, formally known as VC. The thought had her top lip forming into a sneer.

"No need to thank me," he replied down at her, his well-known and well-used cocky grin playing across his full lips, but then he frowned, turning serious. "Though, you blew my cover, and you should have that pretty little ass of yours beat for pulling a stunt like you just pulled. What the hell were you thinking rushing him like that?"

"You're a VC Warrior?" she asked through clenched teeth, looking up at the smug expression on his face and totally ignoring his ass-beating comment.

"Yes, darlin', I am," Sid replied. His frown was once again replaced with a confident grin as he crossed his arms as if waiting for her to bow down and give her thanks and undying love.

With everything she had, she jumped up and punched him in the face, knocking his head to the side. "You son of a bitch!" she shouted, not caring if she sounded like a hysterical banshee. The smug vamp deserved it.

"What the hell was that for?" Sid rubbed his jaw, looking a little shocked that a woman dare hit him.

"We have been through hell. I was knocked out of a tree, dragged across the ground, threatened; plus, I had to watch as a gun was held to my friend's head, and you could have stopped it all at any time, but didn't!" She jumped up and tried to punch him again, but he smoothly moved out of the way.

"I saved your life, lady," Sid growled, a look of confusion on his face. "I'd think you'd appreciate that."

"Appreciate?" she sputtered. "You asshole." Instead of trying to punch him in the face, she snuck a quick punch to his stomach before stomping away, more than ready to get the hell out of there. There was no way she intended to stay around the asshole for any longer than she had to. "VC Warrior, my ass."

"Gun!" someone shouted, and that was all Lana remembered before darkness claimed her.

Chapter 2

Jill walked down the hallway to Slade's office. She dreaded what was to come, but orders were orders, and she had to follow them. Steve was just coming out as she made her way to the door.

"Hey," Steve smiled, giving her a knuckle bump.

"Hey," she grinned back. Steve was always upbeat and had a smile for everyone. "So, how bad was it?" She nodded toward the closed door.

"Not bad at all, mostly questions." He shrugged. "No big deal, but I have to get going. Sloan has a job for me. See ya."

"Yeah, see ya." Jill frowned, watching him go. She really would have liked to talk to him for a while. Anything was better than walking through that door. Ever since she fed from Dr. Buchanan, it had been awkward whenever they were together. Well, it was awkward for her; he just didn't seem to give a damn.

"I don't have all day," his deep voice rumbled from behind the door.

Rolling her eyes, she pushed open the door. "Hi."

He sat at a desk, scribbling something down. "Sit on the table," he replied, not even looking at her.

Jill walked over and lifted herself onto the examination table. Her eyes scanned the room before falling on his broad back. He was a far cry from any doctor she had ever been to. His shoulder-length hair was loose; his large hand kept pushing it back out of his golden eyes. His black t-shirt was tucked into his snug blue jeans. He looked more like a sexy bad boy than a doctor.

Slade stood, grabbing a file before turning toward her, his eyes briefly giving her a once-over before flipping through the papers. “You missed your appointment last week.”

“Sorry, I had something I had to take care of,” Jill replied, keeping the nervousness out of her voice. She actually missed all the appointments. She knew the other half-breeds had already had two visits; she’d had none.

His eyes snapped up from her file, pinning her to the spot. “I was here all day.” His tone was stern, as if talking to a child. “Don’t miss again.”

She had to bite her lip from snapping back a reply she would probably regret. She didn’t want him to look over her personal information. Her infatuation with this huge vampire was out of control, and it scared her. She had done her best to stay away from him, but it seemed every time she turned around, he was there. Now, he was going to touch her, ask her personal questions. This was a cruel fate she had to endure. She just prayed she didn’t make a fool of herself by wrapping herself around his rock-hard body like she had done when she fed from him. Nope, she couldn’t do this…not yet.

“Don’t get off that table,” his tone deepened when she started to slide off. “How are you feeling?”

“Fine!” Jill snapped, scooting back on the table. He made her feel like a child, and it pissed her off.

“Any problems you need to discuss?” His eyes didn’t leave her file.

“No.”

He cocked his eyebrow at her short answer, but kept his eyes on the file. “Is your full name Jillian Robin Nichols?”

"Yes."

He scribbled something in the file. "You're eighteen-years-old?" He looked up when she didn't answer.

Jill squirmed, looking everywhere but at him. "No."

"No?" The discomfort in his voice was evident. "Nineteen?"

She shook her head, peeking at his handsome face, which looked strained.

"Younger or older?" This time he snapped his question at her.

"I'm twenty. I'll be twenty-one next month." Embarrassment heated her cheeks.

"Didn't you go to high school with Adam and Steve?" Slade put the file down, crossing his arms.

"Yes," Jill sighed, not wanting to talk about this. "Next question."

"You just graduated?" He didn't let it go.

"Yes," she nodded, not wanting this man to know what a failure she had been. "I graduated with Adam and Steve as well as Jeff."

"This doesn't add up. Why are you so much older than them?" He was like a dog with a bone; he wouldn't let it go.

"Is this part of my examination, because if not, next question." Jill squirmed on the table with agitation.

He seemed to hesitate, but of course, he wasn't going to drop it. Jill sighed in exasperation when she saw he was going to continue playing twenty-questions. "Answer the question, Jill. How is it a twenty-year-old just graduated from high school?"

"Because I failed two years of grade school." Jill hated to be drilled, and dammit, if it wasn't for wanting to be a Warrior, she would tell him to shove it up his sexy ass. She was mortified. The last thing she wanted was for the guy she had the hot's for to know her failures.

Slade didn't say a word. He remained in place and stared at her with an unrelenting focus.

"Don't you need to write that down in the file?" Jill reverted to her smart-ass self, trying to hide the hurt she felt at her humiliation.

He ignored her comment, but still remained silent for another pause. His arms were still crossed as he assessed her. "You're dyslexic." He finally looked away to pick her file back up.

"How did you know that?" she asked surprised. She knew he couldn't read her because she had so many blocks up he'd need dynamite to bring them down. No way was he going to read her thoughts, ever.

"Because you're intelligent; and that is the only reason I can see you being held back for two years," he replied, while writing in her file.

He sounded so sure of himself she wanted to lie, but decided against it. "Do you have to put that in there?"

"No one will see this but me," he assured her. "Being dyslexic is nothing to be ashamed of."

"I'm not ashamed," she bit out a little too quickly. It was true; she wasn't ashamed, but her disability had always bothered her family as if they were embarrassed, so she didn't like making a big deal about it.

She dealt with it, end of story. "I just don't see how that information is important." Jill felt her anger start to get the better of her.

"How do you do with your reading today?" He seemed to ignore her statement.

"Struggle, but I do okay." Jill really wanted to move on. Being dyslexic had always been an issue in her home life. It had put a burden on her family with teacher meetings and constant homework help, which she heard about daily. Being a burden to anyone rubbed her the wrong way. She coped with it, and that was that, end of story. "What does this have to do with my being a Warrior?"

"As long as it does not put you or another Warrior in danger, then it has nothing to do with it. But as your doctor, it's my responsibility to make those determinations." Slade's tone was stern.

"It won't be a problem." She made her voice just as stern.

He nodded. "Are you still having your monthly menstrual cycles?"

"Excuse me?" Jill about came off the table. "What the hell does that have to do with anything? Did you ask Adam and the rest of them the same question?"

A half-grin tipped his sexy mouth as his eyes crinkled. He didn't smile often, so it took her by surprise and made her brain turn to mush.

"No, that is one question I didn't ask Adam or the others." Humor laced his words. "If I had to ask them that question, Sloan would have more problems than he realizes."

A frown creased her forehead as she thought about what she said. God, she was an idiot, but the question totally shocked her. He openly laughed at her with rare humor in his eyes. "You know what I mean,"

Jill snorted, rolling her eyes.

He nodded, his smile fading, which she immediately thought was a shame. "So, are you?" he asked, back to business.

"Yes." She felt her face heat again. She was going to make sure she was busy the next time her appointment came around, because no way was she going through this again. He'd have to come looking for her.

"Are you sexually active?" The question came out with a growl. He cleared his throat as his eyes came up to meet hers, his light golden eyes darkening slightly.

Finally, he looked uncomfortable, and didn't that make her day. "Not at the moment," her reply was a little smug, liking the tables turning. She didn't know why he was uncomfortable; all she cared about was making *him* squirm a little.

"That's obvious, Jill." Slade frowned at her. "Are you a virgin?"

"No." She watched his eyes darken even more at her response. "Is Adam? No, I bet Adam isn't a virgin, but I'd bet my favorite pair of boots Steve is." She grinned at her teasing of her friends.

"How many partners have you had?" His eyes narrowed; his body language turned as threatening as his tone.

Jill watched the transformation in awe and wanted to see if she could push him further. He was amazing when he was calm, but angry, he was mesmerizing. God, was she crazy wanting to anger this man? Yeah, she was one-hundred-percent nuts, she decided.

"How many are on a football team?" Jill asked, biting her bottom lip as if deep in thought, but her eyes stayed on him and she got what she wanted. She had definitely angered the beast.

"This is not a joke, Jillian." Slade was in front of her in two angry strides, slamming her file down on the examination table next to her. "I'm not playing games here."

"Neither am I." Jill shot back. "I just don't understand what my being a virgin, whether I've had a period or how many guys I've done it with makes a difference to being a Warrior. I mean seriously, Slade, look at it from my point of view. Have you asked Adam how many girls he's screwed?"

"I don't care how many girls Adam screwed." His breath caressed her face; his eyes burned her soul. Her breath hitched at his admission. "You are the only one at the moment at high risk to be abducted and sold to the highest bidder. Have you not been paying attention? You are primed to be a breeder for those bastards out there, and would bring a grand price to anyone who sold you. I am also the doctor to the Warriors, and I need to have personal information to make sure you are progressing in a healthy way as a half-breed. Nothing more, nothing less."

Her pulse rate accelerated with his anger, but her heart pinched. "Why do you hate me so much?" Jill tilted her head slightly, not looking away. She was a little shocked that she questioned him aloud. It was too late to pull her words back.

Slade's head snapped back in surprise. "You really think that?"

"Yes, I do," Jill whispered with a small nod. She kept her eyes on him, wanting to see his reaction. His eyes, which were a dark golden hue, were lined with thick black lashes, and they seemed to look into her soul. He was so handsome, it hurt. Knowing she would never be enough woman for this Warrior made her heart bleed, but she would find her way past it. She didn't have a choice. Her survival mode needed to kick in and quick, because being rejected would be a mighty blow to her already-damaged heart.

They continued to stare at one another, neither looking away. Even as

Slade's phone began to ring in the holder against his hip, he didn't move his body or eyes.

After a few more rings, Jill looked away to the phone on his hip. "You going to answer that?"

Reaching down, he plucked the phone from the holder, bringing it to his ear, his eyes still watching her. "Buchanan." His voice was rough. He finally looked away, grabbing his bag off his desk. "What happened? Okay, text me the directions. I'm on my way."

Concern had Jill forgetting anything else. "What happened?" She hopped from the table. "Do you need help?"

"No." He opened the door, but stopped before walking out. With his back to her, he continued, "I don't hate you, Jillian." With that, he left quickly, closing the door behind him, and left Jill feeling confused and a little afraid. Being hated was easier than being not wanted.

Chapter 3

The burning in his shoulder had Sid cursing. Growling, he lifted himself off the soft woman beneath him. Rolling her over gently, he pushed her black silky hair from her pale face. Her clear blue eyes stared up at him.

“You okay?” His eyes searched hers when she didn’t answer right away.

“Yes, I think so,” she whispered, her voice shook with nervous energy.

Sid reached down, taking her hand, which; it felt small and soft. He slowly pulled her up, but didn’t let go until he was sure she had her footing. “You sure?”

She nodded, loosening her grip to stand on her own. “Yeah, thanks.”

Sid bowed his head, and when he looked back up, his face was a mask of anger. His eyes left hers as he looked over his shoulder to make sure the bastard was contained. Seeing the odd angle of Vincent’s neck and Damon standing over him had Sid cursing again.

“Really, Damon?” Sid spat. “What the hell is wrong with you?”

“His head’s still attached.” Damon glanced down at the dead vampire, not looking one bit sorry.

“Where the hell did the gun come from?” Seeing that there was no threat, Sid turned completely around to walk to where Vincent lay.

“You’ve been shot.” Lana cried out, grabbing his arm and stopping him.

“You worried about me?” A slow, sexy grin made another appearance on his handsome face.

“I may think you’re an asshole, but that doesn’t mean I want to see you hurt or dead,” Lana frowned, lifting her hand off his forearm as if she was burned.

“I’m fine. It wasn’t silver. I will live another day, which probably doesn’t make you very happy.” Sid’s eyes darkened, but the grin stayed firmly in place. She was a hot little number, and any other time he would be taking her further in the woods for some one-on-one time. However, at that moment, he had things to take care of, like one very dead vampire who had answers he needed. “Stay put.”

“I’m not a dog,” Lana spat, her eyes narrowed at his command.

“No, you’re not, but you did blow my cover.” Sid leaned down by her ear. “And that needs to be dealt with. So don’t even think about moving that sweet ass of yours.”

“That’s very unprofessional for a VC Warrior,” Lana lashed out, but looked like she had been taken off her game a little.

Sid leaned away from her with a laugh. “Honey, who told you we were professional?” He gave her a warning stare before walking away.

Jared was leaning over looking at Vincent. “Yeah, he’s really dead this time. His damn head is hanging on by a thread.” He glanced up at Damon. “I really think we need to send you to anger management, big guy.”

“Don’t piss me off, Jared,” Damon growled.

“God forbid.” Jared threw his hands out, his eyes wide.

"Did you get any names or information out of the son of a bitch?" Damon asked Sid who was staring down at Vincent.

"No." Sid frowned before slamming his hands together. "Shit! I was so close."

"What the fuck happened?" Sloan came tromping through the woods with Slade behind him. Stopping over the dead vampire, Sloan's eyes shot to Damon. "Dammit to hell, Damon."

Damon just stood there taking the heat. "When my brothers are in danger, people die."

"Please tell me you got some information from him." Sloan glanced around at all the Warriors, his eyes landing on Sid. "And from the pissed off look on your face, I take that as a no."

"And his cover is blown." Duncan nodded toward the two women who were standing close together.

"Yeah, VC is no more." Jared shook his head sadly.

Sloan opened his mouth, and then snapped it shut looking at Jared. "VC?"

"That was his undercover name." Jared grinned when Sid flipped him off. "Bet you can't guess what his last name was."

Slade, who had been quiet until now, laughed, "You have got to be kidding me." Glancing down at the dead vampire, Slade's grin widened. "And he didn't put two and two together?"

"Never asked for my last name," Sid stated with a nonchalant shrug. "Now, can we stop gabbing like a bunch of old women so Doc can get this damn bullet out of me?" Sid whipped off his ruined jacket, followed by his shirt, and found a downed tree to sit on.

Everyone was quiet as Slade began working on getting the bullet out of Sid's shoulder before it healed over.

"Too bad dead men can't talk," Sloan mumbled. "This is the closest we've been to retrieving information."

One by one, each Warrior looked toward Lana, who was watching in stunned surprise as Slade removed the bullet from Sid.

"This dead man just might," Jared grinned. "Seems we got us a bona fide talker of dead things in our midst." Jared wagged his eyebrows at her.

"Listen, I really…" Lana stopped when Sid's eyes shot from the ground to her.

"Don't tell me you believe she can really talk to the dead, Jared?" Sid snorted as his eyes ran up and down her body. By the way, she refused to be used by Vincent, even with a gun pointed to her friend's head, Sid knew she needed a little pushing, and well, he was brilliant at that. He pushed everybody.

"But—" Again, she was interrupted.

"What? You don't think she can?" Jared frowned at Sid then looked down at the very dead Vincent. "He sure thought she could, and her friend said she could."

"I don't believe in people like her," Sid shot back, trying his best to be serious, but the outraged look on her face had him smelling victory, and damn, wasn't that sweet, almost as sweet as her female scent that wouldn't leave him. "Smoke and mirrors, my friend. Just smoke and mirrors."

"And I didn't believe in vampires, but oh, look…" she threw her hand up like Vanna White showing the next puzzle on the lit board, "here you are."

"No, she really can." Amy took a step toward Lana. "I saw her do it once."

"Shut up, Amy," Lana hissed at her loud-mouthed friend as she glared at Sid.

Amusement curved Sid's lips even as Slade plucked the bullet from his shoulder. He didn't even flinch. "It's just a way to make money off grieving individuals. Isn't that right, lovely Lana?" *Oh yeah, that should do it*, Sid thought to himself trying not to laugh at the different expressions of rage playing across her beautiful face.

"Screw you, fang boy." Lana pointed at him. "You know nothing about me."

"Fang boy?" Sid faked a frown, grabbed his shirt and pulled it on. "I don't believe for a minute a human can talk, read or whatever with a dead person. It's bullshit, so much so that I'm calling bullshit. No, actually, I call *total* bullshit." His eyes dared her to continue.

"Let me tell you something, you oversized blood-sucking Thor-looking wannabe." Once Lana's temper took over, there was no going back.

Sid was actually impressed at her comeback. She was a beautiful woman who had mastered the art of controlling her facial expressions, but when she was angry, she was absolutely stunning. He couldn't take his eyes off her. Her long raven hair had come loose from the braid she had tried to contain it in. A strand teased the corner of her mouth, and his hand itched to caress it away.

"Thor?" Duncan, who was standing next to Amy, finally spoke up.

"What is a Thor?"

"It's a guy in her favorite movie," Amy whispered out of the side of her mouth. "I actually think he looks more like Brad Pitt, but…" Amy clamped her mouth shut when Lana's head snapped around toward her, making Amy take a huge step back.

Having a sudden urge to touch her, he walked up, grasping her chin in a strong enough grip that she couldn't pull away, but gentle enough not to hurt her. With his thumb, he brushed a strand of hair away that was caught in the corner of her mouth driving him absolutely fucking crazy. "Honey, if you want to insult me, come up with something new," Sid's voice took on a husky vibration. "Although, the Thor thing is a new one, the rest is just unoriginal."

"Who the hell do you think you are?" Lana glared at him, finally able to pull away from his touch. "I've been through total hell that you could have stopped, because, well, that's your damn job. As a matter of fact, I'm going to report you."

"You're going to report me?" Sid laughed, looking at Jared. "She's going to report me. Get in line, babe," She definitely had fire, and he wondered briefly how high that fire flamed behind closed doors.

"Do not call me babe," Lana growled standing her ground. She was too pissed to be scared at the moment. "You're a poor excuse for a Warrior."

"Oh, shit." Those words were harmonized by every Warrior present.

"Honey, I'm the only reason you're able to stand here and insult me right now. If it wasn't for me, you and your friend would be on display to the highest bidder, and once bought, raped repeatedly until you became pregnant with a half-breed." Sid's whole attitude changed as he leaned back down toward her, making eye contact. If there was one thing he took seriously, it was his job, not even a gorgeous little lady with a body made for him, and him alone would insult his abilities. Not only that, but the thought of what could have happened if he hadn't been there, had his blood boiling.

Lana stood toe-to-toe with him. His breath was hot on her face, his dark golden eyes seared into hers as he towered over her.

"And if you fail to become a breeder, you are whored out or bled out to anyone with a fat wallet." Sid searched her face before leaning even closer to her, so close their faces almost touched. "You're welcome."

******

Lana watched him walk away before her eyes landed on Vincent. He was right. He did save her life in the end. She and Amy could have ended up in a far worse position, but she wouldn't admit that to the arrogant ass, no matter how much he looked like Thor.

"You going to do it?" Amy whispered, stepping closer. "Or are we going to get the hell out of here?"

"Yeah, I'm definitely doing this," Lana nodded, pulling off her jacket. The Warriors were involved in their own thing and not paying much attention to them. Once again, her eyes went to Vincent, who was lying still on the cold mucky ground.

"Just be careful." Amy bit her lip anxiously.

"Don't let them pull me away until I'm finished," she instructed Amy as she hurried to Vincent, tossing her never-to-wear-again jacket over his half decapitated head.

"I won't." Amy stood behind her, taking a quick glance around.

"Oh and Amy," Lana turned giving her a hard glare, "never ask me to go on a double date with you again," Lana said loudly, glancing at the Warriors.

"Never." Amy looked at her oddly, and then glanced over to see one of the Warriors watching them. "I just have a man problem. I think my 'asshole' radar is broken."

"You've never had a radar," Lana hissed. "You have the worst taste in men."

"True." Amy frowned, crossed her arms and then whispered, "Hurry the hell up."

Rolling her eyes, Lana knelt down. Cold wetness seeped through her jeans. Breathing in deeply, she reached out to grab Vincent's wrist but stopped. Saying a quick prayer, she grasped the cross hanging from her neck in a tight grip before grasping his wrist with her other hand which was shaking uncontrollably. Within seconds of making contact, she knew she had made a horrible mistake.

Flashes of cruelty hit Lana like a brick wall. She wanted to let go, get away from it all, but knew she couldn't. She had to see it through to the end, or she could be lost in the mind of this madman. She was reliving the last day of this man's life in flashes, and it made her horribly sick. All of her senses worked except for hearing. Smells, sights and emotions were all intact. She could feel his emotions, which could only be described as cruel excitement.

At the end of the dingy hallway was a large room; the smell of urine and fear overwhelmed her senses. Small cages lined the wall and inside were women in different states of emotion. Some were reaching through the bars in anger and fear, others were curled on the floor, their faces hidden as their bodies shook in pure terror. Men and women both went from cage to cage, being careful of the grasping hands reaching out begging to be saved.

Even though Lana couldn't hear a sound, she felt vibrations and could tell by the actions of the screaming women that they did so in outrage or pure terror. She felt each emotion as if it were her own. She also felt the sickening satisfaction the monster she was touching had felt at that time. She wanted to break from this nightmare, but knew she couldn't. When she saw a large man at the back of the room wearing a red hooded cape, which covered him from head to toe, she knew by Vincent's emotions, this was the man responsible.

Lana tried to tune out the horror around her to focus on the caped man whose head snapped up suddenly. His face didn't show because of the dark hood pulled low; she urged Vincent to move closer, which she knew was useless. This event had already taken place; she was just watching the replay. Dammit, she needed to see who was under the cape. The conversation didn't last long, and before Lana was ready, Vincent was turning to walk away.

Before Vincent walked out the door, he turned. The man in the cape was brutally pulling a woman from one of the cages, tossing her on a bed of filth. Standing over the woman, he pulled the hood down in a hard jerk. The complete helplessness on the woman's face was one Lana would never forget. The man began to turn to show his face, but then suddenly, everything froze and she could no longer breathe.

Another man stepped into view, walking forward. An immaculate black suit hung on his tall, thin body. His eyes were the same golden hue of the Warriors, but there was an evil wicked light behind them. They sunk into his thin long face. His head tilted as he looked down at Vincent, but something told her he wasn't looking at Vincent, but seeing her. Lana began to panic. Something wasn't right, and as that thought crossed her mind, his eyes turned blood red as his mouth opened, showing sharp fangs.

"I see that you will not be joining us this evening, Ms. Fitzpatrick." His voice was deep. "It's a shame, because I was so looking forward to it."

Lana couldn't believe it. She could hear him. He knew she was there. Never had this happened before. She pushed her fear away to study his face so she could describe every detail.

Shaking his head, the odd man made a tsking sound. "I can't let that happen." He stepped closer. "Such a waste of your talent that you have, and such a shame I will not be able to explore them further, but I cannot let you tell anyone what you've seen here, especially the Warriors."

Lana tried to release herself from Vincent, but she couldn't move. She was frozen like everyone else, except she could hear, see and feel. This was impossible. Thank God, he could only read her present thoughts.

"It's very possible, silly girl. Are you hiding something other than your gift?" His long bony fingers rose in front of Vincent's face into her line of vision. "Together, we could have been unstoppable. Unfortunately, because of Vincent's failure, there is nothing to do, but say goodbye."

His hand reached for Vincent as a tightness gripped her throat, squeezing all airflow off. With every bit of strength she had, she fought again to release from Vincent, but it was no use. She was trapped with no way out; she was going to die inside Vincent's mind. Blackness seeped into her blurring vision. Her last thought, before darkness totally claimed her, was, one way or another, this bastard was going to pay. Chilling laughter was the last thing she heard before she was lost.

Chapter 4

Sid stood talking to Sloan giving him all the information he had found out during his short undercover stint, thanks to the sexy little number who packed a hell of a punch. A grin split his lips as he rubbed his jaw. She had shocked the hell out of him, and he liked it. Women didn't hit him. Women loved him.

Turning his attention toward her, his eyes roamed her body. He was usually into tall, leggy blondes, but there was something about this short, raven-haired woman that got his blood pumping. He would love to have that hair wrapped around him. Her eyes were so round and blue, he had found himself staring at her a little too much when they first met, making him forget what the hell he was doing for a minute.

"I'll be damned. It actually worked." Sid snapped out of his fantasy of what she'd be like in bed, when she headed toward Vincent. Taking off her jacket and tossing it across Vincent's head, she knelt beside the dead vampire, and grabbed onto the dead man's wrist, her body going stiff as her head lifted toward the sky. He took off at a run. "What the fuck?"

"Don't touch her!" Amy shouted, standing protectively over Lana.

The rest of the Warriors hurried over, standing in a complete circle around the two women.

"Okay, that's enough." Sid took a step forward when Lana's body jerked as if she'd been shocked; no sound escaped her parted lips. Her eyes were wide without blinking. Even though he pushed her into this, he didn't know exactly what would happen; he felt like he'd made a big mistake.

"If you break her away now, she could be lost inside that man's memories." Amy grabbed Sid, trying to hold him back. "Please, don't do that to her."

Sid glanced around at his fellow Warriors as they watched in fascination, and that was saying a lot for this group. The small woman knelt in the muck holding a dead man's wrist in a trance that couldn't be faked. If there had been any real reason to doubt her before, no one was doubting her now.

"Can she be harmed?" Sid felt his protective instincts kick in, but was at a loss; he had no idea how he could protect her. Dammit, he could kick himself in the ass for possibly putting this woman in danger. What the hell had he been thinking?

"Not that I know of, but I do know if she is brought out before it's over, she can be lost." Amy looked down at her friend. "It's the one thing she is frightened of."

"Then why does she do it?" This came from Jared, who looked up from Lana.

"She doesn't do it much because…" Amy frowned when Lana jerked again. Her back was tilted back in an odd way, as if she was trying to get away from something. "I've never seen her do that before, though."

Sid watched, fighting every instinct he had; something didn't feel right, and his instincts had saved his own ass many times. Her body became deathly still, her eyes still unblinking. Frowning, he bent closer.

"Son of a bitch," he hissed as bruises formed on her throat.

"Don't break her contact!" Amy cried out, trying to block Sid.

"Fuck that!" Sid grabbed Lana around the waist, pulling her away, but breaking contact didn't work. "Lana! Dammit, Lana!" He shook her, his eyes not leaving the bruises that were darkening around her delicate neck.

Slade ran over, nudging Sid out of the way. “Move!” Slade opened his bag, grabbing something.

“What the hell is going on?” Sid watched as Slade grabbed her shirtsleeve, pushing it up and jabbing something in her arm. “What are you doing?”

“Lana!” Slade’s voice was firm and loud as he jammed the needle back into her arm. “I need to shock her out of whatever in the hell has a hold of her.”

“Jesus, Slade.” Jared stood watching, feeling as helpless as Sid looked.

Every Warrior stood ready for battle, but against what, they didn’t know, and that didn’t set well with any of them. Cursing filled the air as their protective instincts kicked in a hundred percent, with no relief.

“If you stab her with that one more time, I will kill you,” Sid growled when Slade started to jam the needle back into her arm.

“If I don’t shock her out of this state, she’s dead.” Slade started to jam the needle in Lana’s arm again when she gasped for breath, her hands flying to her neck, prying invisible fingers from her throat. Her own nails dug deep bloody grooves into her soft skin.

“Lana, stop!” Sid grabbed her hands, but she fought him.

“Sit her up,” Slade ordered, grabbing one arm while Sid grabbed the other, keeping her hands away from her neck.

Lana kicked away from them, still fighting for breath as she coughed and gagged. Sid took control, grabbing her and holding her close. “Lana, stop!” he ordered, holding her arms tightly against her in a bear hug, pulling her between his legs. “You’re safe.”

Her haunted eyes shot to his, calming slightly as she saw who had her. She tried to say something, but nothing came out. Her eyes watered and she blinked, trying to clear them. She tried to speak again, but a ragged slip of breath was the only thing that escaped.

"Just give it a minute," Sid whispered, watching her closely. As she calmed, he loosened his hold on her. "Do you feel like you're breathing okay?"

Nodding, Lana pried her arm out from his, rubbing her throat; her hand moved lower and stopped. "My cross." Her voice was raw and harsh, but the panic was clear. Pushing away from Sid, she frantically ran her hands through the cold soft mud and leaves. She coughed and gagged again as her breathing sped up in the haste of her search.

Sid watched as Amy also looked around where Lana had been. Sid watched her for a second longer before looking toward his fellow Warriors. They all looked as confused and helpless as he felt. Not able to watch her shuffle around in the mud any longer, Sid grasped her arms, helping her to her feet.

"What happened, Lana?" He didn't like the vacant fear in her eyes. What the hell happened to the strong woman who punched the hell out of his face?

Taking a second, Lana seemed to pull herself together. She looked around at each Warrior, then to Amy, then finally back to Sid.

"There were so many women in cages." Lana's lip quivered at the memory. She had seen some bad stuff in her life, but never anything like what she just witnessed. Before she could continue, she was pulled behind Sid, the sound of guns cocking.

"You stupid son of a bitch!" Sid shouted, putting his gun back under his jacket. "You are not supposed to be here, Adam."

Adam ignored him as he went behind Sid, getting in Lana's face. "Did you see a blonde girl my age?"

Lana shook her head. "I don't know. There were so many."

"How long have you been here?" Sid frowned, realizing that none of them had picked up that Adam was around.

"I followed Sloan." His eyes never left Lana.

"What are you doing here, Adam? You were ordered to stay away from this mission." Sloan stepped up, grabbing his arm, but Adam pulled away ignoring him.

"Her name is Angelina," Adam continued desperately, his focus never leaving Lana even with Warriors bearing down on him. "Her hair is pale-blonde to her waist. She has light sky-blue eyes."

"I'm sorry." Lana shook her head. "I don't remember seeing anyone like that, but I wasn't trying to find anyone, so I didn't pay attention."

"What kind of cages were they in?" Adam hissed with barely-controlled anger. "Were they being taken care of?"

Lana didn't answer. If he had lost a loved one to these people, it wouldn't be her telling him what she was going through.

"Answer me!" he shouted in her face.

Sid grabbed Adam by the neck, tossing him away from Lana. "That's enough!" He put himself between Adam and Lana.

Adam rolled to his feet and rushed Sid, but was stopped when Sloan grabbed him. "You best stand down, son," Sloan ordered, his voice full of authority. "You are already on report. Don't make me cut you from the program or let Sid teach you a lesson you won't soon forget."

Every Warrior present was ready as they watched Adam struggle. Sid was pumped and ready. If Adam made one move toward Lana, he was going to be very sorry. He understood, but the young half-breed needed to learn control, and so far, that had been a big failure since Angelina had been sold.

"Okay," Adam replied. After visibly fighting his anger, he calmed down. When Sloan was slow to let go, Adam jerked away. "I said okay."

Sid took a step closer in warning. "You make one more move toward her or raise your voice again, you *will* regret it. Now, get the fuck out of here."

Adam nodded, looking around before his eyes landed on Lana. "I'm sorry," he sighed as if the weight of the world was on his young shoulders. "I just have to find her."

"She was taken by these people?" Lana asked, her voice a little clearer, but still hoarse.

Adam waited a second before answering. "She was sold." His eyes pleaded with her. "I have to find her."

Sid watched different emotions flit across her already-burdened features. When her eyes went to Vincent, he started shaking his head.

"Maybe if I try one more time, I could see if I find her, but I don't know the location even if I did." Lana put her hand to her throat, clearly indicating touching Vincent again was the last thing she wanted to do.

Sid's respect for the woman tripled at that moment, but there was no way in hell he would put her at risk like that again. "Not happening. Take him back." Sid took Adam by the arm, handing him off to Jared. When Adam glared at him, Sid nodded. "As soon as we're finished here, I'll come straight to you with any information. We're going to find her, Adam." Sid remembered saying those same words to Duncan not long ago when they were looking for Pam. Sighing, he watched Jared lead Adam away with the rest of the warriors following, other than Sloan.

"Lana, you're bleeding." Amy broke the silence.

Sid turned to see blood trickling from her nose, the sweet scent burning its way into his senses. "Are you okay?" His voice took on a harsh, raspy tone; his eyes darkened.

Reaching up, Lana touched her nose, feeling wetness. Bringing her fingers away, bright blood colored the tips. "I'm fine." Lana didn't make eye contact as she took a Kleenex from Amy. "But I have to find my cross." Her grandmother had given her that cross, and she wasn't leaving without it.

Sid looked around, spotting a golden chain by Vincent's hand. Walking over, he reached down, snatching it up. The chain was broken as if it had been ripped off her neck.

Lana rushed up beside him. "Did you find it?"

Glancing down at her, he reached around, lifting the hair off her neck. He could see the marking where the chain had bit into her skin. "How did this get broken?"

"I don't know." Lana grabbed for the cross, but he held it back out of her reach.

He reached out, touching her neck. "I don't know much about what you do, but I have a feeling this isn't normal." His fingers caressed the darkening marks on her neck, making her shiver.

"It's not normal." Amy, who had walked closer, frowned at Lana. "Her sister—"

"Amy." Lana glared at her shaking her head.

Sid's eyes narrowed at Amy. "Her sister what?"

"Is no one's concern." She grabbed the cross out of his hand, holding it in a tight fist. "Now, do you want to know what I saw or not?"

Sid's eyes shot from Amy to Lana. "Yes, I do." He removed his hand from her neck. "I also want to know how those bruises appeared on your throat out of nowhere."

Amy opened her mouth to say something, but Lana took a step, landing on her friend's foot. Amy let out a squeal instead of what she was about to blurt out.

"Damn, Lana, that hurt." Amy leaned against the nearest tree, rubbing her injured foot.

"I'm sorry, Amy." Her voice sounded remorseful, but her eyes shot her a warning. She turned back to Sid. "To answer your question, I bruise like a peach. I probably grabbed my own throat while I was seeing things that were horrifying and choked myself."

"No, you didn't." Sid shook his head, his eyes watching her every move. "Why are you lying?"

"Listen, I'm cold." Lana changed the subject rubbing her arms. "And there is no way I'm putting my jacket back on after it was laying over him. So can we get this show on the road?"

Sid continued to stare at her, knowing she was lying through her pretty white teeth framed with luscious red lips. She had calmed down, but he could feel the fear rolling off her. Taking off his jacket, he wrapped it around her. “Now that that’s taken care of, why are you lying to me?”

“I’m not lying,” Lana lied. “Who’s in charge? I think it would be better if I talk to him.”

“Why, so you can lie to him?” Sid could get on anyone’s nerves when he wouldn’t let go of something. He knew she was lying, and she was going to tell him the truth whether she knew it or not.

“You’re annoying.” Lana frowned up at him.

“So I’ve been told.” His lip twitched, but didn’t spread into a grin.

Lana stared at his mouth before snapping her head away. Spotting Sloan, she pointed at him. “Is he in charge?” When Sid didn’t answer, she turned to look at him. “Stop staring at me!”

“He’s my boss, yes, but I’m in charge of this investigation, so stop lying and…” this time he did grin, “let’s get this show on the road.” He cocked an eyebrow at her after throwing her words back in her face.

“Ass,” Lana mumbled under her breath, and turned back toward Sloan.

“Liar,” Sid mumbled loud enough for her to hear him.

“I am not a liar,” she lied again. God, if he only knew.

“What happened to your neck?” Sid pushed, which is something he did best. He pushed people to the point they wanted to tear his eyes out, and she was getting close to that point.

"Do you want to know what I saw or not?" Lana pushed back. "I have things to do and don't have time to stand in the damn woods all night."

"Yes, I do, after you tell me how those bruises appeared out of nowhere." Sid liked sparring with her. Her facial expressions were all over the place.

"I told you," Lana shot back. "Why do you keep pushing the issue?"

'Because your friend is trying her best to block me, but she's having a hell of a time." Sid glanced at Amy, who looked really nervous.

"You're reading her?" Lana frowned, slapping her hands on her hips. She then slapped his arm hard, and shook her hand with a pained expression. "Well, stop it."

"No." Sid narrowed his eyes, first at Lana, then at Amy.

"Empty your head, Amy," Lana ordered her friend.

"It usually is, but it feels weird." Amy put her hand to her head.

Sid grinned at Amy's answer. "Just relax, Amy. It will only take a minute, and please stop thinking about the last guy you dated," Sid grimaced. "It's kind of grossing me out."

"Stop it." Lana pushed Sid, who didn't budge an inch. "Leave her alone."

"No," he responded with the one word that seemed to get on Lana's nerves, so he made sure he used it often.

"Keep thinking of that guy, Amy." Lana pointed at Amy as an evil grin broke across her lips. "Think of him naked."

Sid glared at Lana, but inside he laughed. She was so much like him it was scary. That is exactly something he would have said. "That's so not cool, Lana."

"What the hell is going on?" Sloan walked up, looking at all three of them. Lana and Sid were glaring at each other, while the other girl, Amy, was holding her head with a goofy grin on her face.

"I'm trying to get the truth out of her." Sid pointed at Lana, and then he tilted his hand pointing, his thumb toward Amy. "And she's thinking of her last date naked, which in truth, she could do much better."

Amy popped her eyes open, looking at Sid. "He's pretty hot."

"But he's hung like an ant," Sid snorted, shaking his head.

Shrugging, Amy stood with a thoughtful gleam and nodded her head.

"You're disgusting," Lana hissed at Sid crossing her arms.

Sid nodded with a large smile. "Sticks and stones, baby, sticks and stones."

"Don't call me that," Lana hissed.

Sloan looked like he was ready to explode. "Sinclair, you are pushing it. Do your damn job and stop…." Sloan sputtered, not knowing what the hell to say, "doing whatever you're doing."

"Okay, boss." Sid held back from saluting Sloan. He didn't need to push it that far.

"Take them back to the compound," Sloan grumbled, turning to leave.

"I'll be there as soon as the coroner gets here."

"Right away, sir." Sid grabbed Lana's arm, leading her out of the woods. "Guess since everyone else left, I'm riding with you ladies. Stop thinking of naked men, Amy, and come on," Sid called out over his shoulder.

"Where we going?" Amy, who was the tall bubbly-blonde type Sid usually went for, plucked her way through the wooded area behind them.

"To the VC Council interrogation room," Sid replied with an evil grin as he winked down at Lana's shocked face.

"Shit," both women whispered at the same time.

Hearing them, Sid frowned, wondering what else these two women, who appeared out of nowhere, were lying about.

Chapter 5

Jill sat at the compound playing with little Daniel. With Pam being a half-breed and the birth coming way sooner than nine months, Daniel was perfect and growing at a normal weight. Slade kept a close eye on him, and so far, he seemed like a normal, healthy baby boy.

"You're good with him," Pam smiled, watching Jill with Daniel. "And he likes you."

"He likes everybody." Jill laughed when Daniel's little fists shot into the air as a toothless grin spread across his lips. "I don't think I've ever seen a happier baby."

"And he has every Warrior wrapped around his little finger." Nicole bent down, tapping Daniel on the nose. "Especially Sid, who steals him away from everyone."

"Duncan's already teaching him the ways of a Warrior," Pam smiled. "I'm going to have gray hair very soon, I'm afraid."

"With all of these Warriors, you don't stand a chance, Momma." Tessa walked in, hearing their conversation. "Jared thinks he is going to be a great Council leader."

"Well, I hope that's the case, because then there might be less fighting." Pam replied.

They all looked at each other and laughed knowing how ridiculous that statement really was. "Don't think you're going to be that lucky," Jill chimed in.

Hearing commotion outside in the entryway, the women watched as their Warriors walked in, each going to their mates except for Slade, who stood back.

Daniel turned his little head at the sound of Duncan's voice.

"Guess my time's up." Jill stood, handing Daniel, who began squirming his way toward Duncan.

"How's my little Warrior?" Duncan held Daniel up with a proud grin. The women looked at each other knowingly before they started laughing. "What?" Duncan frowned.

The loud buzzing from the front door broke the ease of the moment. The men went into Warrior mode. With the women being left regularly at the compound alone and with the addition of Daniel, the doors were locked at all times with a high tech security system in place.

Without a word, Damon took the lead and walked out.

Jill glanced at Slade, who was smiling as he watched Duncan and Daniel. His eyes turned toward her and his smile faded slightly. To say that didn't sting a little would be a lie, but Jill shoved it aside, trying not to allow his indifference to bother her. She was getting used to pushing her feelings aside.

"Someone here to see you, Jill." Damon's voice quieted the room.

Jill's eyes shot from Slade to a tall, muscular man dressed in black leather from head to toe. His dark brown hair hung to his shoulders, but was brushed back away from his handsome face. He had a duffle bag slung on one wide shoulder and a helmet in his hand. Jill had no clue who he was, and it clearly showed on her face.

"Can I help you?" Jill asked puzzled. Not that she wasn't mildly interested as to why this handsome man would be here to see her.

"I'm Corbin Tomblin." His golden eyes brightened as they roamed up and down her body, clearly liking what he saw. Setting his helmet and bag down against the wall, he stood to full height and made his way toward her. Taking her hand, he kissed it softly, his eyes still on hers. "I was sent by Sid Sinclair." His voice was deep with a sexy twang.

"Ah, okay. But why?" Jill still had no clue what was going on, but she could seriously get used to handsome men kissing her hand like she was a special lady. Wow, just wow.

He looked around at the eyes on them. "Can we go somewhere private?" He looked back down at her, his smile charming.

"This is about as private as you're going to get." Slade took a step forward; the snarl matched the growl in his voice.

The man's eyes darkened as he shot a glare at Slade. Bringing his attention back to Jill, he smiled, "I'm here as your blood donor." His eyes once again caressed her body.

Jill gasped, pulling her hand away. "My what?"

Before a word could be spoken, someone else buzzed the door. Damon again went out and came right back with another man following. "You have another visitor, Jill." Damon couldn't wipe the grin off his face.

"Oh, my God," Jill whispered as the door buzzed repeatedly. Before she knew what was happening, there were six of the most handsome men she had ever seen standing before her, and all of them were there for her; she had never felt so humiliated in her life.

"You and Daniel go upstairs," Duncan told Pam.

"Duncan, he's fine," Pam whispered, watching the scene unfold as well as checking Jill's choices, which weren't bad at all. However, Duncan was watching Slade and things could get ugly real fast.

“Now, Pam,” Duncan ordered as he nodded toward Slade, who looked ready to tear the place apart.

“Okay, darn it,” Pam kissed Duncan then waved at Jill, but not before pointing to the guy she thought Jill should pick. She gave Jill a thumbs-up before exiting the room.

“I think you and Nicole need to go ahead and leave too,” Jared told Tessa.

“Not on your life,” Nicole shot back. “I am so wanting to see how this is going to play out, so I’m not leaving this spot. I don’t have a precious baby on my hip.” Nicole just smiled when Damon growled at her.

Jill watched Duncan order Pam out of the room. One of the men stepped into her vision, and for the life of her, she couldn’t remember his name. Not to be outdone, the other five surrounded her and started talking at once. She was overwhelmed, and so out of her league, her stomach trembled with nausea. She glanced over at Slade, who leaned against the wall, arms crossed, staring at her and glaring at them.

“So, Jill,” one of the men, Chaz she thought was his name, smiled down at her. “What’s wrong with you that Sid had to call us in to be your donors?”

That question snapped her head back around. “Excuse me?”

“What the hell is wrong with you, man?” Another man, who she definitely couldn’t remember his name, gave him a little push.

“I’m just being realistic.” He pushed back, his voice raising. “She’s fucking hot, but there has to be a reason no one here wants her to feed from them. We have a right to know.”

"There is nothing wrong with me," Jill replied, anger beginning to burn in her veins, her nausea forgotten. She was going to kill Sid. "And I'm not the one who called you."

"Hey, calm down, baby." One reached to touch her face, but she dodged his touch.

"Get the fuck out!" Slade's angry voice boomed through the room. "Get the fuck out now!"

Jared and Damon pushed Nicole and Tessa a safe distance away, but not before Damon slapped a fifty in Jared's palm. At Tessa's frown, Jared grinned. "I bet Damon that Slade would blow within fifteen minutes, and well, I won."

"Asshole," Damon growled, but his eyes stayed on the situation unfolding.

"What?" The first guy who showed up frowned at Slade. "I didn't come all this way just for the hell of it."

"Yeah, you did," Slade replied, his eyes glowing black. "Now, get the fuck out."

"No, I'm not leaving without…"

Slade was against the wall one minute and in the guy's face the next. "It's not in your best interest to piss me off any more than I already am." Slade towered over the guy. "Now get your leather-wearing ass out of here, and take your friends with you."

"I said I'm not leaving…" He couldn't finish his sentence because he was laying on the floor, knocked out cold.

"Anyone else not leaving?" Slade looked them each in the eye.

The other four backed down quickly, but the one who hadn't said much looked at Jill. "I'd really like to call on you sometime." He held out a piece of paper. Everyone in the room stared at it like it was an explosive device. "It's my phone number," he added, pushing it toward Jill.

"We know what it is, dumbass." Slade grabbed the paper, wadded it up and tossed it on the ground.

Jill watched the battle between the two men. Even though this guy had been quiet, he had a fire in his eyes as he stared up at Slade. Glancing around, she saw Jared and Damon had moved a little closer. Damon was serious as usual, but Jared had a mischievous half-grin as he watched everything unfold. If Sid were here, she'd kick his ass. Well, okay, she wouldn't kick his ass, but she could cuss him out better than anyone. Sick of being humiliated anymore and wanting to spare having blood spilled because of her, which she'd be blamed for and probably kicked out of the program, she stepped between the two vampires who were having a pretty impressive staring contest.

"Listen....ah..." Dammit, why couldn't she remember his name? "Ah, I appreciate you all stopping by, but Sid was mistaken and shouldn't have called you."

"Well, I'm glad he did. I will definitely be calling to ask you out, whether you need a blood donor or not, but it would be my absolute pleasure to give you every drop of blood I have, or anything else you might..." Breaking eye contact with Slade, he winked down at her with a sexy grin, "...need."

Slade's grin was evil as he shook his head. "You were warned." His grin faded as he grabbed the guy and threw him through the nearest wall.

Everyone stood frozen in shock except for Slade, who stepped through the hole, heading for the guy who was trying to stand up. Jill was the first to jump into motion. Quickly stepping over the guy, who had been knocked out, she ran past Slade, blocking him and helping the guy to his feet.

“Are you okay?” Jill’s eyes were wide as saucers, but narrowed at Slade. “What is wrong with you?”

“Get out of the way, Jill.” Slade grabbed her and pulled her aside.

“No, I won’t get out of the way,” Jill glared at Slade before turning back to the men. “You need to leave and take him with you.” Jill pointed to the man in leather who was finally waking.

Damon walked out into the entryway holding leather-guy up by the arm. Jared followed, looking at the hole in the wall, then to Slade. “Damn, dude, and I thought Damon’s temper was bad.”

“What the hell is your problem, bro?” The one who sailed through the wall took an aggressive step forward.

“I’m not your bro, motherfucker.” Slade’s eyes were burning black as coal. “If I ever see you around here again, I will break you in half.”

Jared stepped in the guy’s line of vision, blocking him from Slade. “I know what you’re thinking, and I *think* what you’re thinking is going to get you worse than a trip through a wall. I suggest you tuck your man card in your wallet and walk out while you still can.”

“Get out!” Jill pointed to the door. She was so done. When no one moved, but just stood staring at each other in a battle of who had bigger balls, Jill lost it. “Get the fuck out!”

Drywall Guy turned his head to look at her, causing a dusty cloud of drywall flying in the air; his golden eyes darkened and narrowed in anger. “Honey, you best learn your place,” he sneered. “For someone who has to have other people find you a blood donor, you’re turning out to be more trouble than you're worth. You best watch that mouth of yours before I find better use for it."

"Well shit!" Jared stepped out of the way as soon as the last word was spoken; he knew the Slade train was making a stop on this dude's face.

Jill watched in horror as all hell broke loose. When the other four stepped in to help their guy, Damon, Jared and Duncan grinned, jumping into the fight.

"No!" Jill yelled, but it was no use. The whole entryway was getting demolished, and she was going to get blamed for it all. Glancing over in panic at Nicole and Tessa, who had come closer, she knew by the look in their eyes she was screwed and not in a good way. "Dammit!"

"Jill, no!" Nicole shouted when Jill jumped into the middle of the fighting men.

Jared was pounding away at one when another was rushing him from behind. Jill took off, tackling him from the side and taking him to the ground. The guy turned, landing a fist to the side of her face and knocking her half way across the room. When people said they saw stars, they weren't lying; she saw freakin' stars, stripes and little floaty things. Shaking her head, she went up on her elbows trying to clear her vision. *Damn, that hurt.* Not one to cower *and* the fact that she was a Warrior in training, she jumped up, swaying a little, but took a step forward to jump back in.

Everything had stopped. Damon had one guy by the neck; Jared straddled one on the floor, Duncan had one in a headlock and Slade just stood with his foot on another's chest, holding him down. They all stared at her, even the six blood donor recruits. "What?" Jill frowned, looking behind her then back at them.

An inhuman roar rattled the walls, or what was left of them. Damon, Jared and Duncan dropped the guys they were beating the hell out of, and as one, they grabbed Slade, taking him to the ground.

“I didn’t know it was her.” The guy who hit her watched wide-eyed as Slade tossed the three Warriors off him, making his way toward him.

Damon scrambled back to his feet, grabbing Slade in a bear hug while Jared dove for Slade’s legs, taking him down again. Duncan ran to the guy, who looked scared enough to piss himself, pushing him out the door. “Get the fuck out of here. We were just going to give you an ass beating, but if he gets ahold of you, you’re dead.” He looked behind him to see the others rushing toward the door looking back at Slade, who once again was tossing Jared and Damon off him.

“Go!” The one in leather pushed the others who were in front of him toward the door. They stumbled over each other in their haste to get away from Slade. “Jesus! Go!”

Once they were gone, Duncan stepped in front of Slade, stopping him, barely. “They’re gone.” Duncan gave him a shove. Slade simply growled, trying to push his way past. “Stand down, Slade. I said they were gone, and if I have to knock you the fuck out, I will.”

Slade’s head snapped to Duncan, his eyes black with murderous rage. “Get out of my way.”

“He didn’t know it was her.” Duncan pushed him hard. “Now, stand down.”

“Is she okay?” Slade asked through clenched teeth.

“Yeah, she’s fine.” Duncan glanced around Slade and winced when he spotted a large lump on the side of her face, which was already bruising. “She’s good, Slade. Just calm down, bro.”

Slade nodded, and then turned without looking at anyone, disappearing toward his office.

Jill stood stone-still, the side of her face throbbing horribly, but she knew it would be gone in the next day or two. She healed fast, not as fast as a full-blood, but faster than a human, and it wasn't that bad. Jared walked toward her, staring at the side of her face with a pained expression. Maybe it was worse than she thought.

"Way to take a hit, kid." Jared nodded his respect, but then frowned. "What the hell were you thinking?"

"The guy was coming up on you from behind." Jill frowned back. "It's what I'm supposed to do, isn't it? Have your back. It's what you have taught me, so I did my job. I had your back."

Jared was silent for a long time, just staring at her before he clasped her shoulder. "You're going to make a good Warrior, Jill," Jared finally broke the silence.

"Wish everyone felt that way." Her eyes moved to where Slade disappeared.

"Yeah, well, it's hard for us to see a woman take a hit. Warrior or not, you are a woman, and it's going to take some getting used to," Jared replied honestly.

Jill nodded and then looked around at the mess. "Yeah, well, after Sloan sees this place, I may not be with the program any longer."

Jared shook his head. "Sid is responsible for this mess."

"Yes, he is," Damon added. "And I'm going to kick his ass."

"Get in line." Duncan replied, putting his arm around Jill, and leading her over chunks of drywall that was scattered all over the place. "Now,

I think we all deserve a beer. You did good, Jill."

"Thanks," Jill nodded, a sadness creeping through her heart as her eyes once again sought out the one person who she wished would be proud of her.

Chapter 6

Lana reluctantly followed Sid up the steps to a huge door. She had sat in the back as Amy handed over her keys and sat in front talking to Sid like he was an old friend. Sid hit a code on the keypad; the door buzzed then clicked. He held the door open for Amy and then let her walk inside. Amy thanked him; Lana didn't.

Once inside, both women stopped at the sight they walked in on. What Lana would have once called a large entryway, was a mess of broken drywall scattered all over the floor. Holes in the walls, pictures hanging crooked and the railing on the stairs broken in half.

Sid pushed both Lana and Amy behind him, pulling out his gun. "Stay here," Sid ordered. "Don't move."

Jared walked out from behind the wall with the large hole and stopped. "Good, you got your gun," Jared glared at him. "You're going to need it."

Putting his gun away, Sid looked around, confused. "What the hell happened?"

"You happened." Jared pointed at him then glanced at Lana and Amy. "What are they doing here?"

"Sloan wants them here." Sid said, still looking around at all the damage. "Why is this any of my fault?"

"Seems Jill has become a hot item, thanks to you." Jared crossed his arms.

Understanding flashed across his face. "Man, I forgot about that." Sid looked behind Jared trying to look into the room. "Who did she pick?"

"Look at this place!" Jared threw his arms wide. "Does it look like it went well?"

"Slade?" Sid's eyes widened as a large grin spread across his face. "I knew that big bastard had a thing for her."

Lana stood beside Amy watching, but not understanding what was going on. One thing she did notice was that she kept taking deep breaths through her nose. She still wore this man's, Sid's, jacket and it smelled so damn good. She could smack herself; she was up to her ass in problems, and all she could think about was how this man's jacket smelled. Movement from across the room stopped her in mid-smell. A young woman walked out with both hands on her flared hips. Her short dark hair was tipped in darker blue. She also had large black and purple bruising on the side of her face from her temple to below her cheek. Her bruised face was pinched with anger, which was directed toward Sid Sinclair. Lana liked her instantly.

"Are you crazy?" Jill walked over broken drywall, kicking bigger pieces out of her way. "What were you thinking?"

Sid opened his mouth to respond, his eyes snapping to the side of her face. "What happened to your face?"

She ignored his question. "You humiliated me, Sid," Jill hissed.

"How in the hell did I humiliate you?" Sid frowned, clearly indicating he didn't like that thought. "I was trying to help you. Now, tell me what happened to your face." His voice didn't rise, but his tone had turned deadly.

"How in the hell are you helping me by inviting strange men here for me to feed from?" Jill's lip quivered. She cursed, looking away from him. "Just stay out of my business, okay? I got this and don't need help from any of you."

Everyone was silent as Jill stomped out of the room. Lana looked back at Sid and was surprised at the real remorse shadowing his features, but as fast as it was there, it was gone, replaced with a rage that actually had her and Amy stepping back.

"Did you even check these guys out?" Jared glared at Sid.

"Yeah, I checked them out." Sid looked away from where Jill disappeared and back to Jared, his eyes darkening. "What happened to her face?"

Jared glanced at Lana and Amy before looking back at Sid. "Things got a little out of control, obviously. While I was pounding one guy, another was coming at my back. Jill took him down before he could get to me." Jared grabbed Sid's arm before he could turn to head out the door. "The guy struck without knowing who took him down. He didn't know it was her."

"I don't give a fuck." Sid snapped his arm away. "Which one was it?"

"It's taken care of," Jared responded, but Sid continued to glare at him. "I'm not telling you, Sid. It's over and done with."

"The hell it is." Sid turned, walking past Lana and Amy. "I'll find all six of them."

"She's going to be a Warrior." Jared shook his head. "I wanted to kill the son of a bitch myself. Slade almost did. The guy really didn't know, but we're going to have to stop looking at her as a woman. We have to start looking at her as a Warrior."

Sid stopped, knowing Jared was right, but it still didn't help the rage he felt.

"Why don't you take care of your business, and then help us clean up this mess." Jared looked around and sighed. "After that, you can talk to Jill, but I'd give her a minute to calm down."

"That girl is a Warrior?" Lana couldn't help but ask.

"She's in training." Jared grinned at their surprise. "She's going to make a good one. You would have been proud of her." He glanced at Sid.

A slow smile spread across his face. "She had your back, huh?"

"She was all over it, bro." Jared's voice was full of pride.

"What in the hell happened there?" Sid walked over to the large hole in the wall.

"The Slade train," Jared shook his head.

Lana had no clue what that meant, but when Sid leaned his head back letting loose a genuine laugh, she had never seen a more handsome man in her life. His strong features softened when he let down his guard. She liked this side of him and found herself smiling.

"Wow…" Amy sighed, her eyes on Sid.

"Put your tongue back in." Lana elbowed her.

Amy made a little growling noise. "I know where I'd like to put my tongue."

A sudden urge to claw her friend's eyes out hit Lana, surprising the crap out of her. She didn't even know this man, yet she was ready to mangle her friend over him. *What the hell*?

"Son of a bitch, what the fuck have you guys done now?" Sloan's voice boomed through the room, making Lana and Amy jump.

Sid and Jared both looked at each other and smiled. "The Slade train."

******

Sid leaned against the wall watching as Lana answered Sloan's questions. He was actually impressed with her explanation of the details she had seen. Pretty damn impressed. If he wasn't mistaken, her explanation of detail seemed professional, as if she'd been trained. Interesting. Beauty, body and brains, what more could a man ask for? Sid frowned, wondering where that thought came from.

"So how far back in a person's memory can you go?" Sloan sat back in his chair watching her closely.

"It depends," Lana replied sitting up in her chair, looking very uncomfortable with the question. "I have no control over where I go in their memories, but for me, it has always been, from what I can tell, hours before their death."

"What do you mean 'for you'?" Sid asked. "There are others that can do this?"

"I'm sure there are." Her vague answer amused him.

"Anyone close to you?" he pushed. She was hiding something, and he wanted to know what.

"Yes." She didn't elaborate as she finally looked his way with a glare.

Sid had to give her credit. She didn't crack under pressure.

“I don’t see what that has to do with anything.” She turned back to Sloan. “There was also a man, other than the one with the long cape and hood. I got a good look at his face. I know a guy who can draw up a sketch from my description. He is usually dead-on what I describe.”

“Jill can do it.” Sid looked at Sloan who nodded, grabbing his phone.

“Can you estimate how many women were there?” Sid asked, his tone turning dangerously low.

Lana closed her eyes, trying hard to recreate the scene she had witnessed. “At least fifteen from what I could see.”

“Is there anything that could give us a location?” Sid knew it was a long shot, but had to ask.

“No,” Lana shook her head. “I’m sorry.”

“Jill said she could do it.” Sloan tossed his phone on the desk. “She’s on her way.”

Sid turned his attention back to Lana, whom he caught staring at him. When he gave her a knowing smile, her face flushed a sexy shade of red as she straightened, looking away. “So while we wait for Jill, why don’t you explain how those bruises appeared on your neck?”

Lana sighed, “We’ve been through this.”

“No, you’ve avoided answering the question, and I’ve been continuing to ask.” Sid tilted his head, his eyes moving from her neck to her eyes. “I’m a born pain in the ass. I can keep this up forever.”

“That is very true.” Sloan rolled his eyes. “So damn true.”

The only sign that Sid heard Sloan was a half-grin.

A knock sounded on the door before Jill walked in carrying her sketchpad. She walked straight past Sid without looking his way. Taking a seat, she flipped to a page and held her pencil ready to go.

“Hello, Jill.” Sloan glanced at her, eyes filled with question.

“Hi, Sir,” Jill responded business-like.

Sloan glanced at Sid who simply shook his head. “Okay, well, this is Lana Fitzpatrick.” Sloan introduced them, and both women nodded their greeting. “She is going to describe a man, who we are hoping you can capture in a profile pic.”

“I will do my best, Sir,” Jill nodded to Sloan. Her eyes met Sid’s for a split second before looking down at her paper.

“Are you okay?” Sloan frowned, not bringing up her bruised and swollen face, since the others had already briefed him.

“Dandy.” She gave her best fake smile, shifting her position before looking at Lana. “Ready when you are.”

“Amy, why don’t you come outside with me?” Sid walked over, holding out his hand. “It might help if we aren’t here to distract them.”

Sid watched both women closely as they shared a look. Something was definitely not right. “Ah, okay.” She gave him a half-smile, taking his hand.

Sloan’s cell phone rang; he answered, walking out ahead of Sid and Amy.

Before closing the door, Sid turned and tossed Lana a slow wink along with a sexy grin filled with promise.

Chapter 7

Lana glared at Sid as he walked out behind Amy, whom she prayed kept her damn mouth shut. “Dammit.”

“What?” Jill asked, glancing up from her sketchbook.

“Is he always so…” Lana frowned, trying to find the right word.

“Annoying? Pain in the ass?” Jill glared at the door, rolling her eyes. “Yes, he is, but what’s most annoying is he’s a good guy. One of the best.”

That surprised Lana. “How so?”

“He will go out of his way to help anyone. He will moan, groan and complain about it, but he will help anyone,” Jill sighed with a huff.

The word moan caught her attention in a very vivid way, but Lana mentally shook the word right out of her head. Hearing that vamp moan was the last thing she needed. “Was that evidence of him trying to help you?” Lana nodded her head toward the door.

“Yeah. I know he meant well…I think, but it hurt more than it helped.” Jill sat in thought and then shook her head. “Being a half-breed sucks, but being a woman around here sucks even more.”

“Why? Are you the only woman?” Lana asked, increasingly intrigued by Jill. She looked so small and fragile, yet she was training to be a Warrior.

“In the program, yes,” Jill grumbled. “The Vampire Council supplies blood donors to the Warriors, but they’re women.”

"So you're supposed to take blood from women?" Lana scrunched her nose. "That would be awkward."

"Exactly." Jill threw up her hands. "Especially when they don't want to have anything to do with you."

"So, the one that hit you was a blood donor?" Lana frowned looking at her face, which was still swollen and bruised.

Jill snorted, "Yeah, plus five other guys."

"Wow." Lana's eyes popped open. "Six guys? Well, were they cute?"

"For a human, you seem to be taking this blood donor stuff and me being a half-breed pretty well." Jill eyed her. "It doesn't freak you out?"

Lana thought for a minute before she laughed. "I read dead people." Among other things, but she didn't say that out loud. "It takes a lot to freak me out."

This time Jill's eyes popped open wide. "That is cool. Creepy, but wicked cool."

They both laughed. "Jill, I think we could be great friends."

"I'd like that," Jill nodded with a genuine smile. She could do with some more women on her side.

"Now, these guys, were they wicked hotties?" Lana grimaced. "I didn't use that word right, did I?"

"Ah, no," Jill laughed. "But yeah, actually they were, but it was so humiliating, and then Slade got all mad, but I was handling the situation…" Jill frowned and then laughed, shaking her head. "Why am I telling you all this?"

"Sometimes, it's nice to talk to someone not closely involved." Lana smiled back. She really liked this girl. "So what happened?"

"Slade happened." Jill frowned. "He got mad, started yelling and throwing guys through the wall. Now, he's mad at me, and it was Sid who sent them here."

"Who's Slade?" *Boy, there sure were a lot of Warriors with a name that started with an S,* she thought. How confusing was that!

"The doctor here." Jill didn't elaborate, but her mood soured. "Okay, let's get going on this before Sid comes in here being all bossy. Just give me all the details you can, and we can make changes as we go if I'm not getting it right."

Lana was surprised they had their own doctor and really wanted to know more, but figured Jill was finished. She started her description of the man. "I'm not sure how tall he was, but he was taller than me. He was very thin, almost skeleton-like. His face was long with prominent cheekbones, and his eyes were sunken and golden, but they turned red." Lana shivered, thinking of that moment.

"Red?" Jill glanced up.

Lana nodded. "When he first appeared, his eyes were golden like a vampire, but then he opened his mouth showing large fangs, and his eyes went from gold to a swirling red."

After a few seconds, Jill went back to sketching. "What color was his hair? Was it long or short?"

"It was black and short, but it was slicked back, and he has a receding hairline," Lana answered, and then sat quietly, wishing so badly she could talk to her sister. She suddenly felt way out of her league, but she had the chance to help the women who had been taken; she would do whatever she could. No one deserved what the women she witnessed through a dead man's eyes were living. It was a nightmare.

"Is this close?" Jill turned her book around showing the drawing.

Gasping Lana's hand went to her throat. "My God." She stared at the picture and felt true fear; his eyes stared at her from the page, giving her an eerie, creepy feeling. "That's him to the very last detail." Her voice shook as she stared at the picture. The drawing was so realistic; it seemed as if his bony hand could reach out and grab her again. She swallowed hard to keep the bile from rising into her throat at the uncanny resemblance.

"He's pretty creepy looking." Jill looked back at the drawing. "He do that to your neck?"

"Isn't that the question of the day?" Sid walked in, grabbing the picture and studying it before turning it to Lana. "This is the man you think is in charge?"

"Yes," Lana nodded, her eyes traveling from his large hands, up his muscled forearms and then up to his broad shoulders. Damn, he was built. She could feel the power radiating off him. A funny fluttery sensation that she hadn't felt in a long while hit the pit of her stomach and that was so not good.

Sighing, he put the picture down on Sloan's desk. "Jill, thank you." Sid finally took his gaze off Lana. "But I need to talk to Ms. Fitzpatrick."

Jill nodded and stood. "It was nice meeting you."

Lana smiled up at her. "Thanks, Jill. You're very talented. Maybe someday you can show me some of your other drawings that don't involve creepy men."

Jill laughed, "I would really like that."

"I'll talk to you in a few minutes, Jill," Sid said to her retreating back, but she didn't respond and closed the door behind her.

"Tell her you're sorry. She'll forgive you." Lana actually felt a little sorry for the huge vampire. She could tell by the long sigh that escaped he felt bad. "But my advice is to stay out of her business when it comes to guys."

Sid nodded, but didn't comment.

"Am I free to go now?" Lana stood, and then realized she still had on his jacket. When she started to remove it, he stopped her.

"Keep it." Sid frowned down at her. "Just get it back when you can."

"No, I can't." She pulled it off, handing it to him, already missing the warmth and delicious scent. Okay, she had to get over that real fast. "Where's Amy?"

"She's waiting for you." Sid turned, grabbing a pen and paper. "If you think of anything else, call." He handed her the paper.

"I will." Lana took it and slipped it into her pocket. No way in hell would she be calling him. *Not going to happen*, she thought.

"I warned Amy, and I'm going to warn you. Be careful. Don't be going out with guys you don't know," Sid warned, his face set in a stern mask.

"I usually don't," Lana frowned. "But Amy has a way of talking me into stuff. Tonight is a good example of that."

"Even though my cover is blown all to Hell, I'm glad she did." Sid picked up the picture again. "We are closer to finding the major player. I'm just sorry you were hurt in the process."

"It happens." Lana shrugged, nervously wondering what Amy had told him.

"She's a good friend," Sid grinned. "She wouldn't tell me anything, and I tried. And all she would think about was naked guys, and well, I can only take so much of that, so I stayed out of her head."

Lana laughed in relief. "Amy's head is the last place I'd want to be."

Sid smiled before looking at her neck, his smile fading. "You sure you're okay?" His voice held real concern.

"I'm fine," she lied. She was far from fine, but she would deal with it. She really didn't need anyone else looking at her as if she had lost her mind. She was already wondering that about herself. It was never easy doing what she did, but this time was different, and she felt so alone. She had to suck it up, as always.

Walking to the door, Sid opened it for her. "Thank you, Lana."

"You're welcome." She wondered at his sudden change of attitude. One minute he was calling her a liar and the next, he was thanking her. She was seriously confused by his mixed messages, her mixed emotions and her desire to kiss him goodbye. *Holy shit, where the hell did that thought come from?* She cringed. Clearing her head, she walked out of the room, finding Amy talking with Sloan, who also thanked her. As they made their way to the door, she turned. Sid was leaning in the doorway watching her; his intense gaze holding hers. A slow smile tilted his lips, causing her heart to skip a beat and making her step on Amy's heel.

"Damn, Lana." Amy jumped, hopping out the door. "What the hell is it with you and my feet tonight?"

Embarrassed, Lana practically pushed Amy out the door as a deep rumble of laughter followed her out.

"Damn, sexy-ass vampires," she muttered.

******

Sid watched the women leave and had a strong feeling that wasn't going to be the last of Lana and Amy. Something with those two women didn't add up.

"This is him?" Sloan sat behind his desk holding the picture Jill drew.

"Ugly son of a bitch, isn't he?" Sid walked up and sat in the chair Lana had been sitting in. He could still smell her fresh womanly scent.

Sloan nodded, staring at it for a minute longer. "I'll fax this out and hopefully get a hit. I'd say he won't be hard to miss." Sloan headed toward the fax machine. "Did you find out what happened with her neck?"

"No, but I will," Sid replied with confidence. "I believe those two have some big secrets that we need to know about."

"I'll do a check as soon as I fax this out." Sloan tapped in a number, sending out the picture. "I need a damn secretary to do this shit." Sloan tapped in more numbers, before hitting send.

"I know a few who would be qualified." Sid glanced at his phone, checking his texts.

"After what I saw and heard tonight with Jill and your picks, I don't think I trust your expertise on whose *qualified* and who's not." Sloan sat down behind his desk giving Sid a disgruntled glare.

"Hey, none of that was my fault." Sid frowned, thumbing toward the demolished entryway.

"As a matter of fact, get Jill and the guys in here. I need to find out what the hell happened out there," Sloan ordered, ignoring Sid's case of innocence. He knew Sid far too well to believe he was an innocent bystander.

"How the hell can I get blamed for something when I wasn't even here?" Sid stood and walked toward the door. "Changing my damn name to Sid 'Scapegoat' Sinclair."

******

Lana slammed the car door as hard as she could. "Are you crazy?"

The car started and took off. "That Warrior Sinclair got me all messed up. And look who's talking. You hit a damn Warrior. Punched him right in the face."

Looking at her partner, Lana rolled her eyes. "Don't even go there. You gave my real name." She tried to keep her anger in check, but this was bad. "What the hell were you thinking?"

"I'm sorry." Susan, aka Amy, sped down the road while lighting a cigarette. "I messed up. Why in the hell did you run?"

Lana wanted to smack the side of her friend's head. "Because VC….*shit*…Sinclair…whatever in the hell his name is, kept asking questions, questions that made me think he was on to us. I had to do something to make it legit."

"Yeah, he was getting a little weird," Susan frowned. "That should have clued us in when he started questioning us like a cop."

Lana cursed, "What a damn mess."

"But we did pull it off." Susan blew a long stream of smoke, and then grinned, pulling her wig off. "What was that shit all about not double-dating with me you were spouting?"

"These Warriors are smart. I figured they were listening, so I didn't want them suspicious of us whatsoever." Lana rolled down her window, letting the smoky air out. "And you do have the worst taste in men."

Susan shrugged, not really disagreeing. "Yeah, you're right about that."

"And never mention my sister again. She is *off* limits." Lana frowned at her, grabbed the rest of her cigarette and threw it out the window.

"Hey!" Susan cried out. "Those cost money."

"Yeah, well, you need to stop bumming money off me, so I say you can't afford to smoke." Lana frowned, and then cursed. "And next time, give me time to disguise myself. Dammit, Susan, how could you use my real name? This is going to bite me on the ass."

"I'm sorry," Susan repeated, pulling into their parking lot. "I'll take the heat for this one."

"Yes, you will." Lana looked at her, surprised that Susan thought she would take the blame.

Susan parked, turning off the car, but neither moved to get out. "What happened when you touched that vampire, Lana?"

Lana stared out the window. "The man who I saw, whoever he is, is very strong." She swallowed hard, her throat tender. It was hard to admit aloud, but deep inside, she wondered if they weren't in over their heads.

Susan pulled into a busy parking lot, parked and turned off the car. Both women just sat staring at the building.

"Well, guess it's time to face the music." Susan grabbed her bag taking the keys.

Lana got out of the car, impending doom settling around her. "Let's just hope he's in a good mood."

"Have you ever seen him in a good mood?" Susan snorted, unbuttoning two more buttons on her blouse.

"What are you doing?" Lana's eyes shot from her blouse to her face.

"We fucked up big time." Susan pushed her boobs up as she looked down at her handy work. "We need all the help we can get."

"There is no way…." Lana's tone was outraged until she glanced back at the building and frowned. "Better undo one more button. Have a feeling this is going to go very badly."

Chapter 8

Jill had just arrived at her room when her phone buzzed again. Sid had sent a group text wanting everyone to meet in Sloan's office. "You have got to be kidding me."

Tossing her sketchpad on her bed, she flopped down, lying back with her arms spread wide. Closing her eyes, she blindly reached for her sketchpad. With eyes still closed, she opened it to the page she knew by feel, by heart.

Slowly, her eyes opened to Slade's handsome face looking back at her. She captured him, as she would like to see him, smiling at her with that slow sexy smile. Her phone buzzed again, causing her to slam the sketchbook closed.

Grabbing her phone without looking at it, Jill stormed out of her room, heading down the hall toward Sloan's office. In no time, she had arrived. Walking in without making eye contact with anyone, she made it to the back of the room and leaned against the wall. Adam spotted her and made his way to her along with Steve.

"Damn!" Steve's eyes bugged out when he saw her face, but didn't ask anything else when she shot him a 'don't ask' look.

Adam just glanced at it. "You okay?"

She nodded without saying anything. Her eyes moved up, and of course, landed right on Slade. It was as if her eyes shared a special bond with the man. He wasn't looking at her, but his face was hard as stone, his eyes cold as ice, and it hurt to look at him.

Sloan walked in with his phone, which seemed to be attached to his ear. He didn't look too happy. "You better believe you will make this right!" Sloan yelled into the phone. "We've worked too hard to get this far to have you people screw this up." He scribbled something down, clicked his phone off and threw it on the desk. Looking at it for a minute, he picked it back up and threw it in a desk drawer, slamming it closed.

“Was that Hong Tong’s apologizing for messing up our order yesterday?” Sid grinned from his position in the chair next to Sloan’s desk. “I swear you can’t find good fast food today.”

“No, it wasn’t Hong fucking Tong’s, you dumbass,” Sloan growled, indicating he was not in the mood. He looked around at everyone and decided to save that conversation for last.

Even though she was mad at Sid, he always made her laugh, and now wasn’t any different. Glancing at Slade, she saw a small grin tip his lips.

Sloan seemed to get his thoughts together before he spoke. “Jared explained a little of what happened out there.” Sloan thumbed toward the entryway. “It *will* get cleaned up by tomorrow. It *will* look exactly as it did before.” It was an order. His voice allowed no room for debate.

“I got a crew coming first thing in the morning,” Sid replied where he sat sprawled in his chair.

Sloan ignored Sid, which he did frequently. His eyes landed on Jill, then scanned to Steve before finally resting on Adam. “I am going to say this once and once only.” Sloan’s tone had a final edge, indicating he was done with the bullshit. “I have no problems transferring any of you out of here. You are not in charge of anything.” His eyes stayed on Adam. “The next time you decide to disobey orders, I will put you on report. If you are already on report, your ass is gone, and it will not be a transfer. Do you understand me?”

“Yes, Sir,” the three answered in unison.

“Good, now get the hell out of here.” Sloan’s eyes stayed on Adam as an extra warning.

Jill was more than happy to get out of the room and moved quickly, not looking at anyone.

“You stay, Jill.” Sloan’s voice stopped her instantly.

“Shit,” slipped out of her mouth before she could stop it. Sid’s chuckle reached her ears which pissed her off, because whatever she was about to get chewed out for, was his fault. Back-stepping, she found the wall again.

“Is there a problem between you two?” Sloan glanced between her and Slade.

Jill hesitated before shaking her head. “No, Sir.” Glancing over, her eyes met Slade’s.

“Slade?” Sloan pushed.

Slade turned his eyes away from her to Sloan. “Any problems between Jill and me are between us and will be taken care of by us.”

The temperature in the room dropped considerably. Sloan slammed his hand on the desk, making Jill jump. “Putting a hole through my wall and beating the hell out of someone is not taking care of it.” Sloan glared at Slade then Jill. “You need to feed. We have blood donors already in place. Use them. I don’t want to hear another word about this issue. Is that understood?”

“Yes, Sir,” Jill replied, wishing she would have kept her damn mouth shut about the whole situation.

“Get your anger in check.” Sloan turned his attention to Slade. “I need you here and would hate to have to send you packing because of something like this. It's not worth putting a blemish on your record."

Those words hit Jill hard. Her eyes hit the floor, her insides shaking as nausea burned her stomach. At that moment, she knew that no matter what she did, she could be a blemish on someone's record.

"If anyone attacks a fellow Warrior with words, or physically, I will do whatever I have to do." Slade's voice was deep as he looked around to every Warrior there except her. "I would expect the same from any of you. So put whatever you want on my record."

Sloan remained quiet as he and Slade stared in a battle of wills. Sloan finally broke the silence. "But she isn't a Warrior yet."

"No, but she is a woman who deserves respect, and I will uphold that as I know everyone in this room would." Slade straightened off the wall. "So if you have a problem with that, then you best kick me out now."

Jill's eyes flew from the floor to Slade. "No." Jill took a step forward. "This wasn't his fault."

"So it's yours?" Sloan's eyes pinned her to the spot.

"No, it's mine." Sid shook his head. "I will kick my own ass later. So can we stop and put the blame where it is? Jill had no idea about any of this. It won't happen again."

"Make sure that it doesn't," Sloan growled the warning. "I don't have time to deal with this shit. We have too much going on and we're spread thin. I can't afford to lose anyone because they're thinking with their cock."

Jill's eyes narrowed and she had to bite her tongue…hard.

Sloan glanced her way. "You better get a tough skin, little girl." Sloan eyed her with warning. "If you want to be a Warrior, you better be prepared to be treated like one."

Digging deep, Jill found the courage to open her mouth. She was pissed. "I have never asked to be treated differently. I was handling the situation on my own. I didn't need anyone with a…" Jill swallowed hard, "cock to step in. I may not have a cock, but I have more heart than any of the trainees with a cock."

Everyone had turned to look at her, but she kept her eyes on Sloan whose mouth quirked at the corner.

"It seems others in this room have a problem that I don't have a cock, and that's their problem, not mine." Her voice was strong and just below a shout. Jesus, how many times had she said cock? She couldn't stop staying cock. Her eyes burned fire. "It doesn't take a cock to be a Warrior, and I'm going to prove it. I'll feed from one of those bitches if I have to knock their fake asses out to do it. So this issue is finished, done and taken care of without the help of anyone with a cock. Now, am I dismissed?"

Sloan's eyes crinkled at the edges, but he didn't say a word, just nodded.

Knocking into chairs, she walked with purpose to the door that seemed a million miles away. Jill slowed down as she reached Slade. Reaching up, she pointed in his face. "Stay away from me and my business. I don't need your help, and I *will not* be blamed for you getting thrown out of here."

Slade stared down into her eyes; no grin lit his face, but respect gleamed in those golden eyes. When she went to move past him, he grabbed her arm. "We will have a discussion as soon as I'm done here, so do not leave." When she went to pull her arm away, he pulled her closer, leaning down, not caring if everyone was watching. "I, for one, am glad you don't have a…cock."

As soon as Slade loosened his grip, Jill was out the door, wondering what the hell his words had meant. Damn him and his touch, which still tingled on her arm. Walking across the demolished entryway, Jill kicked a piece of drywall, sending it sailing through the air against an undamaged wall, damaging it. “Why the hell did you have to open your mouth!” Jill cursed at herself. “Cock…really? Oh. My. God.” She put her head in her hands letting her feet find her room.

******

It took every bit of control that Sid possessed not to bust out laughing. His respect just grew for that little girl. For her to stand in front of them all saying her piece without breaking down into tears, but standing straight and proud, was a sight to see.

Looking around at everyone, he grinned. “How many times do you think she said cock?”

At that, everyone did laugh, even Sloan.

“Damn, you guys are bad enough.” Sloan rubbed his eyes, chuckling and groaning at the same time. “But now I have a little wisp of a girl running around wanting to be one of us, and so far, she’s proving up to the task. This may actually be what kills me.”

“Well, at least me and my cock won’t be to blame. Which will be a first.” Sid smacked his hands together, standing up. “Now, if that’s all, I’ve got shit to do.”

“Sit your ass down,” Sloan demanded. “I just got off the phone with the Campbell County Sheriff Department’s Special Unit.”

“Ah, didn’t know they had a special unit,” Jared frowned. “They’re a small department.”

"They are a small department, and no one knew they had a special unit except for the special unit." Sloan leaned back in his chair. "Seems our Ms. Fitzpatrick and her partner Amy were also working undercover."

"You're shitting me!" Jared frowned. "They totally ousted our cover."

"Exactly, and that's why I have demanded they give us any information they've obtained to this point and disperse the unit. If they are not working with us, they are working against us," Sloan informed them. "After a few threats, they saw it my way when I informed their leader I would be calling the Feds to investigate their investigation. It's too dangerous for us to be out there, not knowing who is on whose side."

"So let me get this straight." Sid had leaned forward, his eyes intense. "My cover was blown all to hell because someone in the Campbell County Sheriff's Department decided to set up their own sting without informing the area departments or us?"

"Pretty much sums it up," Sloan nodded.

"So is the profile pic legit?" Sid's tone didn't have the easy-going edge it usually did.

"Yes. It seems that one of our undercover girls does have the ability to read the dead, but that's not the best part." Sloan smiled for the first time since he started chewing ass. "The dead seem to search her out, and she has had contact with some of the women who have been killed, but something is blocking them once they make contact. This is the reason they decided to start their sting."

"And she's a cop?" Sid frowned. He knew all the cops in the area, or at least thought he did.

"Didn't get into the details, but it seems so." Sloan replied, glancing at his phone. "Waiting for a call back from the Chief."

Sid sat back to soak the information in. If it didn't piss him off so badly, he'd be laughing, but to have his cover blown when he had been so close was something he didn't find amusing.

"I'm going to change things up a bit." Sloan eyed Sid for a few seconds. "You're in charge of the investigation. No more undercover work. I'm surprised, with all your press photos from a month ago, you haven't been made out yet."

"Who's going to be undercover?" Sid looked around.

"Slade, if we need him," Sloan informed everyone. "He is our best bet because not too many people know about him yet. He's been low-profile."

Nodding, Sid looked to Sloan. "So you want me to take care of the Sheriff's Department?"

"Be my guest." Sloan scribbled something down, tossing it to Sid. "But don't make me regret putting you in total charge."

Sid grinned, "I'll do ya proud, Dad."

"God, what a scary-ass thought," Sloan shook his head. "Now, get the fuck out of my office, and get that shit out there cleaned up."

Sid was the last to leave. "So I can pull any of their people to work with us?"

"It hasn't been confirmed, but that is what is going to happen, so if you have any problems with that let me know." Sloan picked up his phone, tapping in a number, and dismissing him.

"Perfect," Sid's smile was a little evil as he walked out. He had been trying to decide the best way to get to Lana Fitzpatrick, because there was no way he was letting her get away without getting to know her better. As luck would have it, they were going to be partners. Sid laughed as another thought entered his head. Fuck the partner thing. He was going to be her boss.

******

Adam waited until the Warriors had left Sloan's office before he stepped out of the shadows. He stepped inside to find Sloan behind his desk with his head leaning back on the chair.

"What is it, Adam?" Sloan didn't open his eyes, didn't move his head.

"I want back on the case." Adam stopped in front of his desk.

Sloan sighed, lifting his head, and slowly opening his eyes. "You're too close to this case. You've already proven that."

Adam looked away for a split second before looking back. "I know what I did was wrong."

"Do you?" Sloan crossed his arms, leaning back. "You defied my orders by going in alone to interrogate Jeff, who was close to breaking. Instead of staying back and learning from Sid, you decided to take matters into your own hands, which didn't end very well. The only person who knows where Angelina's is, is now dead, because you couldn't control your rage."

Standing straight, Adam nodded. "I know that, Sir, but I've learned from my mistake, and it will never happen again."

"You haven't learned shit." Sloan eyed him, not pulling punches. "Just tonight, you defied me again and followed. Then, you about got yourself killed because you went after a woman who may or may not have had answers about Angelina. So no, you are off this case."

“This is bullshit!” Adam’s one golden eye turned black.

Sloan stood, placing both hands on his desk. “Don’t push me on this, Adam. Your rage is putting you and everyone else in danger. Until you get it under control, you are in training only. After tonight, you will no longer be advised on the case.”

“Fuck this.” Adam turned, heading for the door. “And fuck this program.”

“If you think for one minute we won’t hunt you, Adam, you’re wrong,” Sloan called out.

Adam stopped, and turned his head to stare at Sloan. “What does that mean?”

“If you leave, you’re out of the Warrior program. If you fuck up out there, we will be hunting you down,” Sloan warned. “I would seriously think about what you’re doing.”

“I’m not going to sit here and do nothing. None of them would either, and you know it.” Adam turned away to leave, but added, “I quit the program.”

Heading to his room, Adam felt his rage building. He knew he was on the edge, and anything could put him over. He hadn’t meant to kill Jeff, even though he wanted the son of a bitch dead, but Jeff always knew what buttons to push with him, and he pushed him too far. Without thought, Adam’s hand had beaten the hell out of him, and then with no memory of doing it, he’d ripped Jeff’s heart out. That was how Jared and Sid had found him: kneeling next to Jeff with his heart in his hand.

He squeezed his eyes shut trying to shake the memory. Slamming open his door, he went to his closet, grabbing a duffle bag and tossing it on his bed. Grabbing whatever clothes his hands touched, he shoved them in the bag. He ignored the knock on the door and walked into the bathroom with the bag, shoving whatever he could inside.

“Adam?” Tessa had let herself in, her eyes going to the bag as he walked out of the bathroom.

“Go away, Tessa.” Adam didn’t even look at her. Grabbing his jacket, he headed toward the door, but she stepped in his way.

“Where you going?” Tessa tried to get him to look her in the eyes. “Adam, what’s going on?”

“I’m leaving.” Adam’s tone was level, no emotion. “I quit the program.”

“You what?” Tessa frowned; anger furrowed her brow. “Why in the world would you quit the program?”

“Give Gramps a kiss for me.” Adam went to step around her, but she stepped in his way again. “Tessa, get out of my way. Nothing you can do or say will change my mind on this.”

“I’m not going to let you do this, Adam.” Tessa grabbed his bag. “You need to stop acting like this and grow up. Take responsibility for your actions.”

“You don’t know what the fuck you’re talking about!” Adam screamed at her. He pulled his bag away from her grip. “It is my fault Angelina is gone, and now, I’ve been forbidden to help in the search for her.”

Tessa, being a redhead and the older sister, didn’t know when to back down. “Then you should have followed the rules.” She pointed at him. “You killed Jeff. Jared was close to getting him to talk, yet you went in there and killed him. You’re lucky all they did was take you off the case."

"You have no clue what happened, so just shut the fuck up," Adam hissed then, without another thought, pushed her into the wall out of his way. Her head slumped forward as she slid down the wall.

Adam watched in horror as his sister sank to the floor. "Oh, God!" he cried out grabbing her before her head hit the floor. "Tessa!" He shook her, but she didn't wake. Checking, he found a pulse.

Tessa moaned, but wouldn't wake.

"I'm so sorry." Adam placed a kiss on her forehead. Grabbing his bag, he ran out the door sending a text on the run, praying his sister would be okay. She had to be okay. If she wasn't, he would turn himself in to Jared, because his life would be over anyway. But first, he had to find Angelina.

Chapter 9

Lana frowned, twirling her finger around the rim of her glass of water. It had been two days since she'd had her ass chewed because of the fiasco. Their whole operation had been scrapped. She and Susan had been put on leave, which was okay at the moment; she'd been informed her new boss was going to be VC Warrior Sid Sinclair, and he would contact her when she was needed. She actually moaned at the thought.

"Are you okay?"

Jerking, Lana almost knocked over the water. Her eyes shot to Doug Lawson, her date. "Oh, yes." Damn, she forgot where the hell she was for a minute. She had already cancelled on him twice, and almost forgot about their date tonight. "Hunger pain," she smiled, and then rolled her eyes at her explanation when he turned to wave down a waiter.

They had already ordered, but he asked the waiter for a few rolls until their meal came. Lana studied him with a critical eye. He was handsome, had wonderful manners and seemed nice enough. He was a lawyer for a firm in Cincinnati. He had kind, gorgeous green eyes; his raven black hair was business short. When he had taken her hand to help her out of the car, his felt too soft. Staring at him, she wondered what sex would be like with him. She'd bet her last dollar it wouldn't be as exciting as sex with Sid Sinclair. She'd bet everything she had that sex with that Warrior would be an experience not easily forgotten. God, she was awful, sitting with a man who would be perfect for her, but thinking of sex with another. She had always been a sexual person, but this wasn't right.

"I'm really glad you accepted my invite, Lana." He smiled, taking a sip of his wine.

He wouldn't think that if he knew she was comparing sex with him and another man. Not really knowing what to say, Lana smiled, taking a sip of her wine. Her phone buzzed in her purse, making her strangle on her wine. Grabbing her napkin, she covered her mouth as her eyes watered.

She waved him down when he started to stand to help her. “I’m fine.” She cleared her throat. “I’m fine, but I’m sorry, I have to get that. I’m on call.”

Doug nodded, but didn’t look happy.

Digging for her phone, Lana prayed it was Susan texting her about a bad date or something stupid. Taking a deep breath, she clicked it on.

To whatever your name is, aka Lana Fitzpatrick.

555 Apple Lane. Take a right onto dirt road. Stop at the hill. I expect you in the next 15 minutes. Your time starts, now.

Sincerely, your boss,

Sid Sinclair

“Shit!” Lana looked at the time on her phone. There was no way she was going to be able to make it back home, change and get to this address in fifteen damn minutes. “What an asshole!”

“Excuse me?” Doug glanced around, giving a nervous smile to the older couple next to them.

Dammit, she’d forgotten where she was again. This date was a total failure. She was pretty sure this would be the last time Doug asked her out, and what she was about to ask him would surely make that a fact. “I need a favor.” She gave him her sexiest smile, hoping it would do the trick.

*****

Sid stood staring at the bodies of two young girls. He had always been able to separate his feelings when it came to cruelty, but this was a little too much. Flashes from the crime scene camera illuminated the woods. Sid looked away to the time on his phone. Glancing up the hill, he watched a car pull to a stop.

"Make sure you send a copy of those to me, Dana." Sid turned and started up the hill, but stopped. A man he didn't know got out, walking quickly around to the passenger side. Opening the door, he helped a woman in a tight, black short dress and 'fuck me' shoes out of the car. Her hair was silky black, smoothed back on one side and hanging loose to her breasts on the other. The V of her dress dipped low, exposing enough cleavage to make a man go to his knees. She turned sideways, and Sid's eyes slid down her body then back up in a slow appreciative slide. Her voice made its way to his ears, and he immediately knew who it was. "Jesus." Sid felt his body respond. A growl rumbled in his chest as the man slid his hand to her lower back as she looked around.

"Okay, got the shots. Pretty much finished, so when the coroner gets here, they can do their thing." Dana said, walking up next to Sid. When Sid didn't respond, he glanced up the hill. "Damn man, who is that nice piece of ass?"

Sid didn't even look his way; he couldn't pull his eye off her. "You like your job, Dana?"

"Ah, yeah." Dana frowned, looking away from the woman.

"Then watch your fucking mouth." Sid looked away long enough to shoot the skinny crime scene photographer a warning. It didn't matter that he was thinking the same thing, but now that he knew who it was, he didn't like anyone else thinking it, and didn't that just surprise the shit out of him.

Dana didn't say a word; he knew better, so he headed in the opposite direction.

Jared, who just finished walking the crime scene, passed Dana, who looked like he was ready to piss himself and stopped next to Sid. "They weren't killed here?" When Sid didn't respond, Jared glanced up the hill and laughed. Knowing right off who it was, Jared shook his head. "Oh, shit. Sid has left the wooded clearing." Jared walked away, knowing Sid was on a mission to score with the hot little number up the hill.

Sid didn't look his way, but continued to watch her. Finally, she spotted him, and then looked at the hill with a frown. Grabbing onto the man's arm, she took off one shoe then started for the other. Sid cursed and climbed the hill quickly.

"Who the fuck are you?" Sid eyed the man who was busy looking at a nice display of shapely leg.

The man's eyes shot from her legs to Sid, who stood intimidatingly close. "Doug Lawson." The man looked Sid over from head to foot, a frown forming across his face. "Her date. Who are you?"

Sid cocked his eyebrow at that. "Her boss. Sorry to cut your night short," Sid grinned, indicating he wasn't sorry at all.

Lana just stood watching the men, not sure exactly what was going on, but the air crackled with testosterone.

"Take your time." Doug smiled down at Lana, who was pulling his donated sweater over her breasts. "I'll wait here for you unless you need me."

"I think we got this, Dan." Sid nodded, stepping over the railroad tie, holding his hand out to Lana.

“It’s Doug.” The man’s eyes narrowed.

“Whatever.” He helped her step over the railroad tie and decided to take it a bit further. “We’re going to be a while. I’ll make sure she gets home safe.” With that, Sid picked her up and headed down the hill.

“What are you doing?” Lana squirmed, wanting down. She looked over his shoulder at Doug, who was staring at them. “I’ll call you. I’m sorry about this. Thanks for a wonderful evening.”

“Dave is a douche,” Sid growled, setting her down as soon as he heard the car pull away.

“His name is Doug, and he’s not a douche.” Lana frowned, pulling her dress that had ridden up to her thighs down. “He’s a nice, successful lawyer.”

“Lawyer?” Sid snorted. “So he’s a successful douche who is an expert liar.”

“Did you do that to make him mad?”

“Yes.” Sid smiled, showing his sharp fangs. “But since you took off your ‘fuck me’ shoes….”

“My what?” Lana’s head snapped back.

“‘Fuck me’ shoes.” Sid grinned.

“That’s sexual harassment.” Lana eyed him, crossing her arms, which inadvertently pushed her breasts together. The sweater Doug had tried to cover them with had parted.

“So is that dress, but you don’t hear me complaining.” Sid looked her up and down, an appreciative gleam in his golden eyes.

Lana rolled her eyes. “I was on a date, and you didn’t give me time to get home and change into work clothes.” When he started to say something, she continued quickly, not giving him a chance to speak, which made him smile. “So what was so important that you needed me so quickly?”

“Two dead girls, which I believe are connected to all the missing reports.” Sid nodded down the hill. “I was hoping you could use your voodoo hoodoo stuff to see if you can get any information.”

Lana frowned up at him. “I don’t do voodoo or hoodoo. I’m a medium.”

“Whatever it is, we need you, but is it safe?” Sid glanced at her neck. She wore a pale red silky scarf as a choker around her bruised neck, and damn if that wasn’t sexy as hell. He wanted to tear it off with his fangs.

Lana stared at him for a long time. “I guess since I’m working with you, I need to be honest.”

“That would be a great start to our working relationship,” Sid agreed with a nod. “But if doing this is going to be a repeat of what happened before, we will find a different way to find out information.”

“I think it will be fine,” Lana replied. “Lead the way.”

Sid bent down, picking her up to carry her the rest of the way. “Next time, keep a change of clothes in your car with a pair of shoes.”

“Next time, don’t call me while I’m on a date, or at least give me enough time to change,” Lana shot back.

Sid frowned. "Until this is over, your dating life is being cut short." At least, he was going to make sure she was too busy to date. When Sid saw something he wanted, he became territorial. He decided as soon as she stepped out of that car, that he wanted her. Hell, who was he kidding? When she had punched him in the face, he had wanted to grab her, throw her down and take her in so many ways it even shocked him. Okay, that wasn't true; it didn't shock him at all.

"You may be my boss now, but that doesn't include my off time." Lana frowned at the side of his face.

"Wanna bet?" Sid's response was confident and final.

******

Lana wanted to respond to Sid's cocky remark, but as he slid her body down his to put her down, her complaint disappeared. He had a wicked gleam in his eye that caused her heartbeat to pick up and her mouth to malfunction. Oh boy, she might be in a little trouble where this huge vampire was concerned; she wondered briefly if the trouble would be worth it. The heat in his eyes and the tingling between her legs told her it would be very worth it.

"What do you need me to do?" Sid asked, his eyes never leaving hers.

And wasn't that a loaded question. Getting naked would be a start. "About what?"

A sexy grin tipped his lips as if reading her mind. "As soon as we are finished here, I will be taking you somewhere that I can really answer that question, but right now, we need to focus on work."

That snapped Lana out of her horny thoughts. It had been way too long since she had sex with a man and not her well-used vibrator, Thor. Yes, she named her vibrator. "That's what I meant. I was talking about work. What do you mean what do I want you to do…about work?"

Sid chuckled. “I’m going to enjoy you.” Sid’s eyes crinkled at the corners, but the heat in his eyes burned her to her very soul.

Not knowing what the hell to say and afraid of opening her mouth for fear of what would come out of it, Lana looked around. Spotting the police tape a few yards away, she frowned, pushing thoughts of Sid naked to the back of her mind.

“Who found them?” Lana headed down a clean path, easier for her feet to take, toward the girls.

“Two hunters.” Sid watched the ground, making sure the path was clear. “Be careful, there’s some thorns.”

Lana avoided the prickly thorns, totally surprised by his consideration. Taking a glance at his strong profile, her stomach did that weird jittery jump indicating that she was in deep trouble. Inches from the tape, Lana stopped and grabbed onto Sid’s arm, her eyes going blank and staring straight ahead. “They’re here,” Lana whispered.

“Who’s here?” Sid’s body went on guard as he looked around, his body ready to protect. “Who the fuck is here, Lana?”

“Them. The girls.” Her eyes cleared as she looked over at the bodies. “The brown-haired girl is Megan Cooper.”

Sid’s eyes widened slightly. “She told you that?”

Lana shushed him, but didn’t let go of his arm. “Dammit.” Lana’s body tensed.

“What?” Sid looked around for a threat.

“Someone is trying to block me from connecting with them.” Lana’s face was pinched. “Come on, girls, fight. Tell me more,” she demanded.

"I seriously don't know if I like this." Sid, still in warrior-mode, looked around, ready for anything that came their way.

Jared had made his way next to them, hearing the conversation. "Honestly, it creeps me the fuck out."

Lana ignored them both. Letting go of Sid's arm, she rushed to the girls. Saying a prayer to keep her safe, she calmed herself with a few deep breaths as she knelt next to their bodies, taking a real close look at each of them.

"My God, they can't be any older than eighteen." Lana frowned, looking at the girls, trying to be professional and keeping her emotions out of it. Forcing her emotions aside, Lana really looked as a cop would look at the crime scene. "I don't think they've been raped."

"What makes you think that?" Sid knelt down next to her.

"No marks. Their clothes are perfectly fine. Not a rip on them. Has everything been processed?" Lana frowned, looking over the girls carefully.

"Yes," Jared answered, also looking them over.

Lana reached out, lifting one of the girl's short skirts up slightly. "No bruising." Looking around the area with a cop's eye, she spoke to Sid. "They weren't killed here."

"No, they weren't," Jared answered with respect. He was impressed that this woman, who had just arrived, knew that with one sweep of her eyes.

"Don't break me away once I touch them," Lana warned both men.

"If what happened last time happens, I'm not going to sit here and watch you get attacked or whatever the hell happened." Sid's tone implied he wasn't going to budge on that.

"Just please, try not to do that." Lana looked away. "I really don't want to get stuck in their last memories of life."

"Then don't do this." Sid shook his head. "If it's not safe for you, we will think of something else."

"Nothing we do in our line of work is safe, but I have an opportunity to find out information we could never learn otherwise. It's worth the risk," Lana argued. "Just don't break me away."

Sid started to say something else, but Lana quickly grabbed onto Megan's cold, lifeless hand. She was now reliving Megan's last hours of life.

"Shit!" Sid cursed, his eyes on Lana, ready for whatever was to come.

Both men watched as Lana's spine straightened; her head flipped to the sky with eyes wide open. A slow smile spread across her wide red lips and stayed for a few minutes until it started to fade into a frown. Her body jerked once, her hand raised slowly out in front of her in a gesture of confusion and fear. Sid could feel the emotions radiating off her.

"Is she okay?" Jared asked. His stance was firm as he stood over her, watching with concern.

"I don't fucking know, but I don't like this shit," Sid hissed, ready to pouncc. "I can't tcll if she is in trouble or not."

Suddenly, Lana let go, falling back, but Sid stopped her from landing on her ass. A loud gasp escaped her throat as she blinked her eyes, quickly trying to focus.

“Are you okay?” Sid brought her face to his. “Hey!”

Lana finally focused on him and nodded, “I’m good.” A small smile of triumph reached her eyes. “They were last at a motel in Alexandria. I know the place.”

“Let’s go!” Jared was already leaving the area, barking orders to uniformed officers who were left guarding the area until the coroner came.

Sid helped Lana up as a uniformed officer walked over. “You get something, Lana?”

Lana turned, glancing at the officer. “Yeah, Fred,” she nodded. “Finally.”

“Good, these people need to be stopped.” He nodded to Lana then Sid before turning his sad gaze to the girls.

Sid watched Lana give the officer the information to pass on to the coroner. She had at least obtained one name, so it shouldn’t be hard for them to find out who the second girl was so their families could be contacted. Once she was finished, he picked her up and headed up the hill, a new respect for this woman filling him along with the need to possess her.

Chapter 10

Slade ran to Adam's room, practically running Damon down in the process. He heard heavy boots behind him. He was sure with the urgency on his face he didn't have to explain anything to Damon.

He passed Jill, who had opened up her door, sticking her head out at the noise of them running down the hall. He practically busted the door off its hinges as he flew into Adam's room.

Damon followed, spotting Tessa on the floor. "Dammit!"

Jill stepped into the room and gasped. "Tessa." She ran over, but Slade stopped her.

"Don't touch her," Slade ordered, going down to the ground. He put his fingers to her neck, feeling for a pulse. Relief shadowed his face as he checked each eye. "Tessa!"

A sigh of relief filled the room when her eyes fluttered; a low moan escaped her lips.

"What the hell happened?" Damon asked, looking around trying to figure it out.

"I'm not sure, but I got a text from Adam saying she was in his room unconscious." Slade glanced at Jill. "Get me a cold rag."

Jill scrambled to her feet, running to do as ordered. Rushing back, she handed him a cool, wet washcloth. "Here."

"Tessa, open your eyes. Come on. Open them for me. I know you hear me," Slade urged her.

“Where’s Jared?” Jill asked, watching Tessa trying to focus once her eyes were open.

“He’s with Sid.” Damon walked away. “I’ll call him.”

“Don’t tell him anything other than he needs to get back right away.” Slade leaned down in Tessa’s vision and held the cool washcloth against her neck.

“I’m not going to have to say anything.” Damon frowned walking out of the room. “He’s going to know.”

Tessa finally became aware and tried to sit up. “Whoa, Tessa.” Slade stopped her. “Not so fast.”

“Listen to him, Tessa,” Jill urged when she continued to struggle. “We need to make sure you’re okay.”

“Do you have any pain?” Slade watched her closely. “Can you move your fingers?”

“Yeah.” She squeezed her eyes shut, moving her fingers. “My head hurts.”

“I’m going to try to sit you up, okay? Tell me right away if anything hurts.” Slade leaned down, wedging his arm under her shoulders. Slowly, he set her up against the wall. “You okay?”

Tessa nodded slightly, but winced. Her shaking hand went to her head. After a minute, her eyes popped open, still slightly unfocused, and searched the room. “Where’s Adam?”

“Did he do this?” Slade asked, anger edging his words.

"He didn't mean to." Tessa's eyes filled with tears. "He's messed up right now. He didn't mean to hurt me."

Slade cursed under his breath as his eyes met Jill's. Picking her up carefully, Slade stood. "I'm going to take you to my office for a little while so I can keep an eye on you, okay?"

Tessa didn't say anything as tears flowed down her cheeks.

"Can I do anything?" Jill asked, following them out of Adam's room.

Slade turned meeting her stare. "Try to get in contact with Adam." He frowned. "But stay away from him."

Jill nodded, pulling her phone out of her back pocket.

"I mean it, Jill," Slade warned. "Don't go near him. Just try to find out where he is."

Slade waited until Jill nodded her understanding, before he walked out the door, meeting Damon. "Did you get Jared?"

Damon was staring at Tessa who had stopped crying; she had her eyes closed against Slade's chest. "Yeah, he's on his way."

"Good. I'm taking her to my office." Slade moved past him. "I'm pretty sure she has a concussion, but and I want to keep an eye on her."

"I'll tell him as soon as he gets here." Damon's eyes flared. "Did Adam do this?"

Slade's eyes darkened as he nodded. "He needs to be found." The words and warning in Slade's eyes were enough for Damon to understand they may have a rogue on the loose.

******

Lana, Sid and Jared stood outside the rundown motel, which only totaled one floor of six rooms. The white paint peeled from days of harsh weather and neglect.

"This place looks shut down," Jared frowned, looking around.

"It is." Lana moved to the last room on the end, staring at it. "You have a flashlight?"

"No." Sid passed her, walking up to the door. "We see perfectly at night and don't need them. Is this the room?"

"Are you sure this is right?" Jared walked up behind them. "It doesn't look like this place has been used in years."

Lana smiled. "I'm sure." She nudged Sid out of the way. Leaning down, she reached behind a thin, leafless bush, pushing a large rock out of the way.

Sid backed up, watching her tight dress slide up her thick, firm thighs. "Damn," he mumbled, his eyes heating as they moved down her legs and back to her ass again. Adjusting himself, he tried to stay focused.

"I can't believe it's here." Lana turned around with a huge smile and a key. She caught Sid's eyes roaming her lower half while Jared stood silently laughing. "What?"

Jared just shook his head, grabbing the key and unlocking the door.

Sid stopped Lana before she could go inside. "Do not wear that dress again when on duty," Sid growled, the heat in his words searing her to the spot.

A feeling of power over the gorgeous vampire set Lana on fire as she watched him move past her, following Jared inside the room. "Then give me more time to dress appropriately for work," she shot back, and then followed them inside.

"What the hell is this place?" Jared frowned.

"It's a place teenagers come to do…" Lana lit a candle that was on a small damaged table, "things."

"Such as?"

"Make out; drink, you know, teenage stuff." Lana held the candle up, looking around. She found more candles and began lighting them so she could see. Finally, the room was aglow with candle light.

"Did you do teenage stuff here?" Sid glanced at her.

"Oh, yeah," she grinned. She had actually lost her virginity here with Mason Barton, but she kept that piece of information to herself.

"By the look on your face, I'd say you did more than make out here," Jared chuckled.

"I'll never tell," Lana chuckled. "I can't believe kids still come here." By the look of the place, they still took care of this room just like they did when she was young and foolish, looking for a place to experiment the joys of growing up.

Going over beside the bed, she picked up a small trashcan, pouring the contents out. Rubber wrappers and beer cans scattered across the bed.

"Find anything?" Sid asked walking over.

"No, not really." Lana took off her shoe, using the heel to poke around in the trash.

"They weren't killed here," Sid observed. "It's too clean, and I don't think whoever killed them would stay around and tidy the place."

"No, they weren't killed here, though I wasn't sure from her memories. I haven't been in this room for over ten years, but I know they were here." Lana used her shoe to push the trash back in the can. "As soon as I connected with Megan, they were walking out of here. I was just hoping we would find something here. I did get a look of the guy they were here with. Maybe Jill can do a profile pic."

"Did it seem like they were forced from here?" Jared asked.

"No, not at all." Lana frowned. "When I do a reading, sometimes I see events as they happen and sometimes it's scattered in no certain timeline. When I read Vincent, it was a total replay of his hours before death. With this girl Megan, things came in flashes. I saw the outside of this motel and knew they had been here, but wasn't sure if this is where they were killed. It can get very confusing and sometimes none of it makes sense. Before they take their last breath is when I'm released."

"Did you see this room just as it is?" Sid asked, leaning against the wall.

"Yes. They were laughing and having a good time. There was another guy here, a little older than them, but they seemed comfortable with him. I know they left this room alive because of this." Lana walked over and pointed at a carved initial in the doorframe by the lock.

Sid watched her running her finger over the initial when she turned quickly. "What?" He pushed himself from the wall.

"Damn, I almost forgot." She hurried past Sid, heading toward the small bathroom. Across from it was a small closet. Throwing the door open, she took the candle from the table, holding it up to the wall. Hundreds of names were scribbled across the walls of the closet. Looking for the area that had free space, she began to search and found what she was looking for. Touching the name Megan Cooper, she smiled when underneath was yesterday's date. Next to it was the name Ben Foster with the same date. And underneath those was Amanda Turner. "They were here yesterday. I would say. The other girl's name is Amanda Turner, and it looked like they were here with a Ben Foster."

"What is this?" Sid looked at the wall of the small closet.

"Whenever you used the room, you signed in." Lana shook her head. "And it looks like the tradition stuck."

"Is your name on the wall?" Jared teased.

Lana looked around and found it. "Right there." She pointed to her name with a large smile. It had been so long since she went down memory lane. "And that was my boyfriend at the time, Mason Barton."

"Mason?" Sid grunted with a frown. "What kind of name is Mason?"

Putting the candle on the shelf, Lana grinned at Jared. "He was the quarterback on the football team. Took the team to state as a matter of fact."

"Yeah, he's probably gay," Sid snorted.

She made a purring sound. "Oh, he was far from gay." Lana bent over, looking at more names, her ass sticking in the air.

"Damn, man, I'm wanting to tap that." An unknown voice filled the room.

Sid, Jared and Lana all turned, aiming their guns at the voice.

"Whoa, shit!" The guy's hands went straight up in the air.

"Don't move a fucking muscle, asshole," Jared growled as he made his way toward the guy, gun still aimed.

Once Jared had him up against the wall and patted down, Sid and Lana relaxed.

"Where in the hell did that come from?" Sid stared at her gun, putting his own gun in the waist of his jeans.

Lana put her foot up on the bed, lifting her tight skirt high. Strapped to her firm thigh was a holster. Looking over her shoulder at Sid, she grinned as she re-holstered her gun. "I never go anywhere without my gun."

Sid watched as she put her foot back on the ground before she shimmied her skirt back down. "Son of a bitch." Sid shook his head, trying to clear the image of that holster strapped to her thigh. "It's a damn good thing we aren't alone in this room."

Seeing the heated look in his golden eyes had Lana swallowing hard, and it wasn't her stomach tingling this time. Her whole body tingled as her nipples hardened under his stare. "Why is that?" *Oh, Lana, you did not go there,* she mentally scolded herself.

His eyes moved from her body to her face in a slow, mind-blowing glance. "I'll show you later." His voice was deep and serious, but the sexy smile that spread across his perfect lips promised things that made women weak in the knees. "That's a promise."

Before Lana could comment, which was not the easiest thing in the world for her to do at the moment, Jared's voice broke her thoughts of hot, dirty images floating around in her mind.

"Hey!" Jared had the guy by the neck. "We gotta go. Damon called and said we need to get back now."

"Why?" Sid eyes stayed on Lana as she started blowing out candles. "What's up?

"He wouldn't say, so I know it's not good." Jared frowned, pushing the guy to Sid. "I'll drive, but let's go. Something's wrong."

"You got any handcuffs up that dress?" Sid glanced at Lana, who was coming up behind him.

"Nope, no room," Lana smiled sweetly. "Sorry."

"Looks like you're going for a ride," Sid told the guy as he led him out the door. "So don't try anything stupid."

"Who are you?" he asked, looking at each of them, fear evident in his shaking body and voice. "Where you taking me?"

"To VC Headquarters." Sid opened the door, putting him in the back seat, and climbed in beside him. "We just need to ask you a few questions, and if things check out, you can be on your way."

"I need to call my parents," he said, looking terrified.

"How old are you?" Lana turned as she spoke from the passenger's seat.

"Seventeen."

"Is he who you saw?" Sid asked.

"No," Lana replied and looked back to the kid. "What's your name?"

"Chris Feldman," he answered without hesitation.

"Do you know Megan Cooper or Amanda Turner?"

"Megan's my girlfriend." Chris frowned, looking between Sid and Lana. "Please don't tell Megan what I said about wanting to…you know?"

Lana ignored his plea. "Do you know a Ben Foster?"

"Yeah, he's Amanda's boyfriend." Chris looked nervous again. When Sid and Lana looked at each other, he paled slightly. "What's going on?"

Before they could ask any more questions, Jared pulled into the compound and was out the door at a run.

"They're dead, aren't they?" Chris started to shake uncontrollably now. "I told them it wouldn't work. I told them." His eyes searched around frantically as he tried to pull away from Sid, who was leading him inside.

Chapter 11

Slade stood over Tessa as she lay on the table. The only light in the office was a small desk lamp. The overhead light was off because of Tessa's sensitivity to light. Jill had found a pillow for her and was also standing on the side of the table. Their eyes had only met briefly, and there was an uncomfortable tension in the air.

Hearing boot heels pounding the floor, Slade slipped out the door, stopping Jared before he could bust inside.

"She's going to be fine." Slade stood before the door like a brick wall. "You need to take a deep breath and calm down before you go inside."

"Get the fuck out of my way, Doc." Jared's eyes were black with rage and worry.

"She's already upset, and if she sees you like this, it's not going to help her." Slade understood Jared's rage, but his concern was for Tessa. "She needs to stay calm. She has a concussion and is very sensitive to noise and light."

"What the hell happened?" Jared kept his voice as low as he could.

"I got a text from Adam." Slade pulled out of his phone, bringing up the text, and then handed it to Jared.

Please get to my room. Tessa is hurt. I didn't mean it. I'm so sorry. Make sure she is okay.

Jared cursed, handing the phone back to Slade. "Okay, I'm calm," Jared sighed, but his eyes were still black as night. "Now get the fuck out of my way."

"Don't upset her," Slade warned before stepping to the side, following

Jared.

Tessa had her head turned toward Jill. When the door opened, she turned, spotting Jared. She tried to raise her head, but groaned.

"Stay still, babe." Jared was at her side, brushing her hair from her forehead. "I'm here."

"He didn't mean to hurt me, Jared," Tessa whispered, a tear escaping the corner of her eye. "You know how he doesn't know his own strength. Please don't hurt him."

Jared glanced up at Slade, who was giving him a look of warning. Looking back down at Tessa, he kissed her forehead. "Don't worry about anything, Tessa." Jared rubbed her cheek with his thumb and wiped away a stray tear.

Slade glanced at Jill, nodding toward the door. "I want her to stay here for a while longer before we move her. I'll be back."

Jill followed Slade out the door, but kept on going. "Wait." Slade grabbed her arm. "We have some unfinished business."

"No, we really don't." Jill tried to pull her arm away, but he wouldn't let go. "I heard Sloan loud and clear. I am going to feed off one of the blood donors and everyone will be happy."

"But you won't." Slade frowned.

"I'm not disobeying Sloan's orders," Jill snorted, looking at him like he was crazy.

"No, I meant you won't be happy," Slade corrected her, watching her closely.

"Oh," Jill replied, a little shocked, before shrugging her shoulder. "I'll live."

"Come on." Slade held out his hand.

Jill looked at his hand like it was a disfigured alien ready to take a bite out of her. "What?"

"You're going to feed." Slade kept his hand out, waiting for her to take it. "It's been a while and I know you're ready."

Her eyes shot from his hand to his face in disbelief. "From who? You?" Jill shook her head. "No thanks."

"Why the hell not?" He dropped his hand, taking a step toward her.

"Why the hell would I?" she countered. "The time I did feed from you, you acted like you'd rather have your head decapitated by Damon than have my lips anywhere near you. I'd rather take my chances with the blood bimbos."

Slade didn't say a word, just stared at her.

"Listen, Doc, you're off the hook," Jill assured him. "I've got this. You can go on and take care of whatever it is you take care of. I don't want different treatment. I shouldn't have even brought the blood stuff up in the first place."

"I said I didn't hate you." Slade's voice held a hint of frustration.

"Good to know." Jill's phone buzzed, and she looked too happy to grab it out of her pocket to read her text. "Gotta go. See ya, Doc."

Slade watched her walk away, his eyes sliding down her tight body.

She was thin and firm, but rounded in all the right spots. Her words said one thing, but he could tell by the slump of her shoulders he had hurt her deeper than she was willing to admit, and dammit, he didn't know what to do about it.

"Fuck!" He went to punch the wall, but stopped. Jared was right; he needed to get his temper under control. He turned, stomped down the hall and out the door for some fresh air, slamming the door behind him. If she knew his real feelings for her, she'd probably run screaming. She was too young for his appetites, and what he wanted to do to her. "Fuck!" he roared his frustration, sending a stray cat running for its life.

******

"Okay, Chris, we need to ask you some questions," Lana said after finally calming the kid down. "When was the last time you saw Megan?"

Chris sat at the table in the interrogation room, staring at her with wide-scared eyes. "Last night."

"At the motel room?" Lana sat down; her feet were officially killing her. She was going to burn her shoes as soon as she got home.

"No, my house," Chris frowned. "We had a big fight."

"About what?"

"We had been trying to get money together to go to Florida for spring break. Ben said he knew how we could make enough money to go." Chris fidgeted in his chair. "It was a bad idea, and I told them so. I didn't want any part of it. I just started dating Megan, even though we've been friends for a long time."

"How was Ben going to get the money?" Lana pressed. She had a bad feeling she knew.

"He said some guy approached him during a football game. Said if he could bring him a couple of girls, he would give him five hundred apiece for them." Chris shook his head. "Am I in trouble?"

Lana glanced at Sid, who was leaning against the wall with his arms crossed. "No, Chris, but we need to know where Ben is."

"He wasn't really going to do it. He was going to take Megan and Amanda, but then once the money exchanged hands, they were going to take off."

"You haven't heard from them since then?" When the kid shook his head, Lana sighed. "Have you tried to contact any of them?"

"They aren't texting me back. At first, I thought they were just mad because I didn't go along with them, but now, I don't know." Chris put his hand to his head, looking like he was about to freak out again.

Sid grabbed a pad of paper and a pen from a small table and put it front of Chris. "Give us their cell phone numbers."

Chris took the paper and scribbled their numbers down.

"Why did you come to the motel tonight?" Sid took the numbers looking at them.

"I was hoping they were there." Chris took a drink of water Lana had gotten him. "That's where they met up before they were to meet that guy."

"Did Ben tell you this guy's name or where they were to meet him?" Sid frowned down at the kid, knowing they weren't going to get that lucky.

"No, and I don't even think Ben knew his name. I know they were going to Metropolis because Megan was mad I wasn't going with her, but I'm not sure that is where they were meeting the guy." Chris looked at his phone that lay on the table. "She's dead, isn't she?"

Lana knew she couldn't give that information out until the family was notified and was glad when Damon opened the door.

"His parents are here," Damon informed them before leaving quickly.

"Thanks." Sid headed toward the door. "I'll go talk to them. Bring him out in a few minutes."

"Are you four in high school still?" Lana made a few notes.

"Yeah, except for Ben. He graduated last year."

"Campbell County High School?" Lana asked, trying to get as much information before the kid left.

"Yeah."

"Do you have Ben's address?"

"He lives on Washington in Alexandria. I don't know the number or anything, but it was right by the church in the small white house." Chris rubbed his eyes as tears formed. "You don't want Megan or Amanda's?"

Lana sighed, knowing they would get that information soon enough. "No, that's it for now. Just make sure if you remember anything at all to call Sid or me. And definitely let us know if you hear from Ben.

You have both our numbers."

Chris just nodded as tears fell. "I shouldn't have let her go."

"This isn't your fault, Chris." Lana patted his arm. "And you were smart to stay out of it."

Sid came in with Chris's parents who went straight to him.

"Is he free to go?" His mother looked at Lana, her eyes red from crying.

"Yes, we have all the information we need for now. But we may need to talk to him again, so please stay in town." Lana gave the woman a sad, understanding smile as she watched Chris and his parents walk out.

"Thank you." Chris's father shook Sid's hand.

Once they were gone, Sid closed the door, turning to Lana. "So what do you think?"

"I think you owe me dinner," Lana replied with a groan, leaning down to rub her feet.

"What makes you think that?" Sid's sexy grin appeared.

"I think that because you rudely interrupted my date before I could take a bite of food." Lana sat straight again then stood. "I haven't eaten since this morning, and I'm starved. I want to eat, go home, take this dress off and then sit by the fire I'm going to start by burning these damn shoes."

"Even though I love the thought of you getting out of that dress, we still have work to do. Though, if you'd like to do it out of the dress, I won't complain. I believe in employee rights." Sid's teasing remark was said lightly, but the searing heat in his eyes warmed the room. "Jill has to do another profile pic and…"

Being in the police force, Lana was used to these kinds of remarks, but none ever gave her that fluttery feeling she experienced with his words. Usually, she just had a comeback that shut the men up real quick. But this Warrior was different. The way he looked at her, as if he was seeing the real person behind the mask she tried so hard to hide behind, was throwing her way off. "I believe I will do my job fully dressed, Mr. Boss Man. I do have rights, which I believe so strongly in, and I will fight for them. I am officially off. Now feed me before I turn into a moody bitch who even I can't stand," she replied, hoping her voice didn't betray that she would love to be standing in front of him completely naked. Jesus, she was doomed.

Sid simply stared at her for a few silent seconds before laughing, "You are something else, Lana Fitzpatrick." Sid went to open the door, looking at his watch. "Not much is open this time of night."

"That's what's great about White Castle," Lana ignored his first comment as she tried to pass him to walk out the door without making contact, but he was big, which didn't leave her much room. As their bodies touched, she tried to hide her reaction to his closeness. "They never close and have the best damn coffee."

"I'm not going to White Castle," Sid shook his head, his inner cook cringing at the idea.

"You owe me." Lana didn't let up.

"For what?" Sid opened another door for her, but stood in her path, blocking the exit.

She looked up at him and frowned. "For messing up my date." Then she tapped him on the chest. “Moody bitch is breaching the surface.”

Sid’s head fell back as he laughed. “Yeah, well you should thank me.” He moved out of the way. “Denny wouldn’t know what to do with a woman like you.”

“His name is Doug.” Lana rolled her eyes as a small smile slipped across her lips when she looked over her shoulder. “And he’s a nice man.”

“Who you’d eat alive and spit out,” Sid snorted. “You’d be too much of a challenge for lawyer boy. You need a man who isn’t afraid of a challenge.”

“Oh, really.” Lana frowned, stopping at the car they rode in. “And who would that be? You?” she laughed. She immediately wished she could pull the words back in her big mouth at the look he gave her.

Sid’s smile grew as he reached for the door handle, but pushed his body against hers, pinning her to the car. His head leaned so close she could feel his warm breath on her face. “I’m always up…” he cocked his head, his eyes intense, “for a challenge.”

As Lana instinctively leaned in toward him, he moved, opening the door for her, his cocky grin plastered on his face. Acting like she hadn’t been leaning toward him, she quickly leaned toward the door and plopped in. When the door slammed, Lana let out a string of curses knowing that, in truth, this Warrior wouldn’t have a challenge at all since she was ready to do him right there in the parking lot of their headquarters.

“Calm down and get control, you hoe!” she reprimanded herself before he gracefully slid into the driver’s seat.

“Who’s a hoe?” Sid asked, starting the engine, his eyes pinning her to the seat.

“I didn’t say hoe,” Lana laughed nervously, feeling heat climb up her neck. “I said…I’m hungry so…let’s go…bro.”

Sid sat staring at her for a second before laughing and putting the car in gear. Lana turned her head, looking out the window and making a disgusted face at her reflection; she was screwed in more ways than one. “Bro?” she silently cursed at her reflection.

*****

Sid sat and watched Lana put away two double sliders with cheese, onion chips, a large coffee and was now draining a diet Pepsi. He was impressed. “Feel better?” he asked, watching her luscious lips wrap around the straw of her drink, wishing her lips were wrapped around a certain part of his anatomy.

“Mhmmm.” She tossed her napkin and sat back. “Told you I was starved. You sure you don’t want anything?”

Glancing around, he shook his head. For a Friday night at midnight, he wasn’t surprised that the only customers in White Castle were people going to get their drink on or had already had their drink on. He had picked the booth in a corner with his back to the wall so he could keep an eye on everyone. “I prefer food, but thanks.”

Lana waved her hand over her empty cartons. “What’s this?”

“I have no idea.” Sid made a disgusted face.

Lana rolled her eyes. “Well, if it doesn’t come in a bag or box, I’m screwed.”

“You can’t cook?” Sid’s eyes narrowed as if that was the sin of all sins.

"Nope, but I can whip up a mean mac and cheese," Lana smiled. "Now, my mom can cook like a goddess."

"So how is it you were undercover, but using your real name and identity? Lana is your real name, isn't it?" Sid leaned back, stretching his legs out the best he could under the table.

Lana took another sip of her diet Pepsi. "I was supposed to be Linda Lovelace, but Susan messed up saying my real name, and like you, she didn't give me time to disguise myself."

"Pretty dangerous mistake when undercover," Sid pointed out.

"Oh, like using the name VC Warrior was playing it safe?" Lana cocked an eyebrow.

"I like to live dangerously," Sid grinned. "So how did a beautiful woman like you become a cop?"

"Just like the men. I put my time in, studied hard and went through training." Lana frowned, indicating she didn't like the question.

"So calling you beautiful didn't lessen the harshness of that question, did it?" Sid was pleasantly surprised. Most times when he used the words like 'beautiful', the women were putty in his hands. This was a new experience for him, and he liked it very much. The only women who didn't fall for his bullshit were his brothers' mates, and now this woman sitting across from him, looking sexy as hell, who had a gun strapped to her leg and knew how to use it. Shit he was getting hard thinking about it.

"No, it didn't." Lana relaxed, looking sleepy and totally clueless of his thoughts. "It's a typical question from chauvinistic pigs."

"Touché." Sid's eyebrow cocked a notch.

"Very." Lana imitated him by cocking her own eyebrow.

"Okay, fair enough." Sid laughed, wanting to know more about this woman who didn't seem to fall at his feet wanting to worship him. One would think he would be turned off by that, but the easy conquests who threw themselves at him daily were getting old, and funny thing was, he just now realized that. "So what made you want to become a cop?"

A small smile lit her face. "My father is a retired Sheriff." Her eyes met his. "For as long as I can remember, I have been fascinated with what he did. I would beg him to take me for rides in his police car, mercilessly ask him questions about his day and the bad guys he put away. I was a constant visitor at the station. I drove my poor dad crazy, along with all the other cops in his division when I could corner them."

"I bet he's very proud of you." Sid said as he watched the emotions dance in her eyes.

"Well, he really didn't want me to become a cop, but he knew all along that's what was going to happen." Lana straightened up and rolled her shoulders, which made her breasts jiggle, and she was totally unaware, which was another unexpected turn on. She wasn't trying to be sexy.

Sid groaned low in his throat. It wouldn't look good on either of them if he pulled her across the table so he could latch onto one of those nipples begging to be touched with his mouth. He was pretty sure White Castle would frown on that, and Sloan would have a major meltdown. Sid cleared his throat, forcing his eyes up to hers. "So are you going to tell me about what happened to your neck that night?"

Lana nodded. "Not here though," she replied, glancing at the table diagonal to them. Five guys and two girls were crammed together. The guys were staring at her and making crude comments.

Sid glared at them. “Excuse me.”

“Don’t worry about it.” Lana tried to stop him.

Sid ignored her as he stood and headed to their table. Stopping, he stared down at them. It didn’t matter that he had been looking at Lana the same way these little dickheads were, but it was different when he did it. She was his. Shocked at his thoughts, he didn’t say anything; he simply glared at them.

“What’s up, man?” One brave idiot trying to look cool asked, the smell of beer hovering over their table.

“My foot up your bony ass…” Sid replied, slamming both hands on the table and leaning in the guy’s face. “if you don’t stop remarking about the lady I’m with.” Just to make it clear he wasn’t fucking around, Sid sneered at them showing his sharp fangs.

The table, as one, leaned away from him, crushing each other. “Hey, man, we don’t want no trouble.”

“Hey, man…” Sid mocked with a glare, “good choice. Now, why don’t you sober up before you find yourself in more trouble than you can handle.”

Turning, he made his way back to Lana, who was getting up, making sure she flashed the gun beneath her dress. With a wicked grin, she shimmied the dress down. They all stared at her with wide eyes.

“Good thing he got to you first. Night boys,” She warned. With a wink at their table, she passed Sid, who was holding open the door for her. “Oh, and make sure you don’t drive out of this lot unless you have a sober driver. I just texted my good friend, Officer Beckman. I’d get some coffee if I were you.”

Sid waited until they were out in the parking lot before he started laughing. "That was great."

"I think you scared them back to puberty," Lana snorted. "They about peed themselves when you showed your fangs."

"Did you really text someone?" Sid shook his head as he opened the car door.

"Sure did." She waited until he slid into the driver seat. "I'm sure they're not old enough to be drinking, and I sure don't want to hear about a bunch of kids being killed because I did nothing. It's my job."

"Which you do well," Sid nodded as he pulled out of the parking lot.

Lana looked at him shocked. "Thank you."

"You're welcome." Sid glanced over at her. "So start talking, Officer Fitzpatrick."

Lana sighed, taking off her shoes. "It's kind of a long story and I'm wiped out, so how about the next time we work?"

"Well, that's going to be at nine tomorrow morning, so be ready to talk, because I'm not letting this go," Sid warned, pulling up to a small one-story white house with dark blue shutters.

"I'm not trying to get out of telling you. Just the night that it happened, we were not working together, and you know…" Lana grabbed her shoes then looked out the window. "Hey, I didn't tell you where I lived. How did you know where I lived?"

"I Googled you," Sid smirked, getting out of the car and walking around to open hers up.

“You did not,” Lana laughed when he opened her door. “Guess being a Warrior gives you special privileges to information.”

“Some,” he replied, following her up the walkway to her front porch.

“I didn’t get to learn much about you tonight.” Lana frowned as she stopped at the door.

“Not much to tell,” Sid shrugged, looking uncomfortable. He didn’t talk about himself, ever.

“Oh, I don’t believe that for one second. There’s a story or two I’m sure you can share, and *I will* be getting it out of you,” Lana laughed. Reaching up under her dress, she opened a small pouch on her gun strap, pulling out a key.

“I’m sorry. I know I’m supposed to be your boss, but that is fucking hot,” Sid growled, his eyes heated.

Lana stared at him for a second before her shaking hand finally got her door opened. “Yeah, well it’s uncomfortable as hell, I’ll tell you that. If the strap doesn’t fit right, it feels like it’s sliding down. I hate wearing dresses, but a girl has to do what a girl has to do.” She stood inside her open door. “Thanks for standing up for me with those guys at White Castle. Sometimes, it’s nice to have someone stand up for you.”

“Not a problem,” Sid smiled down at her. “Just because you’re a badass cop doesn’t mean a man can’t be a gentleman when the need arises.”

“You want to come in?” Lana had stood silent before she asked.

“Yes.” Sid stared at her, taking a step closer to her, but stopped. “But I’m not going to.”

"Yeah, I guess we both know what will happen if you do" Lana shrugged as if indifferent, but a sad loneliness that was hard to hide shadowed her eyes.

"Oh, there's no guessing about it, lovely Lana." Sid leaned close. "It will happen, just not tonight. I'll see you tomorrow at nine. I'll text you the address to the warehouse where I'll be. Lock your door. Sweet dreams." He stared at her for a second longer before giving her a sexy smile and wink, leaving Lana at the door panting.

Chapter 12

Jill ran laps, her iPod blaring. She knew Slade had come in, but she didn't make eye contact. She wanted to get her workout going before Sid and the cop Lana came in this morning. Sid had texted her about doing another profile pic. She also knew the blood bimbos were due in early, so she needed to get her 'suck it up' mode going. Something just told her that this day was going to suck like no other.

Passing the window where she had her phone sitting, she glanced to see if she had a missed call or text. Adam hadn't answered any of her calls or texts, the jerk. She'd officially decided she was going to kill him, or at least beat the shit out of his sorry ass. Thank God, Tessa was going to be okay. Regardless, Jared was pissed and stressed to the max. She needed to get to him before Jared or any of the other Warriors did.

She had lost count of how many laps she had run, but sweat poured off her. Slowing down, she picked up a towel, and wiped her face before grabbing her water.

Feeling a tap on her shoulder, her phone flew out of her hand. Juggling it before it fell to the floor, she grabbed it finally and turned. "What?" she yelled, and quickly frowned when Steve pointed to her ears. Looking around everyone was staring at her. Pulling her earphones out of her ears, she looked at Steve. "What?" she asked again, but this time in a normal voice.

Rolling his eyes at her, he glanced around. "I talked to Adam."

"When?" Jill cringed when she spoke too loudly, once again drawing attention to them.

"A few minutes ago, okay." Steve continued as low as possible, "He's okay. He's worried about Tessa, but I told him she was going to be fine. He said he knows everyone thinks he's going rogue, but he's not.

He's on to something and needs our help."

"Why the hell didn't he call me?" Jill hissed. "I called him all damn night."

"I don't know, but he's going to be calling you at noon today so try to be alone." Steve took a drink of water. "He's going to try to do a three-way call."

Jill nodded, glancing at the clock. She had four hours to get done what she needed to get done before then. Glancing toward the back, she saw the blood bimbos walk in, and, of course, they headed toward Slade who stood talking to Sloan. They were having a meeting after they fed. It was Alice and someone Jill had never seen before.

Alice waved a finger at Steve, which put a goofy grin on his face.

"Oh, please," Jill snorted.

"What? She's nice and looks damn good." Steve waved back.

"And you're a douche." Jill nudged him.

He nudged her back. "And you're jealous."

"Of that?" Jill didn't even look toward Alice. "She's a bitch, and you just like her because she has big boobs and will drop her pants for anybody."

"So, what's wrong with that?" Steve grinned.

Jill tried her best to ignore when Slade and Alice walked by heading toward the back. Jill squeezed her bottle of water a little too hard causing the water to spray out.

Steve laughed. "You are so jealous of Alice. Just admit it."

Fire shot out of her eyes as she glared at Steve. Without a thought, she dropped down, kicking his leg out from under him, pounced on him, grabbed his arm and got him in an arm bar. Jill tightened the arm bar, making a funny noise come out of Steve's mouth. "You better tap before I break it."

Steve slapped on her leg, tapping out. Jill let go and rolled to her feet, grabbing the water and her phone she dropped when taking him down. "Damn, Jill." Steve rubbed his arm glaring at her when she sat down on the mat. When she wrinkled her nose at him, he smiled. "I don't care how many arm bars you get me in; you're still jealous."

Jill reached over, grabbing a punching mitt, and threw it, slamming him in the back of the head. When he turned to glare at her rubbing his head, she simply smiled, put her earphones in and then laid back. She didn't want to watch Slade walk from the back with a satisfied look on his face, so she just lay there jamming, letting her mind try to figure out what Adam was up to. Glancing at her watch again, she noticed a shadow falling over her.

Sloan stood over her, his mouth moving. Taking her earphones out again, she turned her iPod down. "What?"

"I hate those fucking things because I always have to repeat myself," Sloan growled. "Get back there and feed so we can get this meeting going."

Jill stood, glancing around, and was surprised to see Slade already out talking to Damon and Sid. Hell, did she fall asleep? Glancing at the clock, she frowned because only about ten minutes or so had passed since Slade went in the back with the bimbo.

Nodding, Jill tossed her stuff off the mat and then headed toward the back. Steve was just walking out as Jill was walking in; he wore a disappointed frown. "Ah, what happened, Stevie? Didn't get your after-meal blow job?" Jill teased as they passed.

"Shut up," Steve glared, and then pouted. "And no, as a matter of fact, I didn't."

Jill laughed when Steve grinned at her. "Poor thing, but at least you're safe from some horrible disease for a while."

"You're so damn mean," Steve accused. "My whole day has been ruined. Where's the sympathy?"

Rolling her eyes, she walked into the back, spotting Alice and the other woman leaning against the counter. Figuring she would try a new approach and be nice to Alice, Jill plastered on a nice smile. "Hi Alice." Then she nodded to the other woman.

"That her?" The tall woman with curly blonde hair eyed Jill up and down.

"Yes, that's her." Alice pushed away from the counter, walking toward Jill. "Disgusting isn't it? I personally think all half-breeds need to be exterminated."

Jill stood still as Alice walked around her. She kept repeating to herself 'keep your cool'. If things went bad with this, Sloan would kick her ass to the curb. She'd been warned.

Alice laughed. "Although Steve could be my little slave, so he does have some purpose for a half-breed. All I have to do is give his cock a little attention and he's all mine. And I can't forget Adam, who is hung like a horse and gets a hard-on every time he feeds, but will only let me blow him. His love for his little human is sweet, and he doesn't want to cheat on her by fucking me, but he is always anxious to stick that big cock in my mouth." Alice stopped in front of Jill, staring into her mismatched eyes. "Men are funny, aren't they, breed? Thinking sticking it in one hole over the other isn't cheating."

"You're disgusting," Jill didn't blink, just stood staring.

The only indication that Alice heard her was the flare of anger in her eyes. "So then that leaves you." Alice tapped a finger to her red painted lips. "And honestly, you have no use whatsoever to anybody. Just a waste of space."

"What is your problem?" Jill asked, still in control, but she felt it slipping, fast.

"My problem, you stupid little freak of nature, is you and those other bitches coming in here thinking you're better than me." Alice, who was, in truth, very beautiful, turned ugly in the blink of an eye. Jealously and rage turned her beauty into something so ugly it was hideous. "I have been taking care of these Warriors for a hundred years. I've been used for my blood and fucked by every one of them, but what do I have to show for it? Nothing. Except watching no-good, low-life bitches come in here stealing them away from me…from us."

"Being a blood donor is a choice," Jill reminded her. "You aren't forced to do it, and if you decide to stop, you are taken care of by the Council for your years of service. I'm sorry, but I have no sympathy for the choices you've made. Being a blood donor was your choice, as is being a Warrior whore."

"Oh, no she didn't." The blonde chick took a step forward, but stopped when Alice held up her hand.

"Listen, and listen good, you half-breed piece of shit." Alice leaned in close to her face. "You may think I'm a whore, but when those Warriors out there need a shoulder, I'm here for them and they talk."

Jill again repeated to herself to stay cool, but with Alice in her space, she was finding it really hard to keep calm. She had space issues, and this bitch was too close.

"And do you know what they say?" Alice's eyes opened wide as if she was ready to tell a secret. "As a matter of fact, after giving your fellow half-breed Steve a good cock sucking, he told me a few secrets."

"And I repeat. You're disgusting." Jill took a step back knowing she had to get her space back. "Stay out of my space, Alice. I'm here to feed, not listen to your pitiful life of blowing my fellow Warriors," Jill warned.

Alice ignored her, stepping closer. "One secret is how you are panting after our new doctor." Alice watched closely for any reaction. "Well, we had a talk, me and the sexy doctor."

A film of rage travelled over Jill's vision; she fought it back, clamping her mouth shut.

"He feels bad for you. He's such a nice man." Alice gave her a look of pity. "But he's embarrassed about how you are always staring at him."

Jill crossed her arms to keep from strangling the redheaded bitch. She could keep control. She had the power to do that, and dammit, she was going to.

"After he pulled out of me and we lay together, he thanked me for being a woman who didn't play little girl games." Alice smiled as if enjoying the memory. "He also asked as a favor to him to feed you, so he didn't have to again."

Hurt slammed into Jill hearing those last words. The film of rage slammed across her eyes. "Fuck it!" Jill growled, punching out at Alice, who moved just in time.

"Oh, did I make you mad?" Alice mocked, her laughter echoing around the room.

With a speed that surprised Alice, Jill tackled her with such force they both went through the wall. They rolled out onto the mat area. Jill landed on top of Alice, pounding her head into the floor while holding onto her red hair. Alice got a punch in, sending Jill off her. Jill rolled, but before she could make it to Alice, she was picked up and carried away like a sack of potatoes.

She felt a jolt then she was crashing to the ground, rolling to her back ready for an attack. She saw Alice on Damon's back trying to get to her, and Sid trying to pry Alice off Damon's back.

"How dare you!" Alice screamed, her red hair sticking out with her makeup smeared making her look like something out of a horror movie. Her fangs snapped at Jill. "You're nothing! Do you hear me, half-breed? You are nothing!"

Jill went for her, but Slade gripped her around the waist. "Stop!" He jerked her a little to get her attention.

"Get off me!" Jill fought him with everything she had, but he was too strong.

Sid had finally got Alice off Damon and was holding her.

Sloan looked at the hole in the wall then at Jill. "Get to my office now!"

"I want her out of here," Alice threatened as she tried to get to Jill again. "I mean it. I won't service anyone else here if she is not thrown out."

"Good!" Jill shouted. "Maybe they can get someone clean in here, so the guys don't have to worry about their dicks falling off, you nasty bitch."

"I swear to God, I'm going to kill you." Alice hissed, flaying her arms and legs, trying to get loose from Sid.

"Can we just let them go at it and get it over with?" Sid asked, avoiding an elbow heading toward his face. "I haven't seen a good chick fight in a while."

Sloan lost it. He picked up a stool, throwing it against the wall next to the large hole. "I said shut the fuck up!" He pointed to Jill. "Go! Now!"

With one last glare at Alice, Jill pulled loose from Slade. When he went to follow her, Jill turned and pushed him back. "Stay away from me!"

"Alice, you are done here." Sloan had turned his attention to Alice and her friend who stood wide-eyed.

"What?" Alice screeched, making each Warrior grimaced. "Are you fucking serious?"

"I'm more than serious," Sloan growled. "I've had more than enough reports on you, but because you have been with us so long, I've made exceptions on your behalf, but not anymore. You are released from your duties, and I will make recommendations against you being taken on by other Warrior Departments."

Alice smoothed her hair down then straightened her clothes. "You *will* regret this," she warned Sloan.

"I doubt that." Sloan didn't take the bait. He just stepped aside. "Get out."

Jill headed out and down the side of the warehouse. She didn't have a damn car, so she was going to have to walk to the compound, which probably was best. Give her time to cool her temper off a little. The bitch's words kept replaying in her head and she didn't want to believe it. She didn't want to believe Slade would talk about her to that bitch, but it seemed he had, and that broke her heart.

Hearing footsteps rushing her from behind, Jill turned just in time to be grabbed by the throat and picked up off her feet.

"You think you won, you bitch?" Alice squeezed Jill's throat tighter. "Grab her arms." Alice ordered her friend who did what she asked.

Darkness edged Jill's vision, but she still fought with everything she had, and just as her eyes started to fade, she heard the click of a gun.

"Let her go. Now," Lana held the gun to the back of Alice's head.

Jill felt the hold loosen on both her neck and arms. She tried to warn Lana.

"You're human?" Alice hissed after sniffing the air. "Another pathetic human."

"With an attitude that matches my gun and silver bullets." Lana's voice was serious and to the point. "Now, let her go."

"Gladly." Alice's smile was evil.

As if in slow motion, Jill felt Alice let go as she raised her hand speeding toward Lana, who Jill knew couldn't take a hit from a vampire. Anger so deep enveloped her body and soul.

"No!" Jill screamed, her hand shooting up at Alice. Without one touch, Alice was flung against the side of the building, held by an invisible force from Jill's hand, which was aimed toward Alice.

Everyone had rushed outside at the screaming.

"Put me down, you fucking freak!" Alice screamed.

Shocked, Jill pulled her hand back against her chest and watched with everyone else as Alice hit the ground hard.

Popping up quickly, Alice growled and screeched at the same time as she started to run toward Jill.

"Freeze!" Lana raised her gun. "Don't even think about it."

"Lana, no!" Sid yelled running up, but knew he was going to be too late.

"Fuck you, human!" Alice's laugh was crazy as she lunged again toward Lana, but Jill threw her hand out, this time sending Alice tumbling across the parking lot.

Jill was pissed and it showed in her every move. She held her hand out, holding Alice down. She didn't know how the hell she was doing it or how long it would last, but she was done with Alice's crap, and it was going to stop now.

When Alice's friend started to rush her, Jill looked her way with a snap of her head. "I have two hands, and I will nail you to the wall if you come one step closer," she warned her even though she didn't know if she could or not.

"Let me up," Alice hissed, but some of the fire had gone out of her.

"I'm going to let you up, but if you try one more thing, I am going to twist you into a knot with my bare hands," Jill growled down at her then dropped her hand.

Alice stood up with as much dignity as she could. "You better watch your back, bitch."

Jill didn't reply, but she did flick her wrist, making Alice jump, before walking quickly to her car, her friend running after her. Once they left the parking lot, Jill looked down at her hands amazed. Turning around, she found everyone looking at her.

"Well, that was new." She lifted her hand and was shocked when everyone hit the ground like she was aiming a gun.

Chapter 13

"Put that thing away." Sid placed his body in front of Lana. Once Jill dropped her hand, he stood helping Lana up. "Hot damn, what the hell was that?"

"I don't know?" Jill stood looking as confused as they were.

"That was freaking awesome." Steve threw up his hand, aiming toward Damon.

"If I even feel a breeze, I will kick your ass," Damon warned Steve with a growl.

Steve pulled his hand back so fast he smacked himself in the face. "Sorry."

Sid walked up to Jill. "You okay?"

"Yeah, I think so." Jill's eyes were wide and a little frightened.

"You better let Doc check you over." Sid wrapped his arm around her shoulder. "You look pretty shaken up."

Slade was already there by her side, but he had been silent, just watching and taking everything in.

"No, I'm fine." Jill didn't look at any of them, her hands shaking uncontrollably. "I just need to…"

Lana walked up, grabbing Jill's hand. "She needs a minute, boys."

Sid watched as Lana took control of the situation, leading Jill inside. "Looks like our Jill has grown up and come into her powers before our very eyes."

"She needs to learn how to control it," Sloan frowned. "I'll call around and see if I can find anyone who has the same power that can help her."

"That won't be necessary." Slade, who had been quiet to this point, spoke up. With a curse, he threw up his hand aiming it toward the dumpster at the end of the parking lot. Within seconds, it lifted and moved a few feet before banging to the ground, all under his complete control.

"Damn, you're like Carrie on steroids." Sid looked impressed.

"What the fuck are you talking about?" Sloan glared at Sid.

Steve stepped up, excitement on his young face. "Dude, I thought the same exact thing when Jill did that to Alice." Steve looked at Sloan. "The movie *Carrie*. Stephen King....*Carrie*. When she goes crazy and kills all those people at the prom. But she didn't use her hand; she just gave this intense stare, and BAM, they were thrown all over the place."

They all watched Steve as he tried to duplicate the parts in the movie. No one found it humorous other than Sid who stood, arms crossed, and grinning.

"She could even control things like a fire hose and electrical cords. Hey, you think Jill can control things like that with her hand? Make anything her weapon." Steve's mouth was going a hundred miles-an-hour, but stopped at the look Sloan was giving him. "Guess you didn't see the movie."

"No, I didn't see the fucking movie," Sloan growled. "And I suggest you stop hanging out with Sid."

Sid ignored the jab, his stare going to Slade. “Well, hell, bro, guess you and Jill are a match made in heaven.” Sid’s grin grew larger. “You can make beautiful holes in the wall together as well as skip a moving crew when you buy your first house together, save a few bucks.”

“Shut the fuck up, Sid,” Slade growled, walking away toward the warehouse.

“Ah, and there it is,” Sid sighed, closing his eyes. “Music to my ears.”

“Why do I even keep you around?” Sloan growled, actually rolling his eyes.

“Because I lighten the place up.” Sid headed toward where Jill and Lana disappeared. “I put smiles on the faces of Warriors, and deep down in your secret place, you love me, boss.”

Sloan glared at Damon, who had a grin on his face. “What the fuck are you grinning about?” Sloan’s face was frozen with frustration. “Don’t you have someone’s head to remove or something? Jesus, if I have to deal with any more shit, it might be mine you decapitate with my wishes.”

“Just let me know, boss,” Damon tossed out a rare teasing when Sloan walked away. “Always happy to help a friend in need.”

Sid, who was just opening the door to the warehouse, laughed loudly hearing the whole exchange. “Nice, Damon,” Sid called out. “I’m going to get that stick out of your ass one day.”

“Fuck you, Sid,” Damon growled.

“Fuck you too, brother.” Sid nodded as he disappeared inside.

******

As soon as Lana and Jill walked into the warehouse, Jill lost it. Tears and hard sobs wracked her body. Lana looked around not knowing where to go. “Come on.” Lana looked back at the door. “Where’s the bathroom?”

Jill headed toward the opposite end of the warehouse with Lana following. After entering a large bathroom with showers, Lana walked over, and turned on the faucet.

“Here, splash some cold water on your face.” As Jill splashed her face, Lana rubbed her back. “Scared you a little, didn’t it?”

Jill raised up, looking at herself in the mirror. “Terrified me.”

“So, obviously that was the first time you’ve ever done that.” When Jill nodded, she turned the faucet off and looked at Lana through the mirror. Lana smiled in understanding. “You know, the first time a dead person contacted me, it scared me so bad I peed my pants.”

“You did not,” Jill snorted, wiping her face.

“True story.” Lana crossed her heart. “Though I was only six-years-old; still it scared me to death. Whenever it happened, I would run and try to hide, but they always found me. No matter what I did, they would find me. I never said a word to anyone. But then when my grandfather died I was at his funeral, I walked up to the casket and he looked like he was just sleeping like he always did in his big chair at home. So I reached out to try to wake him up, just to make sure.”

“What happened?” Jill had calmed down; her tears stopped.

“I relived his last moments of life.” Lana gave Jill a sad smile. “Most of my family thought I was nuts because here I was holding onto my dead grandfather’s hand, staring up at the ceiling in a weird trance. My mom wouldn’t let anyone touch me and the whole funeral was put on hold until I came out of it. I was seven when that happened.”

“So your mom knew what was going on?” Jill seemed to have forgotten her issues for a moment, which had been Lana’s plan.

“Yeah, she did. My grandmother has the gift which was passed to my sister and me,” Lana replied.

“Wow, that’s crazy that both you and your sister can do that,” Jill nodded looking wistful.

“We’re twins,” Lana smiled. “Neither of us knew what the other was going through, and we didn’t know until the day at my grandfather’s funeral. Neither of us wanted to tell each other for fear of the other running and telling Mom and Dad.”

“Well, at least you have someone who understands and you can talk to,” Jill sniffed. “I would love to have that right now.”

“My sister is lost to us,” Lana cleared her throat.

“I’m so sorry.” Jill’s eyes widened.

“It should have been me. She didn’t really like using her gift, but in my line of work, I use it a lot.” Lana looked at Jill, realizing this was the first time she had really talked about her sister to anyone other than her parents. “My sister wasn’t prepared emotionally for the read. One of the officers on the scene thought she was under distress during the reading and broke her away from the girl who had been murdered.”

“And that killed her?” Jill gasped, touching Lana’s arm, sorrow in her eyes.

“It probably would have been better if it had.” Lana grabbed Jill’s hand squeezing it. “She is a resident at the Adult Psychiatric Unit at UC where she relives the last hours of the girl’s life before her death.”

"Oh, my God." Jill hugged Lana. "That's horrible."

Lana hugged her back. "Even though it has only been a little over a month, I miss her so much."

"Aren't you afraid that can happen to you?" Jill pulled back, looking at her. "You shouldn't be doing it anymore."

"It's my gift." Lana shook her head, and then smiled. "I use it to help solve crimes and to help families find closure. I use it to help others, and that is how you need to look at your own gift."

"I didn't use it to help anyone." Jill's face fell. "I plastered someone up against the wall and then sent her flying across the parking lot."

Lana thought for a minute. "If you think about it, you only did that when she was coming after me." Walking over to the garbage can, she grabbed it and moved it to the middle of the bathroom. "Try to move it."

Jill looked at her like she was crazy, but finally lifted her hand. Nothing happened. She dropped her arm, sighed and then tried again. "It's gone." Jill looked confused. "I can't do it."

"Maybe because you were trying to protect me." Lana had no clue if that was the case, but it made sense. "And she was a nutty bitch."

Jill smiled with a chuckle. "Thank you." She hugged Lana again.

"You're so welcome." Lana hugged her. Pulling away, she continued, "Now, get out there and let them know you're okay. You're strong, Jill. I know being a half–breed, and now having this new power, is overwhelming for you, but use it to help others."

"You're right." Jill stood up straight. "I love what I'm doing and no one is going to stop me from doing it."

"You're going to make a great Warrior," Lana said proudly. "Even though you are in with all these alpha men, you've got the power to keep up with them. If not, just plaster their asses to the wall."

Jill laughed at the thought. "I can do this."

Lana smiled with a nod. "Now, go out there and do your thing. Girl power and all that crap."

After she left, Lana sighed, leaning against the wall, feeling a heavy weight slump her shoulders. Even though her sister was always in the front of her mind, she didn't talk about it.

"Girl power?" Sid walked in with a smile, but there was something else in his eyes.

"Damn straight." Lana gave a firm nod. "Nothing more powerful out there."

Sid leaned against the sink, staring down at her. "You are a special woman, Lana Fitzpatrick."

"No, I just understand. Nothing special about that." She frowned, "How much did you hear?"

"Ah, pretty much all of it." Sid cocked his eyebrow at her. "Not only am I the cook, comedian, handsome, witty and charming Warrior, I also excel in eavesdropping."

"That's a pretty long, conceited list." Lana rolled her eyes with a laugh. If she wasn't careful, she could easily fall for this man, and not just in bed, which she knew was going to happen. Why fight the inevitable? She'd already made peace with that, but that didn't mean she had to lose her heart in the process.

“Just stating the truth,” Sid replied with a confident grin, but then his teasing look changed. “I’m sorry about your sister, Lana.”

“Yeah, so am I.” Lana frowned, “It should have been me. I was supposed to be the one, but I was in the middle of a deal and couldn’t make it. I called her to step in for me.”

“I don’t see how that could have been your fault, Lana.” He tipped her chin up. “You didn’t know what was going to happen.”

“She was a school teacher, Sid. She wasn’t a cop and had no business there, but because I asked, she dropped everything and went.” Lana pulled away, shaking her head. “Today’s her birthday, so I have to quit a little early.”

Sid nodded, noticing she didn’t mention that it was also her birthday, but let it go for the time being. “Not a problem.” He glanced at her neck. “Someone attacked you during your read, didn’t they?”

“Yes, and it’s never happened before,” Lana replied with a frown. “It was the man Jill drew. I have no idea how he did it, but he’s strong.” Subconsciously, she began to stroke her neck.

Sid cursed as his eyes were drawn to her bruises, “You need to be more careful.”

“I know,” she agreed as they both stood deep in thought.

Lana’s phone interrupted the silence. “Yeah?” she answered. After a second, her eyes met Sid’s. “We’ll be right there.”

“They found Ben Foster.” Sid knew before she even had time to hang up.

“They found Ben Foster,” Lana repeated, a frown on her face. “Dead.”

“Shit.” Sid pushed away from the sink. “Where’d they find him?”

Lana looked puzzled. “The same place the two girls were found.”

Chapter 14

Adam sat staring at his phone. Fifteen more minutes until he called Jill. Even though Steve was keeping him updated on Tessa, he wanted to hear her voice. He loved his sister and never meant to hurt her. Running through his contacts, it landed on Tessa's number.

"Fuck it." He pressed her number, putting the phone to his ear.

"Where the fuck are you?" Jared answered after the third ring.

Adam cursed, hearing Jared's voice. "Let me talk to Tessa," he demanded.

"You're pressing your luck demanding shit from me," Jared hissed over the phone. "If it wasn't for your sister, I'd be out hunting your ass right now."

"I didn't mean to hurt her, Jared," Adam sighed, exhaustion overcoming him.

"You're damn lucky she's going to be okay," Jared growled in the phone. "Though she is more worried about you than herself right now. That's what really pisses me off. You fucking left her laying on the floor hurt; that is something I will never be able to forgive."

"How can I expect you to forgive me when I can't even forgive myself?" Adam hung up. He knew they thought he was going rogue, but they were wrong. Looking around the dingy motel room, Adam felt more alone than he had in his entire life. He prayed to God, whom he hadn't prayed to since he'd been turned, that they were wrong.

******

Jill walked out of the back and straight up to Sloan. "I tried to leave, but Alice came after me." She purposely didn't look at Slade, who stood right to the side of Sloan. "I also refuse to be treated like that by anyone. That may make me look like I'm starting trouble, but I'm not. I just refuse to be treated like a piece of garbage. I hope to stay on here and I did follow your orders."

"Alice has been let go," Sloan replied, and before Jill could say anything, he lifted his hand to stop her. "She should have been let go a long time ago, but I will warn you to watch your back. She won't take this lightly."

"Thanks for the warning." She glanced at the time on her phone. Any minute Adam was going to call her.

"Now about this new power you seem to have." Sloan shook his head with a rare grin. "Which took us all by surprise, I might add. Slade is going to work with you on controlling it."

"That's okay." Jill absolutely was not going to work with Slade. "I couldn't even do it again in the bathroom, so it might have been a one-time thing."

"It's not a one-time thing." Slade frowned down at her.

"Oh, and what makes you so sure of that?" Jill was trying to keep the hurt and anger out of her voice. She had to separate her feelings for this man, but in truth, she wanted to smack the crap out of his handsome face for screwing that hoe and then talking to the bitch about her afterwards.

"Because I have the same powers." Slade's tone or facial expression didn't change, but his eyes burned into hers.

And that's when Adam decided to call. As her phone played 'Blurred Lines' over and over, Jill continued to look at Slade.

“You going to answer that?” Slade didn’t take his eye off her.

“Hey, I have to call you back,” Jill answered, knowing it was Adam. “No, I’m not…Okay…Yeah, soon. You good?...Bye.” Jill clicked the phone off.

“He okay?” Slade crossed his arms, standing in a relaxed position.

Jill’s eyes flicked to Sloan, who had walked away and was talking to Sid and Lana who had come out of the back. “Who?”

“Adam.”

“That’s wasn’t Adam.” Jill, who couldn’t lie to save her life, lied.

“You need to tell him to get back, Jill,” Slade warned. “He’s out of control.”

“He’s not out of control,” Jill defended him. “And he’s not going rogue. He wants to find Angelina, and the only way he could do that was to leave here. He didn’t mean to hurt Tessa.”

“And you know all of this, but you haven’t talked to him?” Slade frowned. “You’re going to find yourself in trouble.”

“What’s new?” Jill snorted. “It seems like that’s all I can do right around here is get into trouble. The harder I try, the more it gets thrown back in my face.”

Sid and Lana walked over before Slade could comment. “Heard you got some Carrie powers also.” Sid eyed Slade with a grin.

“Carrie powers?” Jill frowned, confused.

Lana laughed. "You did remind me of the movie *Carrie* when you were tossing that chick all over the place."

Jill moaned. "That's kind of creepy."

"No, it's not creepy. It's a gift," Lana reminded her with a wink, and then glanced at Slade. "And now you don't have to be alone. You have someone who shares your gift."

"You can do what I just did?" Jill frowned, wanting to make sure she heard right. She also realized this was just another reason for him to reject her, just what she needed.

Slade didn't say a word, just gave a nod.

"We might have something tonight, Slade, so keep open," Sid turned from teasing to serious. "Jill, we might be needing you also. You ready?"

"I'm ready." Jill's excitement at taking her training to a whole different level was hard to miss in her wide eyes and growing smile. "I am so ready."

"Good." Sid tugged her short hair. "We'll be back at the compound soon and go over everything."

As Sid continued to go over a few things with Slade, Lana leaned over. "He's cute." Lana grinned with a wink. "And that look he gives you, well, girl, your panties should be on fire."

Jill gasped, looking at Lana surprised.

"On…fire," Lana emphasized, and then smiled. "Lucky girl."

Jill watched Sid and Lana walk away before peeking at Slade, who was staring at her with his usual intense emotionless stare. Lana was crazy. If anything, his look was like someone dropping ice cubes in her panties.

Right then and there, she decided he wasn't worth her losing her position here. She would treat him like a brother just as she did with the others. Thoughts of having sex with any of them made her gag. She tried to convince herself that's what she was going to do. Dammit, she could do this.

"I think your type of power may have developed because you fed from me," Slade's deep voice rumbled in the now empty warehouse. "But I'm not a hundred-percent sure about that. So the first thing we need to do is to find out what exactly you can do."

The reminder of feeding from him sent tingles throughout her body. Jill tightened her body, willing the tingles away, and reminded herself that he was like a brother, and having tingles was wrong and totally gross.

"Is that okay, or do you have to call Adam back right away?" Slade cocked his eyebrow.

"No, I don't have to call Adam back because that wasn't Adam." Jill's eyes narrowed as she lied. She hated to lie because she sucked at it and always got caught. But dammit, she did have to call Adam back.

Slade took a step closer, leaning down and bringing himself face-to-face with her. "You can't lie worth a shit, Jill."

God, he smelled so good. The power that radiated off him sent a slow burn through her body and panties. Dammit. Tightening her legs together, Jill winced when the burn became a raging fire from the friction hitting her groin. Swallowing hard, she tried to get it together. She watched as he lifted his head slightly as if smelling the air. His eyes went to instant black as they slammed into hers. His slow knowing smile sent her over the edge, and she knew right then and there, he could smell her desire.

"Are we going to stand here staring at each other all day or are we going to get some work in…bro." The more she looked at him that way, the easier it was going to be to ignore her growing attraction and move on. Damn him.

Slade's eyes widened before he burst out laughing. "You are too much." He turned and headed for the door. "Come on. We'll start outside."

Jill frowned then did something a sister would do to a brother who laughed at her; she flipped him off with not one, but two hands.

******

Sid and Lana pulled up to the same spot where they had found the two dead girls. Activity was in full force. Sid walked around to open the door for Lana before she could.

"Who taught you such impeccable manners, Mr. Sinclair?" Lana teased. "Even though I appreciate the gesture, I'm not used to it and can open the door myself."

"Shut up and get out," Sid grinned down at her. "There is that better? Now, am I more like the losers you've dated?"

"Oh, I didn't know this was considered a date," Lana teased back, actually holding onto Sid as they made their way down the steep hill. "I'm going to have to step up my game."

"Honey, if you step up your game much more, I'll be putty in your hands," Sid replied in a serious tone, but the sexy grin was anything but serious.

"Oh, good to know," Lana grinned, but stopped, her whole body going tense.

"What's wrong?" Sid was on alert, his eyes leaving her to scan the area.

"He's here." Lana also scanned the area, before letting go of his arm. Reaching under her jacket, she pulled out her gun.

"Who are we looking for, Lana?" Sid was calm, but alert and ready.

"The man in the drawing, the General." Lana took a step, her eyes sweeping over Ben Foster's dead body. "Ben is telling me he's here and he goes by the General."

Sid glanced at the dead body in the same exact place the girls had been found. He then searched back around the area. "That's creepy as shit, but ask him where?"

At the same time, they spotted a tall man move out from behind a tree leading into the woods. Sid was down the hill so fast he was nothing but a blur. Lana slid and ran down the hill cursing all the way. Finally making it to the tree, both Sid and the man were gone.

"Shit!" Lana moved deeper into the woods trying to find any clue to where they went. They were long gone. No evidence, nothing. "Shit!"

Hearing a stick crack behind her, Lana turned with gun ready. With a speed she didn't even see, her gun was knocked out of her hand and she was grabbed by the throat; her body was lifted off the ground, not by the man in her vision, but it was the man in the red cape. Sid was chasing the man in the drawing.

Knowing she was going to die, Lana fought with everything she had. Kicking, punching and then trying to pry the man's hands off her throat. Her eyes watered as her airflow was slowly being cut off. With one last effort to survive, she beat at the man's arm then kicked out, making contact with his stomach. Her foot got caught in the cape, pulling it down off his head.

She now knew what horror the woman in her vision had seen, the woman he was going to rape. Lana's mouth opened wide in a silent scream, her eyes staying on the gruesomeness of the man's scarred face, which looked to have been melted.

"Put her down," Sid's voice was hard and loud, the authority ringing through the woods.

The man's hand loosened as his one eye opened wide in surprise, but a snarled smile lifted the less-scarred side of his mouth.

"Put her the fuck down or die, motherfucker." The sound of Sid's guns cocking in the silence of the woods echoed throughout the leafless trees. "I won't ask again."

Lana could feel the man's fury radiate off him as he turned his head to the side. His grip had loosened enough for her to get air. As soon as he turned to look back at her, she knew what was about to happen, but couldn't yell out a warning fast enough. Gripping both hands around the arm and hand that were gripping her throat, she held on so her neck wouldn't be broken.

"Fuck you, Warrior!" The man's gravelly voice hissed as he swung Lana around toward Sid and let go.

Lana's body sailed through the air so hard and fast, when it made contact with Sid, they went flying through the woods until Sid's back made contact with a tree. His body shielded her from contact.

“Son of a bitch.” Sid rolled her over, checking her body. “Lana!”

“Go. I’m fine,” She croaked through her tender throat, and then waved her hand.

“Fuck that.” Sid did glance up to make sure the bastard wasn’t coming after them, but he was long gone. “Can you sit up?”

Lana did, but her body felt battered and her throat burned like hell. “Where in the hell did you go?” Lana rubbed her throat.

“I was chasing the guy, but something told me to come back.” Sid moved her hands to look at her neck, where it was bruised over the faded bruising. He cursed, “Dammit!”

“I’m fine.” Lana rose up to her knees. Her eyes closed suddenly. “Ben warned you.” Her eyes opened in shock.

“What?” Sid knelt beside her.

“Ben warned you to come back.” She closed her eyes again. “He also said you know who the man in the red cape is and that this was all a set up.”

“Who was it?” Sid demanded, not liking any of this.

“He’s gone.” Lana looked up and then around the area.

“Who’s gone?” Sid’s frustration was evident in his voice.

“Ben.” Lana stood with Sid’s help. “Whoever we’re dealing with is strong. If he can block the dead from seeking me out or stop them from talking with me, then his power is very strong. Ben called him the General.”

"Who had you around the throat, have you seen him before?" Sid made sure she was steady on her feet before returning to collect his guns from the ground.

"Yes." Lana couldn't help but shiver. "I didn't see his face before, but now I know why he wears that cape with a hood. And I think Ben is right. I think he knows you."

Sid holstered his guns watching her closely. "What do you mean?"

"I don't know. A feeling, I guess, but when he heard your voice, he at first looked shocked, and then smiled, or at least it looked like a smile." Lana frowned.

"What the hell are you talking about?" Sid eyed her.

"His face was badly scarred. It was hard to tell his facial expressions." She looked up at Sid. "His skin looked melted, like he had been burned badly."

Sid paused, staring at her; she could tell his brain was going a mile a minute.

"Son of a bitch! Come on. We have to go." He grabbed her hand while dialing his phone with his free hand. Putting it to his ear, he slowed down so she could keep up. "Mcct mc at the compound in five. Make sure the women are accounted for and everyone is there."

Lana groaned as her body protested, but she kept pace. "What's going on?"

"It looks like you're not the only one seeing dead people." Sid opened the door, helped her in, and then ran jumping into the driver's seat.

"I don't think he was dead, Sid," Lana frowned.

“No, but he should be.” Sid put the car in reverse. “Buckle up,” he warned as he backed up and took off at a breakneck speed.

Chapter 15

“No way.” Duncan shook his head. Barely controlled rage flew off him in waves. “No fucking way. I sent that son of a bitch to hell.”

“I’m not one hundred percent positive, Duncan, but I have a bad feeling about this.” Sid glanced at Pam, who held Daniel tightly. “Just keep the women close until we know for sure.”

“It can’t be,” Pam shook her head, fear making her shake. “You killed him.”

Duncan walked over to hold her close. “I watched him burn,” Duncan told her, his eyes moving from her to Daniel and then back to Sid. “I watched him burn!”

Sid didn’t know what to say. He wasn’t positive it was Kenny, but the coincidence was too fucking crazy not to take seriously. “I know you did, brother.” Sid gave him a nod, his eyes going to Daniel. “But there is no way we can let this go without making sure. There’s too much at stake.”

“We’ll up security around here,” Sloan nodded. “Phillip is coming back and I’m trying to get a few more Warriors transferred.”

The Warriors silently looked at each other. With the women in the room, they didn’t want to frighten them any more than they were, but each knew this was bad. Really bad.

Duncan leaned down, kissing Pam and then Daniel’s soft little forehead when he started to fuss. “If this is Kenny, which I doubt, I will not let anything happen to you or Daniel.” Duncan hugged her close. “The little guy’s getting hungry. Go on and feed my boy. I’ll be there in a minute.”

"Don't you keep anything from me, Duncan," Pam warned and didn't look away until he nodded. She looked at each Warrior before turning and leaving the kitchen with Daniel, who was fussing loudly.

Nicole pulled Damon down, kissing him on the cheek. "I'll go with her." She stopped next to Jared. "Is Tessa up?"

"Yeah, she was just getting a shower when I came down," Jared replied.

"I'll stop by and check on her." Nicole patted his arm.

"Thanks." Jared smiled down at her. "Tell her I'll be up soon."

"Stay inside unless one of us is with you," Sid gave the warning as Nicole walked out.

Duncan's attention snapped to Sid as soon as Nicole was out the door. "You didn't get a good look at him?

"No, he never fully faced me," Sid replied, the frustration thick in his voice.

"Even if he would have gotten a good look at him, trying to get a positive ID would have been impossible," Lana added, her voice hoarse and harsh from not talking for a while.

Sid cursed, walking away. They were in the kitchen, which was the biggest room they had and would hold them all at one time.

"He was disfigured beyond recognition. Any hair he had was patchy, and one eye was scarred over with skin. The other was a dull gold with a pale white film." Lana wished she had more, but that was it.

"Here, drink this." Sid handed her a mug. "It's hot tea and brandy. It will help soothe your throat."

"Thanks." Lana took the cup, blowing across the top before taking a drink.

"We need a way in." Jared frowned. "And because of all the shit that's happened around here, we are all poster boys for the Warrior Clan in this area. Dammit!"

"Blurred Lines" broke the silence following Jared's curse. All eyes landed on Jill who had been standing to the side with Steve. Steve took a step away from Jill.

"Sorry." Jill started out the door to answer her phone, but Sid stopped her.

"Answer the phone, Jill. I know that's Adam's ring tone because I almost killed the fucker over that damn song," Sid glared at her. "Put it on speaker."

Jill glanced around at all the eyes on her as she answered. "Hello?" She clicked the speaker holding it out.

"Why the hell didn't you call me back?" Adam growled over the phone.

"Because I haven't been alone until now," Jill said the lie as every Warrior in the house frowned at her. "Stop being an asshole and tell me where the hell you are."

"Sorry," Adam replied, sounding just a little sorry. "I need your help, Jill. I've made contact with someone, and I need you to help me on this."

Jill closed her eyes feeling like the biggest traitor in the world. She loved Adam like a brother and she hated betraying him, even if it was out of her control. Glancing at Sid, who nodded to her, she sighed.

“You know I’ll help you any way I can,” Jill replied with a frown. “But don’t you think you should be asking about Tessa?”

Silence echoed over the phone and throughout the room. She knew she chanced Adam getting pissed and hanging up, but she didn’t care. She had to make sure for herself that Adam wasn’t turning into a non-caring blood craving rogue.

“I’ve been talking to Steve,” Adam admitted.

All focus turned to Steve who spread his arms wide open, his mouth as wide as his eyes; then he just slumped his shoulders, glaring at Jill.

“And I talked to Jared, who was being a total jackass. I know how my sister is, Jill, so don’t worry about that,” Adam shouted in the phone.

Jill watched Jared take a menacing step toward her phone, but Damon stopped him with a slap of his huge hand to Jared’s chest. Sloan pointed at Jared in warning.

“Well, I do worry about it, Adam,” Jill said even though Sid was shaking his head at her and rolling his eyes. “Because there is no way I’m helping you do anything if you’re turning rogue, so don’t tell me what to worry about, and if you don’t lose the ‘tude’ I’m hanging up. I’m not your little bitch.”

Sid smacked his hand to his forehead. Jared still looked ready to kill her phone. Damon just shook his head, while Sloan was glaring at her and Slade was actually grinning. Lana, the only other female in the room, gave Jill a thumbs up.

Again, silence, as everyone held their breath, wondering if Adam was just going to say 'fuck it' and hang up.

"Growing some balls are we, Jill?" Adam, sounding like the old Adam, chuckled.

"Bigger every day." Jill couldn't help the grin on her face. "Now stop being a jerk and tell me what you need me to do."

"I need you to meet me at Metropolis Night Club tomorrow night at ten." Adam's tone turned deadly serious. "I need to sell you."

That shocked Jill. "Sell me? What the hell are you talking about?"

"It's our way in." Adam's voice had an excited edge to it. "Please, Jill, I really need your help. I know it's asking a lot, but I swear I won't let anything happen to you. I just need to find out where they take you and then I'll get you out."

Sid and Lana made eye contact. Lana dug into her bag, grabbing a pen and an old envelope scribbling something down.

"To who?" Jill responded, reading what Lana wrote. "Who are you selling me to?"

"He wouldn't give his name," Adam sighed. "I know I haven't given anyone any reason to trust me, but I swear, Jill, I never meant to hurt Tessa. I love her more than anything, but I have to find Angelina. Please understand that."

Sid watched the emotions play across Jill's face as she looked at each one of them. Slade and Steve were shaking their heads no, while everyone else was nodding, urging her to agree. Sid grabbed the paper from Lana, writing something down.

'We will have your back!!'

Jill read Sid's note. "I'll be there, Adam." Jill glanced at Sid, who gave her a wink of confidence. "I gotta go. If anything changes, just text me."

"I owe you one, Jill," Adam sighed heavily over the phone.

"You bet your ass you do," Jill replied, hanging up the phone, and that's when all hell broke loose.

Sid stood back watching everyone cursing and yelling. He glanced at Lana, who also sat back watching. They finally made eye contact both knowing, without a doubt, this was the break they needed.

******

When everyone finally left the kitchen and the plan for the next night was in place, Lana stood ready to leave. "Well, I guess I better get going." She stretched grabbing her stuff. "I need to go see my sister since I won't be able to make it tomorrow night."

"You don't have plans for your birthday?" Sid frowned down at her, not liking the sadness in her beautiful blue eyes.

"No, we usually celebrate with her the day after." Lana rubbed her throat, which was still bruised an ugly shade of black and purple. "I'll have to tell them I can't make it then."

"Why not just do it tonight?" Sid lifted her chin a little, looking at her neck, anger darkening his eyes. When she didn't answer, Sid's eyes slid to hers. "Why don't you celebrate on your birthday, Lana?"

"Because her fiancé will be there and he hates me," Lana frowned. "His whole family hates me actually."

Sid watched as she fought the emotions swirling in her eyes. "Lana, if you want to see your sister then nothing should stop you."

"I know that, but I try to give them their time without drama." Lana looked up at him with a hardness. "Usually, I don't give a damn what people think, but I am responsible and I know that. I just don't want it thrown in my face constantly. I have a hard enough time dealing as it is."

Anger at anyone who would throw something like that in this woman's face pissed Sid off. He dared anyone to throw anything while he was around. "Come on." He grabbed her bag, handing it to her.

"What?" Lana took the bag, looking confused.

"Let's go see your sister." Sid grabbed her hand, leading her toward the door. He would be damned if anyone tried to stop her from seeing her sister.

"You'd go with me?" She looked surprised.

"I am your partner, so yeah." Sid nodded, his expression serious. He was on her side, and he was proving it with his actions.

"Thought you were my boss." Lana glanced at him as they made their way outside to Sid's car.

"When you're stubborn, I'm your boss," Sid explained with a get-this-straight smile. "When you're complying with everything I say, we're partners."

"Thank you," Lana said as soon as they were both inside the car.

"Call your parents," Sid instructed. "I'd love to meet the ones who gave birth to the woman who put me in my place."

Lana laughed. “Oh, I put you in your place?”

Sid loved her laugh. It was open without a hint of anything other than a true genuine laugh. He wasn’t used to that with women and he enjoyed the sound. “Okay, maybe not put me in my place, but made me think twice about crossing you.” Sid worked his jaw back and forth with his free hand. “Who the hell taught you to punch like that?”

“My daddy,” Lana smiled proudly. “Me and my sister could take any boy in the neighborhood.”

“That I have no doubt.” Sid glanced at her once they stopped at a light.

“Do you always have a smile on your face?” Lana teased. “I thought VC Warriors were supposed to be all moody badasses.”

“Oh, I’m a badass.” Sid tossed her a look. “I just like to have a good time while being my badass self.”

Lana laughed. “You certainly seem to do that well.”

“You better believe it.” Sid pulled into the parking lot. “I’ll teach you how to be just like me.”

“Full of myself?” Lana got out of the car with a large grin at the seriousness of Sid’s tone as he got out and walked around to her side of the car.

“Nooo, but you will be the coolest and funniest badass chick on the police force.” Sid replied after opening her door and helping her out.

Lana grinned at him before glancing up at the hospital. “Thank you.” She turned, reaching up to kiss his cheek. “I know we started out on the wrong foot, and I know I don’t really know you well, but just by the past ten minutes, I realize how great a person you are.”

Sid frowned, feeling uncomfortable, which was a feeling he was not comfortable with at all. “Lana, I’m an asshole.”

“No, you’re not. If you were, I would be walking into a grim situation alone.” Lana grinned up at him, grabbing his hand. “You’re a nice guy, Sid Sinclair.”

Even though her words made him cringe, they also warmed him. He didn’t want to see her face this alone. He wasn’t exactly sure what to expect, but he was ready for whatever it was going to be. She may be a cop and tough as hell, but that didn’t make his strong urge to protect this woman go away. If anything, it made her more vulnerable to him.

“Some would definitely argue that to the point of laughing themselves to death, Ms. Fitzpatrick,” Sid winked down at her. “And it could be I have an ulterior motive in being nice.”

“Humm, you ever wonder if all my sweet talk could mean I have a motive of my own?” Lana gave him a slow wink, and was inside the door before Sid could pull her back to find out exactly what she meant.

His eyes roamed to her hips that swayed with purpose. “Jesus, I hope to hell you do.”

A young grunge-looking kid stood just inside the door. “What?”

Sid pried his eyes off Lana’s ass. “What?” Sid glanced at the kid.

“Dude.” The kid was holding an iPod in one hand and an earplug in the other. “You’re freaking me out, man.” The kid’s laugh was goofy as hell.

“I wasn’t talking to you.” Sid glared down at the kid who started following him.

"Hey man, you got a smoke?"

"Don't smoke." Sid again glared at the kid trying to scare him away.

"How about some money so I can buy me some smokes? Come on, dude, help a guy out." The kid didn't back down. His eyes landed on Lana, and immediately he began to pant like a dog. "Oh, yeah. Now, I know what you were sayin'. That's a nice piece of…"

"Okay…*dude*. I'm going to help you out." Sid sneered down at him, stopping at the elevator. "Number one: get a fucking job and buy your own shit. Number two: take your eyes off the lady. Number three: get the fuck away from me."

When the kid let loose another goofy laugh, Sid leaned in his face with a growl, and bared his fangs.

"Ah man, you about made me shit my pants." The kid, who looked scared to death a second ago, was grinning like an idiot. "Those things real?"

Sid ignored the kid as he stepped inside the elevator with Lana. Hitting the close button, Sid watched the door close on the kid who continued to stare at him as the door closed in his face.

"What floor?" He glanced down at Lana who had watched the exchange and was now looking up at him curiously.

"Eighth," she replied. Waiting until he hit the button, she said, "Don't ask?"

"Don't ask," Sid agreed. He still couldn't believe the brief exchange with the kid, who either ate lead paint chips since birth or had scored a bad bag of weed, had even happened.

The elevator stopped at the fourth floor. A pretty nurse with red hair stepped on, and proceeded to squeal when she saw Sid.

"Sidilicious!" She rushed on the elevator with a huge grin following her huge breasts that she stuck out as soon as she saw Sid. Lana stepped away, not wanting to get crushed.

Sid had no other choice but to grab onto her, or they'd both crash into the elevator wall.

She grabbed on tight, practically crawling on him. "Why haven't you called, baby?" she pouted, smacking him lightly on the arm. "The last time you were here and we…"

"Oh, hey, ah…" Fuck he couldn't remember her name. Son of a bitch, he knew his dick was going to get him in deep shit one day.

She pushed away from him, her lip trembling. "It's Diane." Her hand went to her mouth. "You don't even remember my name." The doors opened as she smacked him across the face; she then stomped out without looking back.

"Going up?" Sid eyed the small man in a suit looking surprised as he stood outside the elevator.

"Ah, I'll wait." The man glanced once at Lana then at Sid. "But thanks."

"Whatever." Sid hit the close button.

"Guess I deserved that," Sid cleared his throat, cracking his neck to the left then the right.

Laughter drowned out the God-awful elevator music. "Oh, you *so* deserved that." Lana grinned at Sid's shocked look. "You should have seen your face when you realized you couldn't remember her name."

At that moment, Sid stopped grinning, realizing that this beautiful blue-eyed woman could be the one. He had thought if he ever found a woman who could tame his ways, he would go running for the hills, but he was having the total opposite thoughts. He wanted to stay right by her side. She was so much like him it was damn scary. The door opened to their floor. He waited for her to exit, but she was laughing too hard.

"Oh, no, after you, Sidilicious." She snorted when he grabbed her, pulling her off the elevator, a grin playing at the corner of his mouth.

"Well, I'm glad you're having the time of your life, while your sister is sitting in a chair lost to us." A male voice silenced the hallway.

Chapter 16

"That's not fair, Rod." Lana frowned, her whole personality taking an offensive edge.

"No, what's not fair is her being in there and not you," Rod glared at her, hate coming off him in waves.

"I know." Lana eyes drifted from him. "Don't you think I don't wish for that every single day?"

Sid did his best to keep his mouth shut, but he instantly disliked the man talking to Lana as though she was at fault for her sister's condition. His overbearing way of standing over Lana was making his fist itch to smash into his fucking face. Not to mention how confusing it was seeing this 'in your face' woman turn a one-eighty into a very docile woman who didn't seem to know her own worth. Yeah, he was getting pissed. He would give her another minute to hit this motherfucker in the face herself.

"What are you doing here?" Rod hissed taking a step closer. "This isn't your day."

"I know," Lana repeated again. "I'll wait. It's just I can't make it tomorrow and I wanted to see Caroline."

"Tough shit, Lana," Rod's voice rose. "You should have thought about that when you called her to do *your* job. You knew she hated what you call a gift, but you guilted her into doing it. So I don't care about your issues."

"But I do." Sid stepped up behind Lana. "And if you don't back off, you're going to have your own issues to deal with."

"No, Sid." Lana shook her head, reaching into her bag. "He's right. It is his day."

"Who are you?" Rod glared over the top of Lana's head at Sid.

"Don't worry about it." Lana lifted up a small glass hummingbird; the wings were tipped with different shades of blue. "This is our grandmother's. We used to fight over it when we were little. Grammy wanted me to give it to her. Maybe set it on her tray or in the window. The necklace is from me."

"I don't want anything from you or that woman near her. She is in there because of you and that old woman." He knocked the glass hummingbird and necklace out of her hand.

"No!" Lana tried to catch it, but the sounds of glass breaking on the floor echoed followed by an angry roar.

One minute, Rod was standing there looking satisfied, the next, he was on the floor, his face smashed against the glass.

"You are going to pick up every single piece of glass, you stupid son of a bitch." Sid's hand tightened in his hair. "I don't care how long it takes you. You're lucky I don't kill you."

"Don't even think about it, Fred." Another male voice filled the hallway.

Sid looked behind him to see a man approaching him. Then he glanced up at an older man who was standing next to Lana.

"Let go of my brother," the man behind Sid ordered.

"You best back off or you'll find yourself next to him." Sid warned, pushing Rod's head harder into the glass.

"Let him up, son." The older man, who was gently holding Lana back from going to the glass on the ground, nodded to Sid.

Sid sighed with a curse. "You just got a free ticket, asshole. You see that necklace lying next to your hand?" When Rod didn't answer, Sid pressed down harder.

"Yes!" Rod cried out. "I see it."

"Good," Sid hissed. "You're going to pick that up nice and careful, and then we're going to stand up. You understanding so far?"

"Yes." Rod looked at the necklace. "Hurry up, there's glass in my face."

"Do you seriously think I give a shit?" Sid laughed without humor. "You should be glad that's your only problem at the moment. Now, grab the necklace."

Rod worked his hand over, grasping the necklace, which was a locket on a pale red ribbon. "Okay, now let me up."

Sid stood, pulling the man up by his hair. When Rod started to struggle, Sid kicked his feet out from under him, sending him back to the floor on his face. With his hand still in his hair and a knee to the man's back, Sid leaned down. "This is your last warning, motherfucker," Sid said just loud enough for Rod to hear. "If you don't think I'll kill you on the spot, you're sadly mistaken. Now, let's try this one more time, because all you get is one more time."

Again, Sid stood, pulling him up by the hair. Glass pieces were stuck into his cheek, blood oozing from each wound.

"Now, you are going to hand Ms. Fitzpatrick the necklace with an apology." Sid jerked his head back so Rod could see his black eyes.

"And it better be nice," he warned.

"Here," Rod growled and then hissed when Sid snapped his head back hard.

"Not nice enough." Sid shoved his head back.

"Sid, please." Lana looked around at the crowd that was watching.

"You will not be treated like that when I'm around." Sid's stare softened when it landed on her.

Lana reached out, grabbing the necklace.

"I'm sorry," Rod said, keeping the sarcastic and hateful edge out of his tone.

"Better, but still not good enough," Sid growled then looked back at Lana. "You want to punch him?"

"What?" Lana's eyes opened wide.

"What?" Rod's eyes also widened in surprise.

"I know you want to." Sid nodded toward Rod, his hand still holding him still by his hair. "Go ahead."

"You're crazy." Rod started to struggle.

"You don't even know, asshole." Sid did let go so he could punch him in the jaw, ass planting him in the glass on the floor.

"Honey, why don't you go on inside and see Caroline?" The older man steered her away from Rod and Sid.

Sid stared down at Rod who was trying to pick himself off the floor. Once Rod stood straight, he started toward Sid. "Please make my day." Sid smiled, which stopped Rod cold. "Smart move. Now get the hell out of here before you make the worst decision of your life."

Rod's brother stepped in and grabbed Rod. "Come on. Let's go."

"This isn't over." Rod pointed to Sid and then at the older man who stood at Sid's back. "Miles, we had an agreement."

"Which was Lana's idea, but you better believe that agreement is over." Miles, who was a big man with a military build, took a step forward. "If I ever hear you talk to my daughter that way again, I will do worse than this young man did and stick a 45 up your scrawny ass."

"But you can't do that." Rod's eyes narrowed. "That's my fiancée."

"Exactly. Your fiancée." Miles' voice was full of authority. "You have no rights here."

Rod gave them both one last heated glare before rushing out.

Sid watched him go before turning to who he figured was Lana's father. "I'm Sid Sinclair." He stuck out his hand. "I take it you're Lana's father."

"Miles Fitzpatrick." He shook Sid's hand in a firm grip. "Thank you for what you did."

"No need to thank me," Sid replied, following Miles to where Lana disappeared. "He had it coming and I was more than happy to give it to him."

Miles stopped at the door, looking at his daughters. "You know, Lana is the toughest girl I know. I made her that way. She is actually tougher than some of the men I know, but this has really been hard for her."

"Is that why she did a one-eighty with that bastard?" Sid asked, also watching Lana combing her sister's hair. "Because, in all honesty, I held back at first, waiting for her to unload on him."

Miles shook his head, looking over at Sid. "I guess Lana has explained to you what this is all about."

"Not in so many words," Sid replied, not mentioning he listened in on her conversation with someone else. "But I've filled in some of the blanks."

"She blames herself," Miles sighed. "Her sister never grasped her gift like Lana. Even with them being twins, they are totally opposite, but very connected, if that makes any sense at all."

Sid nodded, glancing back at Lana as she talked a mile a minute to her sister, who just sat staring straight ahead, emotionless, lost in a world they couldn't see. They were not identical, but you could tell they were twins. "Yes, sir, it does."

"So when this happened, Rod was devastated and blamed Lana, who already blames herself." Miles frowned, "They were to be married next month. So Lana goes out of her way to make sure Rod has time with Caroline without her around. Even on the birthday they share, which as you know is today. We were to come tomorrow to celebrate."

"That's kind of my fault," Sid frowned. "We have a case we're working on and—"

"No need to explain." Miles raised his hand. "I'm a retired cop, so I know. And now seeing what I just saw, I know she's in good hands."

"You know she's working with the VC Warriors?" Sid asked, surprised.

"There isn't much I don't know, son, and what I don't know, Lana fills me in," he smiled. "Now, why don't I introduce you to my other daughter?"

Sid followed Miles inside the large room that was set up just like a girl's bedroom would be. "Hey, how's my girl?" Miles leaned down, kissing Caroline on the forehead.

"She looks good today," Lana smiled, putting the brush down.

Sid spotted the necklace on Lana's sister's neck. His eyes met Lana's, and even though there was a smile on her face, the sadness in her eyes almost did him in.

"My Lord, Lana." A beautiful woman walked in the room carrying presents. A younger girl who looked a lot like Lana followed, bringing in a cake. "A little more warning would have been nice."

"Sorry, Momma," Lana grinned grabbing things out of her hands. "But you know how work is."

Her mother rolled her eyes, and kissed Lana's cheek before heading toward Caroline. "Hello, baby." She touched her cheek and kissed her forehead.

"No, I'm good." The young girl snorted. "I got this."

Sid walked over, grabbing the cake out of her hand.

"Ah, who are you?" The girl eyed him then Lana.

“That’s my boss.” Lana grinned when Sid rolled his eyes. “Sid Sinclair. And this is my mother, Melanie, and my younger sister, Jamie.”

“Nice to meet you.” Sid smiled at them then looked toward Miles. “You poor man. Living with four beautiful women. How do you cope?”

Miles laughed. “Son, you have no idea. I’ve built two bathrooms onto the house and I still have to wait.”

“It’s nice to meet you, Sid.” Lana’s mom smiled at him before turning toward Lana. “He’s very handsome.”

“And can hear every word you say,” Lana frowned at her mom.

“As can your husband,” Lana’s dad growled, grabbing her mom and kissing her neck. “Don’t make me beat Lana’s boss up. It could look bad on her yearly review.”

Sid looked at Lana who just shrugged silently as if saying ‘this is my family and good luck.’

“So, you’re a vampire, huh?” Jamie stared at him. “Do you have an urge to kill us and you know—”

“Jamie Marie Fitzpatrick,” Her mother scolded while Lana laughed behind her hand and Lana’s dad laughed outright.

“Not at the moment, Jamie,” Sid grinned. He leaned closer, nodding his head for her to come nearer. “But I will tell you those three are safe. You, on the other hand, would be a tasty treat.” Sid grinned wider, showing his fangs.

Jamie stepped back so fast she fell into her father. “Okay, that wasn’t funny."

"Serves you right for being rude," her mother scolded again.

"I didn't mean to be rude." Jamie looked at Sid. "I was just curious. I've never talked to a vampire before."

"It's okay, Jamie." Sid gave her his jaw-dropping smile.

"Where's Rod?" Lana's mom asked a little nervously.

"Oh, he's gone already." Miles gave her a look that Sid didn't miss.

As the night wore on, Sid sat back, and even though they kept him feeling part of the group, he watched as an observer and was impressed by the love this family had for each other. It was something he had never known. The closest he had ever felt love from another was from his VC brothers, and that in itself could be dangerous as hell. Guess that would be called tough love. But this made him feel something he had never felt before, a craving to belong and feel like part of a family.

Even though Caroline did not come close to acknowledging anything, they all included her in everything as if she were normal. The only one who seemed to catch herself at times was Lana, and he knew exactly when that happened because a look of such sadness enveloped not only her face, but her whole body. Then she would close her eyes for a second, look around at the rest of her family and plaster on a smile, joining back into the mix. It took everything he had not to grab and hold her tightly as he fought her sadness away. One weakness Sid had was women. It had been that way for as long as he could remember, but he didn't remember ever having these types of feelings for one before. Her happiness had risen to the top of his priority list and that was very new to him.

Sid helped clean up, but quietly listened to them laugh and tease each other. He had never had a family of his own. Even before he was turned, he was orphaned, never being adopted out. He had been raised by priests. When he was old enough, he was thrown out on the street where he was turned within two days of being free. His thoughts turned back those hundreds of years ago, surprising him, because this was the first time in all that time, he yearned that things had been different for him.

"Hey, you okay?" Lana stood next to him, taking him by surprise. It had been a long time since he'd been so caught up in his thoughts that he was taken by surprise.

"Yeah." He looked down at her. He stared into her eyes, wondering if he could commit to a life with one woman. Doubt surfaced, but he knew without a doubt, if there was one woman out there he would want to spend his long lifetime with, it would be her. Jesus, he must be losing his mind to be thinking this way. What the hell! He hadn't even slept with her yet. He quickly wondered if this was how his brothers had felt when they found their mates or he was just losing his mind.

"Penny for your thoughts." Lana gave him a warm smile, but there were questions in her eyes.

"Give me a twenty, and they're yours," he said without a smile, but winked at her.

Lana reached into her back pocket, pulling out ten bucks. "I'm ten short. Can I have the bargain version?" she grinned, but her grin slipped quickly at the seriousness in his gaze.

They stood staring at each other while activity bustled around them. Neither smiled, but an understanding seemed to click.

"Sid, thank you again for taking care of my girl." Miles broke the moment, pulling Lana into a bear hug. "It's hard to let go. If I had it my way, all my girls would live under my roof forever."

Sid gave a nod. "She's a handful, but I've got it."

Lana rolled her eyes, pulling away from her dad. "Mom, Dad's being overbearing again." She took on a high-pitched voice as she called out to her mom. Sid couldn't help but laugh.

"Miles, stop it," Melanie ordered, but the adoration in her gaze softened the heat behind her words. She walked over, pinching him on the ribs before looking up at Sid. "I'm not sure what happened before I got here, but thank you. We were rushing to get here and Miles took off to make sure Lana didn't have to face Rod alone."

Sid glanced over at Lana, who was talking to Caroline, softly saying her goodbyes. "Does she come here alone often?"

"Yes." Miles pulled his wife closer. "Because of her work schedule, sometimes she has to drop in whenever she can, but she comes every day. I can only imagine what is said when we're not around, but nothing short of revoking Rod's visiting privileges, I don't know what to do."

"Lana won't let you do that." It wasn't a question; it was a fact Sid knew was true. In the short time Sid had known her, Lana definitely thought of others before herself.

"No, she won't," Melanie sighed.

Sid shook Miles's hand then kissed Melanie's. "It was nice meeting you both, and thank you for allowing me to be a part of your special night." Sid looked over at Jamie, who was staring at him. "Jamie, it was nice meeting you."

She nodded, glancing at her mom and dad who were busy getting their things. "Don't let anything happen to my sister." Her eyes, so much like Lana's, pleaded with him before she grabbed her things and walked out.

Sid turned his head, watching her leave. This family was going through a hell no one deserved. Turning his attention back to Caroline, he walked toward her. Reaching out, he placed his hand on her small cool fingers. A quick flash of something blinded his vision, but then it was gone. He had hoped touching her would allow him to see something but she was totally shut off to him. Adam had that talent, and as soon as he found the pain in the ass he would be bringing him here.

"It was nice meeting you, Caroline," he repeated the words he had said to her family. He squeezed her hand and was surprised to feel a finger twitch. Frowning, he stared down at her hand.

"You okay?" Lana walked up with her belongings.

Knowing he wasn't going to say anything, because he wasn't sure that he'd felt anything and didn't want to get Lana's hopes up, he looked away from her sister.

"Just saying goodbye," he smiled down at her.

Lana smiled back, gave Caroline one more kiss to the forehead, waved to her family one more time, and then walked next to Sid to the elevator. Sid noticed she didn't even glance to see if the glass had been cleaned up, which it had. Thinking about Rod, Sid's instincts kicked in and he became aware of everything. Rod looked stupid enough to hang around and he wasn't going to be caught off guard.

As soon as the door closed, Lana seemed to fold into herself. Her shoulders slumped; her eyes drooped as she leaned against the back wall of the elevator.

"Lana, you okay?" Sid watched her closely.

"Umm hum," she mumbled, her eyes closed. "I don't want to go home."

"Good." Sid leaned back next to her. "Because I wasn't taking you home."

Chapter 17

Lana made it to the car. Thankfully, Sid was quiet on the walk there, because it was taking everything she had to hold her emotions back. Hoping not to see Rod, she had kept her eyes down, almost running into people, but Sid had wrapped his arm around her, leading her out the door without running anyone down.

Once at the car, Lana stopped at the door waiting for Sid to unlock it. His hand slipped under her chin, pulling her face up to his. He didn't have to say a word; just the understanding look in his eyes did her in.

The first tear leaked from the corner of her eye, slipping down her cheek, and another followed from the other. Her lips quivered. "It should have been me," she whispered from somewhere deep, her words so full of hurt. "I should be the one up there, not her."

Sid pulled her into his arms, holding her tight. "Let it out."

His words hit the most wounded part of her soul, making her hold onto him for dear life. For the first time since her sister's accident, she didn't cry alone, but held onto a Warrior who absorbed her pain as if it was his own.

"It hurts so bad," Lana cried the words into his chest. "She was getting married. Her dress is still hanging on the door in her room. It's all she ever talked about when we were little girls. She wanted to get married, have a huge wedding, and I wanted to shoot bad guys."

Sid pushed her away enough to look down into her face. Using both hands, he tilted her face up to his. Sid gently rubbed her cheeks with his thumbs, wiping her pain away.

"She was a school teacher for God's sake. I'm the cop. I'm the one who faces danger all the time." Lana's tear-filled eyes looked up at him, searching for answers. "What made me ask her to do what she hated? Why did I ask her to take the risk?"

"Life is a risk, Lana." Sid's eyes didn't waver. "And being a school teacher is a risk with all the school shootings. You never would have knowingly put your sister in harm's way."

"No, I wouldn't," Lana replied, stepping away from him and wiping her eyes. "But I did, and it's one thing I don't know if I can live with."

"Don't even talk like that," Sid raised her face to his, anger forming each word. "You have a family who has your back and loves you very much. They would be devastated if something happened to you."

Lana nodded, and then shook her head. Dammit, she was losing it. Pouring her heart out to Sid was unexpected, but it felt so right. "I know and I didn't mean it like that. I'm not going to off myself. Shit, I would never…" she cursed once again, wiping her tears away with quick swipes. "I'm not usually this bad. I'm so sorry for falling apart like this, and thank you for the shoulder." She leaned up and kissed his cheek, a habit that she was becoming familiarly oddly comfortable with.

Sid's eyes drank her in as he leaned down, placing a light kiss on her lips. "Never thank me, Lana." Sid pulled away opening the door. "I'm here for whatever you need."

Lana practically melted into the seat. If he only knew what his words meant to her. She had been alone for so long. Even with her family, she had been so lonely. Taking a deep breath, she slowly let it out. Glancing up at the hospital, she knew in her heart that Caroline would want her to go on with life, and she was really trying. God, she was trying. Sid slid in, started the car, and backed out without a word. From the corner of her eye, she watched him and wondered if this man could help her find herself again. She was just as lost as Caroline; the only difference was Lana was hiding the fact behind fake smiles.

The ride was silent, but Sid had reached over, taking her hand with a firm grip. It only took ten minutes to get back to the compound. Lana didn't ask any questions. She didn't want to go home and fall into the depression that plagued her every time she left her sister.

As if by habit, Lana waited for Sid to open her door. Without words, they walked into the compound hand in hand, she taking comfort from his touch. Lana noticed the entryway was almost completely reconstructed, except for a paint job. Sid led her into the kitchen where they were met with Damon and Nicole in a deep embrace.

"What part of Sid's Kitchen Law did you two not understand?" Sid growled, letting go of Lana's hand to take off his jacket, tossing it in a chair.

Damon growled back, but let go of his wife. "You have the worst timing, brother."

"No, you have the worst case of being whipped by your woman that I've ever seen." Sid slid past him, pointing to the small poster board of his kitchen laws he had actually made up. "Read it, learn it, and by God, do it! This is a kitchen for Christ's sake."

Nicole shook her head, arms crossed and smiling when Sid came to her, kissing her on the cheek. "Sid, as many women as you've had, I'm sure you've done it in many a kitchen." Nicole turned, seeing Lana, and grimaced. "Ah, sorry."

"Oh, no. Don't be," Lana grinned, watching Sid squirm.

"See." He pointed a large wooden spoon at Nicole. "I try to bring a respectable lady here and you go and say things like that. I am ashamed of you."

Lana snorted, "Seriously, don't worry about it. He's just my boss and I've already met one of his lovely ladies." Lana's grin widened when

Sid shook his head at her. "Sidilicious seems to be well-known at the hospital, especially by redheaded nurses with big breasts."

"Ah, shit!" Sid glared at Lana with narrowed eyes. "Really?"

Lana nodded, pursing her lips. "Really."

"Sidilicious?" Nicole sputtered. "Oh man, tell me you're not lying." Nicole eyed Lana and threw back her head laughing when Lana crossed her heart.

"Control your woman," Sid growled at Damon, who just looked at Sid in disgusted shock.

"Sidilicious?" Damon glanced at him sideways. "Tell me it's not true, my brother."

"Hey! Hey! Can I help it if the ladies like to nickname me?" Sid threw his arms out wide.

"Sidilicious, Rachel Ray? What's next, G-strings and pedicures?" Damon held his hand up, shaking his head.

Nicole lifted her hand toward Damon for a high five. "I can't breathe," Nicole wheezed. She watched Sid as he opened doors to every cupboard in the kitchen before slamming them shut. "What in the hell are you looking for?" she asked with a hiccup and giggle.

"My manhood," Sid frowned, slamming another draw door closed. "Now, get the fuck out of my kitchen."

Damon and Nicole grinned like fools as they made their way to the door. Nicole stopped and glanced back at Sid then to Lana. "I'm Nicole." She patted Lana on the shoulder. "I'm sure I'll talk to you very soon, Lana."

"Get out!" Sid growled, pointing toward the door with his spoon.

Lana frowned, feeling terrible for teasing Sid. He looked so upset, and she really didn't mean to do that. Getting up, she walked over to him, his back turned toward her.

"Sid, I'm sorry." Lana started to apologize.

"Are they gone?" Sid asked without turning around.

Lana glanced behind her to make sure. "Yeah." Before she knew what was going on, Sid grabbed her, pulling her in front of him. His lips found hers in a long opened-mouthed kiss that had her body on fire in one fast flash. One large arm was around her lower back, the other her upper back as his hand tangled in her hair, cupping her scalp. When she thought she was going to pass out, he lifted his mouth a fraction from her lips; his eyes remained closed as he breathed her in.

"That will teach you to tease me." His eyes opened slowly, burning into hers. His voice was teasing, but his eyes were telling a whole different story.

Lana's lips tilted in a small smile, her eyes searching his handsome face. If teasing him got her this, then she would come up with new ones by the minute. "Rachael Ray? Really?"

His lips smashed down on hers as his hands cupped her ass, bringing her up his body. She wrapped her legs around his waist, her arms around his neck, loving the feeling of being smashed against his hard body. His strength radiated off him in waves and she relished the feeling. She rubbed against his hardness making him moan.

"Think I found your manhood," she grinned against his lips.

"Honey, it was never lost." His growl against her ear sent shivers in places she didn't know she could shiver.

He worked his way to her neck, eating her alive. His fangs dragged across her skin, sending her over the edge.

"Oh, sorry…" A male voice echoed in the room. "I, ah…"

"Shit," Sid hissed, his body going rigid.

"You have got to be kidding me!" Jared actually walked closer, seeing Lana peek over his shoulder. "Hey, Lana."

Lana gave Jared a finger wave over Sid's shoulder, then looked up at Sid, who was staring down at her. "Cover your eyes and don't look, no matter what you hear."

"Why?" Lana asked concerned at his seriousness.

"Because there is about to be a lot of blood." Sid walked a few steps, setting her on the counter. "Jared, get the fuck out of here." Sid adjusted himself before turning around.

"This is fucking classic." Jared leaned against the counter, his arms crossed.

"Hey, guys." Tessa walked in and with one glance at Sid's tense face, she frowned. "What's going on?"

Sid took three steps, kissing Tessa on the forehead, his eyes still glaring at Jared. "How you feeling, Tess?"

"Fine," Tessa replied, still looking between Jared and Sid. "Did I interrupt something?"

"No, I did," Jared's grin widened.

"Tessa, honey, if you like Jared's face that way, you best get your man out of here," Sid warned sweetly to Tessa, but still glared at Jared.

Jared casually pushed away from the counter, walking to the poster board with the kitchen law. "Read it, learn it, and by God, do it! This is a kitchen for Christ's sake." Jared's voice mocked Sid's word by word.

"Yeah, the difference is, dickhead, it's my kitchen." Sid dove for Jared, knocking him to the ground.

Lana jumped off the counter, but Tessa stopped her from getting close. "They're fine." Tessa grinned, shaking her head. "I'm Tessa, by the way."

"Lana." Lana nodded at her, but quickly turned her attention back to Sid and Jared.

"I'm impressed." Tessa looked her up and down. "Sid never brings his women here."

Lana's glanced at her. "Really?"

"Oh, I'm sorry." Tessa bit her lip. "I shouldn't have said that. I mean…"

"It's okay," Lana smiled seeing that Tessa was truly shocked. "I know he's a…."

"Man whore?" Tessa supplied for her.

"Guess that's one way to put it." Lana moved her head back and forth, watching as Sid helped Jared up, then punched him in the stomach.

"And that doesn't bother you?" Tessa's smile faded a little showing that she was truly impressed.

"At the moment, no." Lana laughed when Tessa's mouth dropped open. "I have a past also. We all do. I'm not going to hate a man because he kissed me in the kitchen after he's been with countless women."

She suddenly felt a little sorry for Sid. Since she had known him, everyone gave him shit. Not that he didn't give it back, but sometimes enough was enough. She saw the frown he gave Jared when Jared made a comment and knew it was another dig. This time Sid just turned away, holding his hand to her. Instead of taking his hand, she took two quick steps, jumping into the same position they had been found, kissing him hard.

"What happens if I break your Kitchen Law?" she grinned against his lips.

He turned, totally ignoring the open-mouthed gapes of Tessa and Jared as he headed toward the door. "You're about to find out."

Lana grinned, kissing the side of his neck, and gave Jared and Tessa a finger wave.

Loud laughter followed them out of the kitchen.

Chapter 18

Sid made it to his room finally after a few stops of plastering Lana against the wall, kissing her breathless. She was still wrapped around him, kissing and biting at his neck. It took him forever to open his door; he even had thoughts about kicking the fucker down.

Once inside, he let her slide slowly down his body, loving the feel. Glancing around his room, he frowned. "I'm sorry, but this is the only place I have," Sid apologized, not really knowing why he apologized.

"It's fine." Lana didn't even look around, her eyes on him.

"I just moved here a little less than a year ago and haven't had a chance to find a place of my own." Sid added, wondering why in the hell he was explaining himself to her. Okay, he was definitely freaking himself out. He never explained himself to women; he just fucked them and moved on.

"Sid, what's wrong?" Lana took a step back.

"Nothing," he sighed, running his hand through this hair. "No, that's not true. Jesus, this is new for me."

Lana looked at him a little surprised. "You trying to tell me you're really a virgin?" she teased.

Sid actually grinned at that, and then stared at her for a minute. "Yeah, in a way I am."

"Excuse me?" Lana choked on the words.

"I've never brought a woman here before." Sid glared down at her. "And I have never had second thoughts about screwing her."

"Okay, well that was crude and fuck you, asshole." Lana pushed him aside, making her way to the door.

"Fuck." Sid grabbed her, turning her around. "That came out wrong."

"Ah, you think?" Lana pulled her arm away. "Listen, I need to go anyway. We have a big day tomorrow, and we both need to have our shit together. Not stressing about whether you want to *screw* me or not."

Sid put his hand on the door, looming over her. "You're not going anywhere." Sid caged her in, his front to her back. "What I'm trying to say, with much difficulty, is you're different. I don't want to just toss you on the bed and be done with it."

Lana dropped her hand from the doorknob, but didn't turn to face him. "Go on."

"And I know tonight was hard on you. I don't want to take advantage of you. I don't want to use you like I've done others." Sid tilted his head back, looking at the ceiling, wondering what pussy had possessed him, because the shit coming out of his mouth was not him.

Lana finally turned around, pushing him back. "I'm a grown-ass woman, Sid. Going home and crying myself to sleep is not what I want to do." She unbuttoned the first two buttons on her shirt. "I know what I want. I'm not asking for music or flowers or sweet rhyming words. That's not you, and I knew that when I punched your arrogant face. I know what kind of man you are. Women aren't stupid. Well, at least most of them aren't. I still can't believe the redhead in the elevator is a nurse, but that's beside the point."

Sid's lips twitched. "Go on," he repeated her own words back to her, but neither knew if he meant with her buttons or words.

"I want you, Sid, and I'm not afraid to say it." Lana finished unbuttoning her shirt, slipped it off her shoulders and let it drop to the floor. "So if you're too big of a *pussy* to make the first move, I will."

Sid still had one hand plastered against the door above her head. His ears heard every word she said, but his eyes roamed the fullness of her breasts spilling out of her lacy pale-blue bra. When she reached behind her to take off the bra, he stopped her. "The jeans next." He demanded, his voice deep.

Unbuttoning her jeans, she shimmied them over her hips, down her legs and stepped out of them. Her pale-blue panties matched her bra.

"Turn around." Sid didn't move. He didn't have to. His voice held enough deep authority to demand what he wanted. Her hips were wide, making her panties cup her well-rounded ass cheeks, leaving just enough dipping out, making his mouth water and his cock press painfully against his zipper. "Damn." He brought his free hand up, cupping her ass as he ran his middle finger lightly along her crease.

Lana moaned softly, moving her head to the side, looking up at him from over her shoulder, her eyes heated with desire. Sid had never seen anything more beautiful in his long life. His hand left her ass, traveling to her lower back and then to her stomach, which was rounded, not flat and or concave; it was perfect and sexy as hell. Sid liked his women with meat on their bones. There was nothing sexier than a woman's curves, dips and valleys to explore. His hand splayed wide across her stomach as he pulled her against him. Dropping his other hand from the door, he moved her hair out of the way, kissing her neck, and smiled when she arched her back, pushing her large breasts out.

"What do you want, lovely Lana?" His words were spoken softly against her skin.

"I want you to touch me." She didn't hesitate to answer and wasn't shy when she grabbed the hand that was against her stomach, moving it between both breasts. Her hand dropped as her head fell back on his chest when he cupped one breast, using his hand to massage and squeeze every part except for the nipple that was poking through the thin material, begging for his touch. With his thumbs, he pulled her bra underneath each breast before turning her around.

His golden eyes had darkened to almost black; they roamed her body before meeting hers. With his strength, his gripped her hips, lifting her up and slowly pinning her against the door. Her hands gripped his wrists. He couldn't take his eyes off her. She was beautiful as he held her there for the pleasure of just looking. Finally, he leaned in, kissing underneath one breast then moving to the other. He purposely missed both nipples, knowing he was driving her crazy, which was his plan. He would ruin her for any other man. He would make damn sure of it. He didn't even take the time to wonder where that thought came from.

His arms lifted her higher so that he was able to place a kiss at the edge of her panties below her bellybutton. His lips trailed above her bellybutton and slowly up her stomach, stopping between her breasts. A sexy grin tipped his lips at the pure lust shadowing her eyes as she stared down at him. With the tip of his tongue, he lashed out, wetting her nipple. He had to tighten his hands when she jerked violently. He moved to the other, lathering it with the same attention.

"Sid." The breathless calling of his name had him smiling with pure male pride.

"Yes, Lana." He moved her down slightly to his eye level.

"If you don't stop teasing me, I'm going to shoot you." Her voice was still breathless, but rang true.

"I like to take my time and enjoy, lovely Lana." Sid gave her a slow wink.

"It's been a long time for me." She managed to grab his waist with her legs, pulling herself to him. In a motion so quick, Sid was taken by surprise when she wrapped her legs around him in a tight grip. "And you're killing me. Please, Sid, I can't take much more."

"Honey, we are both on the edge, but believe me when I say holding out will bring greater pleasure." With his hands still on her hips, he moved her up and down against his hardness.

"Screw that," Lana moaned. "Maybe next time."

A deep growl rumbled in his throat as she took the lead and started to move herself against him. He leaned down, latching on to her large nipple, sucking while using his tongue to flick the sensitive nub. Within minutes, her head slammed back as a scream of pleasure echoed through the room. He left her breast to watch as waves of pleasure made her body shake as she shattered in the most beautiful way before his very eyes.

Breathing hard, Lana used his shoulders to pull herself back up. Her eyes were still glazed with desire as they looked at his. Licking her lips, she smiled. "Guess I should have warned you…I'm a screamer."

"Jesus," he groaned. Never had he been this close to losing control. Sid felt emotions run through his body. Rage was at the forefront of those emotions as he thought about another man witnessing what he just experienced with this amazing woman.

"Now, it's my turn." Lana wiggled her way out of his grip. Reaching around, she expertly unhooked her bra, letting it drop where it fell, and within seconds, her panties followed.

Sid watched, fighting his alpha that was clawing to come out. He wanted to be in control. He wanted his hands on her, but he stood still as stone as her hands tugged his shirt off. Her eyes caressed his body, making soft sounds of pleasure as her hands ran down his chest, stopping at his own nipples. With eyes filled with desire, she peeked up at him, rubbing small circles against his nipples with her thumbs. A tiny smile played on her lips before her hands moved across his hard stomach to the buttons on his faded jeans. She unsnapped them, but before going to the zipper, one hand moved playfully around to his back, grasping his gun.

He about snapped when she brought his gun around placing it to her lips, running it down her chin and between her breasts. Because he knew she was as good with guns as he was, he didn't take it away from her. In truth, watching her sexy play was probably the most erotic thing he'd ever seen.

With one hand on the waist of his jeans, she knelt down, placing his weapon on her bra. With a sigh of pleasure, she turned her attention back to his jeans, slowly unzipping them over his growing bulge. The look of womanly appreciation on her face, once she realized he was commando as his cock sprang free, almost did him in.

******

Lana was trying so hard to take her time and be sexy, but it was damn hard when all she wanted to do was have another mind-blowing orgasms. Sid was like no other man she had ever been with. His body was nothing but corded muscle from his neck down to his sexy toes.

As she unzipped his jeans, she moaned as her pussy throbbed when his cock sprang free. A man who went natural under his clothes was the ultimate turn-on, and she was about ready to explode again. Not able to wait any longer, her hands left his jeans at his knees, running up his legs, cupping his sack with one hand as her other wrapped around his girth, moving down the length of his heavy cock. Her eyes lifted to his and her breath caught in her throat. The desire she saw in his black eyes flashed across her body. His mouth was slightly open; his fangs had elongated, and just the thought of him sinking them into her skin made any other sexual fantasy she had ever had seem dull in comparison.

Licking her dry lips, she placed them at the tip of his cock, flicking her tongue around the tip of the head. His groan of pleasure urged her to sink his cock to the back of her throat. With no gag reflexes, she was blessed with the talent of giving great head. Working him with her mouth, she could tell by the tightening of his body he was getting close, and knew it even more when his hand tangled in her hair, controlling her motions. Wanting to please this man more than she ever wanted to please anyone in her life, she fought against the pull of her hair. When her mouth reached the base of his heavy cock, she swallowed.

"God damn!" Sid pulled her away as gently as he could.

"I want to taste you." Lana pouted, licking her lips again as he kicked his jeans the rest of the way off and then picked her up.

"Honey, that's music to my ears, but right now, I am too riled up. And the first time I come is going to be inside that beautiful tight pussy of yours," Sid's voice was filled with sensual authority.

His words didn't embarrass Lana whatsoever; if anything, they turned her on more. Most men were too afraid of saying what was on their mind, but not this man, this Warrior. He knew what he wanted and wasn't afraid to say it, take it. Yeah, he was going to be hard to top after this was over. No man she had ever been with or would find after Sid, would be enough. She pushed the thought away as Sid laid her on the bed, gripping her chin. "I will warn you once, that if I ever feel like you are thinking of another man when with me, I will torture his name out of that talented mouth of yours and kill him."

Lana removed his hand from her chin and kissed him so hard and deep that she became lightheaded from lack of oxygen.

Breaking the kiss, Sid licked his way down her body. "Now, speaking of tasting, it's my turn." He gave her a wicked grin before his lips latched onto her core, sending her straight into another screaming orgasm.

All track of time was lost, as well as the number of orgasms she had, but damn, she probably should call Guinness because that had to be a world record. His tongue and mouth had done things to her that had nearly made her pass out.

"You okay?" He was now positioned over her, looking down with a smug knowing grin.

"I seriously don't know." Lana blinked a couple of times.

"We can stop and take a rest." His grin grew larger as male pride set in.

"Shut up." Lana raised up on her elbows, eyeing him. "You're going to be the one needing a rest."

She knew without a doubt Sid let her roll him over. If he didn't want to be on the bottom, he most certainly wouldn't be on the bottom. Straddling him, she lifted over his cock, sliding down slowly, trying to keep her eyes focused on him, but the feeling of him sliding into her was almost too much. It has been so long; she had forgotten the feeling of a man inside her. She was so tight; it was almost painful, but the pain was pleasurable, and she took a deep breath, sinking all the way down flush against him. Hearing his moan sent her breath out in a soft sigh.

Once her eyes focused, they locked with his as she began riding him slowly at first, stopping just before he slipped out before then pushing herself back in slowly. She repeated the steps and watched, mesmerized at the small tick in his strong jaw. He was on the edge and she knew it, loved it, and wanted to make him shatter like he had done to her countless times.

His hands grabbed her waist setting a tempo faster than what she was doing. Even as she continued to ride him, she pried his hands away. "This is my ride." Lana gave him a sexy smile. "Can't you take it?"

Sid hissed as she slammed down on him. “Oh, we going to play like that, are we?”

“What’re you going to do about it, Warrior?” Lana smirked, slamming down again, loving the power she had over him for the moment. “I’m in control now.”

A moment was all she had. Before she knew what was happening, she was on her back with her arms clasped together over her head, and they were pinned to the bed, and he was still inside her. “Who’s in control?” He cocked his eyebrow in question before biting at her neck.

Lana was in heaven as he pounded into her. When she thought she could take no more, he slowed down, licking and worshipping her breasts. As soon as she came down from the edge of insanity, he began his fast pounding pace, sending her right back to the edge.

“Please, Sid,” Lana panted. She had never begged for release in her life, but the pain of being denied was driving her crazy.

“I’m in control now, Lana.” His words came out in deep breaths. “I could do this all night and never get tired of feeling your warmth wrapped around me.” He grabbed her breasts, squeezing them together. “Are these gorgeous tits virgin?”

Opening her eyes at his words, she looked down at her breasts overflowing his rough manly hands, turning her on even more. “What?” she panted, her mind not working right.

“Has a man been between these tits, Lana?” Sid growled, plucking at her hardened nipples.

Just those words alone sent a sharp tingle through her clit. “Oh God.”

“By your reaction, I take that as a no,” Sid grinned. “Did I shock you,

Lana?"

She moved her head back and forth on the pillow. "Just make me come, Sid."

"Music to my ears, babe." Sid lifted her hips as he pounded into her mercilessly. With one hand, he tapped her clit.

"Please, bite me," Lana urged Sid, but when he only stared at her in surprise, she pleaded, "Come on, please. I want to feel it. Please, Sid."

Sid cursed before slamming his fangs into her neck. Lana screamed as a mind-blowing orgasm consumed them both.

Chapter 19

Sid headed for the kitchen. Lying next to Lana for hours after she fell into a deep sleep was another new experience for him. To say he wasn't shaken by what happened would be a total lie. Two things had happened in his room that had never happened before. Never had he lay with a woman in his arms after having sex, and his fangs had never sunk into human flesh. Her blood was sweet and strong as well as addictive. He already craved more of the sweet taste and her. He was fucked, plain and simple.

Slamming into the kitchen, he was met with knowing and curious stares. Before Jared could open his mouth, Sid stopped him. "If one motherfucker says one thing disrespectful, I will kill you."

"I was just going to ask what's for breakfast." Jared held his hands up. "My stomach is *screaming* for food."

Duncan chuckled, but Damon stood between Sid and Jared. "It's okay, Damon," Sid glared at Jared. "I'll just poison his food. It won't kill him, but it will be painful as hell."

"Ah, come on Sid." Jared got up following Sid. "Why the sour-puss mood? You should be tap dancing to that stove after what we heard last night."

"Definitely getting my own place," Sid mumbled to himself as he grabbed stuff out of the refrigerator to start breakfast, while trying his best to ignore Jared.

Slade walked into the kitchen carrying a folder. "Glad you guys are here." He tossed the folder on the long table. "I got the report from the blood samples I took from Steve, Jeff, Adam and Jill."

"Where's Sloan?" Sid asked, slapping bacon in a large skillet.

"He's out, but I'll fill him in." Duncan filled another cup of coffee.

"So what's up, Doc?" Jared grinned at his own Bugs Bunny joke.

"I really fucking hate that cartoon," Slade glared at him. "Anyway, they all have the same elements in their blood. I won't bore you with all the medical stuff, but there is one element that should not be in their blood, and none of our top lab techs knows what it is."

"So what does that mean exactly?" Sid continued to cook, but his attention was on the conversation.

"Sounds like we don't know any more than we did before we recruited half-breeds." Jared frowned.

"On the blood samples, that's true, but in the research I have been doing, I have documented something I've never seen before. I've asked around to some of the oldest vampires I know and even they are surprised." Slade opened the file, pulling out a paper. "They are maturing. Each one of them have has either gained or lost weight. Steve has grown in height."

"So they are more human than vampire?" Duncan frowned. "But what about Adam and Jill's gifts? I mean, you would think if they were more human, they wouldn't have the power they have."

"That's the thing." Slade pulled out another paper. "According to the blood work-up, Jill and Adam had more of the unknown compound than Jeff or Steve."

"Any half-breed I've ever met has stopped all human characteristics other than a heartbeat. They don't grow and they don't age." Sid added with a frown.

"It's a mystery, but they haven't given up. They are still running tests and want more blood in the next two months to see if there are any changes." Slade set the papers back down in the file. "We have to find who manufactures this stuff."

"Thanks, Doc," Duncan said with a nod. "Maybe tonight we'll get lucky."

Slade glanced at Jared. "Can I talk to you in private?"

"Sure." Jared followed him out.

"I have tried to think of a way to help you and Tessa." Slade checked his phone when it beeped.

"I appreciate that, Slade." Jared slapped him on the shoulder. "But we've got it worked out. We've interviewed a few donors and came to a decision with one that we're both comfortable with."

"Is she still wanting you to turn her?" Slade asked concerned.

"No, we've got it worked out." Jared frowned. "Tessa went through a lot with an abusive father and then an asshole of a boyfriend. She's working on her issues, but in all honesty, I think she's perfect."

"Good to hear." Slade nodded. "Tessa is a very special lady."

"That she is," Jared smiled proudly.

"Well, if things don't work out, I do have a few suggestions that could help you," Slade added.

"I appreciate that," Jared replied. They both turned, hearing footsteps coming down the steps.

Slade and Jared watched as Lana managed her way down the steps and toward the door. They looked at each other with amused knowing smirks.

"Hey, Sid." Jared walked back into the kitchen with Slade right behind him. "Looks like your latest conquest is slipping out the front door."

Sid's head snapped up. "Keep an eye on this," he ordered Jared as he stomped out of the kitchen.

******

Lana woke alone. Flashes of last night sent heat through her body. My God, she acted like a…slut. Slapping her hands on her reddening cheeks, she groaned. She had never been that brazen with a man. No wonder he skipped out on her. Grabbing a pillow, she crushed it to her face trying to suffocate herself. When that didn't work, she got up, looking for her clothes which were scattered everywhere. It wasn't like she had done anything wrong; she knew that, yet in the light of day she was embarrassed as hell. Then the thought hit her, sending her hand slapping against the side of her neck. Jesus, she had asked him to bite her. Asked, hell, she practically begged him to bite her. Running to the bathroom, she looked at the side of her neck to see two small puncture wounds. Her eyes left her neck as she stared at herself. Slowly, she bared her teeth, and then she sighed loudly when no fangs appeared. She wasn't totally sure how one was changed into a vampire; she was sure there was more to it than having your neck bitten by a hot, sexy vampire, but human nature took over making her check it out anyway. Thank God just being bitten didn't do the trick because that was so damn hot. She knew, without a doubt, she was going to be begging him again to slide those teeth back into her.

Leaving the bathroom with a 'you are truly fucked' look at herself, she grabbed her clothes. As she dressed, she looked around, noticing that the room was pretty bare. Nothing in this room revealed that anyone even lived here. It broke her heart. Walking to a dresser, she opened a drawer, finding a bunch of black t-shirts. Picking one up, she lifted it to her nose, breathing in his scent. Catching a glance of her reflection in the mirror over the dresser, she rolled her eyes at herself. "You're pathetic." She stared at herself as she put the shirt in her bag, which made her more pathetic because she wasn't just smelling his shirt, she was stealing his damn shirt. With one last look around, Lana rushed out the door.

By the time she made it down the steps and out the front door, Lana was actually sweating. She didn't want to face Sid. She needed to get her shit together and have an Oprah moment. Oh, who was she kidding? She messed up bad. He was her boss for shit's sake. How professional was that!

"Yes, sir, sorry I'm late, but how was that blow job I happily gave you last night?" Lana hissed, mocking herself.

"You're not late, breakfast is just now ready, and the blow job was the best I've ever had," Sid's growl was right behind her. "Now, where in the hell do you think you're going?"

Lana jumped a mile high, dropping her bag, which of course fell upside-down, dumping the contents onto the ground. And if her luck wasn't bad enough, his shirt she stole lay on top of all her shit. Dropping to the ground trying to shove everything back in her bag before he saw, Lana's mouth silently cursed a string of obscenities. Her eyes closed when a large masculine hand reached in front of her eyes, grabbing the shirt.

"Is that my shirt?" His deep voice flowed over her.

Lie, just lie, Lana. Then he can call you lying Lana. Yep, she was losing it. "Yes," she said, but her head shook no.

"So you stole my shirt and decided to make a run for it?" Sid asked, helping her to her feet.

That sounded better than why she was really leaving. Finally, her eyes rose to meet his. "Yes."

"Stealing is a crime, Lana." Sid held the shirt out. "Didn't you learn that in…cop school?"

"Yes," she answered again, frowning when his lips twitched.

"Why were you leaving, Lana?" Sid handed her the shirt back.

Lana took the shirt, shoving it in her bag with a sigh. "You were gone." She shrugged looking back up at him. "I figured you had that morning-after regret thingy."

Sid eyed her. "Morning-after regret thingy?"

"Yeah, you know." Lana flipped her hand, laughing nervously, and then made a shocked face. "The 'holy hell…what did I do and how the hell can I get out of it' moment?"

Understanding flashed in his eyes. "And because I was gone, you felt I had the 'morning-after regret thingy' going on?"

"Well, yeah, I mean I did act pretty slutty and…" Lana's words started flying out of her mouth fast.

Sid laughed loudly, cutting her off. "Lana, honey." Sid's grin grew. "First of all, last night was the best time I've had in a long time. Everything you did came from you, meaning you were a hundred-percent honest in what you wanted and wanted to give."

"Are you calling me a slut?" Lana frowned. She had, in fact, said she acted slutty, but to have him call her one was a whole different matter.

"Have you ever acted like that with another man?" Sid growled, his eyes darkening.

"No," Lana replied, wondering why he was getting angry.

"Good, because I'd hate to have to kill the son of a bitch." Sid pulled her close. "A woman who can be herself with a man, going for what she wants, is priceless, and honey, last night was priceless. What man in his right mind wouldn't want the woman he was with to act a little…slutty…hmm?"

"But you're my boss for the moment, and that was totally unprofessional." Lana looked at him.

"You're fired," Sid grinned down at her. "Since that's taken care of, come on and get something to eat, then you can act slutty again."

Lana smacked him. "I'm being serious."

"So am I." Sid winked down at her. "I've been around a long time, honey, and let me tell you, last night was the most I've ever been turned on by a woman, and I'm ready for round…."

Looking up at him when he cut himself off, she watched as he seemed in deep thought. "Round what?"

"Shush, wait a minute. I'm trying to count." Sid tried not to grin. "Five, I believe, round five."

Lana, feeling better about the situation, grinned then elbowed him. "It's six."

Sid didn't reply. He pulled her into his arms, kissing her long and hard. Lifting away, he nipped her chin. "I know. I was testing you." He grabbed her hand, leading her back inside. "You definitely keep it interesting, Lana."

"Not a boring minute with me." Lana smiled, feeling better after their talk. In all honesty, she should have just been the woman she knew she was and faced it like she had before, but with Sid, it was different. Not only was he a vampire, which was definitely a new venture for her, but he oozed alpha male confidence and she knew they would clash. She didn't take well to demands from anyone, even drop dead sexy alpha vampires.

Lana's phone rang, and when she looked at it, she grimaced, feeling conflicted. She and Sid did have sex, but was that all it was or was it something more? To her, it was something more. She liked sex, yes, but she just didn't go around spreading her legs for anyone. To Sid it was probably just another sexual encounter, and though that hurt, she was a big girl and knew what she was in for before dropping her panties.

"You going to answer that?" Sid eyed her, his happy mood disappearing quickly. "Who is it?"

"Ah, it's Doug. I'll just call him back." Lana went to put her phone in her back pocket.

"The fuck you will." Sid grabbed her phone, answering it.

"Hey!" Lana grabbed for her phone, but he was too quick.

"This is Sid Sinclair and Lana is no longer available. If you call her again, I will hunt you down," Sid growled into the phone. "You got me, Dennis? Good!"

"Why did you do that?" Lana looked at him with a wide-eyed stare. "And his name is Doug."

"I don't give two fucks what his fucking name is," Sid growled, handing her the phone. "I suggest you block his number if you want him to live."

"What is wrong with you?" Lana stepped back, shocked by his anger, but in all honesty, he was amazing. She'd never had a man act like this by her just talking to another man, and it made her feel…special. What in the hell was wrong with her? She was a cop, a woman who knew who she was and didn't need an overbearing alpha male bending her to his will…or did she?

Sid took one-step, invading her space. "You are mine, Lana." Sid's eyes were black with possessiveness. "I have never said that to anyone in my long life, but you are mine. I don't share with anyone, and I will hunt that motherfucker down if he calls you again."

Lana's stomach was doing all kind of weird flips and flops; her knees felt weak, and all she wanted to do was hold on to this man and never let go. So much for clashing. It was like his alpha side was singing her favorite song, pulling her in and that totally shocked her. But she also had a little alpha in her and she had to make one thing clear; then she could feel that their relationship could go further. "I don't share either, Sid," she responded, taking her one-step toward him. "So make sure you really mean what you're saying. I know how much you love the ladies, and—"

He grabbed her up in his strong arms and kissed her hard, his tongue pushing deep into her mouth. It was a kiss she had only read about in romance novels. Her toes actually curled as he bent her backwards. Finally, he lifted his mouth from hers, staring into her eyes. "I haven't looked at another woman since I met you. And that surprises me more than anyone else," he growled as he nipped her lower lip. "You are mine, Lana Fitzpatrick."

She knew she had a decision to make. No words of love were spoken, but what did she expect? Did she want to be his just until it lasted? Could she guard her heart enough to just have some fun until his eyes moved on to someone else? She knew the answer to those questions before she even asked herself. She wanted this. She needed it. She could handle it. Wrapping her arms tightly around his neck, Lana breathed deeply and then jumped in with both feet. "I'm yours, Sid Sinclair."

They walked into the kitchen hand in hand, and all went silent. Forks stopped in mid-lift. All eyes fell on her and she wanted to step behind Sid; she knew she was a screamer and now everyone in the compound knew it too.

Pulling Sid down, she whispered in his ear. "Are the rooms here sound-proof?"

"No, they're not." Sid winked at her. "Don't pay any attention to them. They're just jealous, and if one of them says a word, I'll kill them."

Surprised at how serious he sounded, she let him pull her toward the food. "Did you make all of this?"

"Yes, so eat up." Sid handed her a plate. "I don't like to see food I've made wasted."

Lana wasn't afraid of food. She loved food. It didn't matter that she couldn't cook, but she sure as hell could eat. Filling her plate with eggs, bacon, sausage, hash browns and a biscuit, she glanced at the table where the other Warriors were eating. Deciding not to go there, she placed her plate on the counter and started to dig in.

"I'm done." Slade stood and took his plate to the sink. "Take my seat."

Not wanting to seem rude, Lana picked up her plate and headed to the only available seat, between Damon and Duncan and across from Jared, who sat next to Jill and Steve. Noticing once again that everyone had stopped eating and was staring at her plate, Lana smiled. They were about to be amazed.

"No way you can eat all that," Jill eyed her plate.

"Oh, I can and will eat all of this," Lana nodded with confidence. "There isn't an overflowing plate I haven't been able to demolish yet."

"How do you stay in shape eating like that?" Jill looked at her then her plate again.

The room grew silent as they all looked at her. Lana met Jared's gaze and she knew for a fact he had heard her last night and was dying, absolutely dying, to say something. Not to sound too much like a bitch, but if things were okay between her and Sid, she really didn't care what others thought.

"A lot of hard and sweaty exercise that makes you scream." She peeked at Jared who choked on the drink of coffee he'd just sipped from his cup.

"Well, you must have been doing some extra-hard exercises last night." Steve stood with his plate. "Cause I heard a lot of screaming."

The room exploded with laughter. Lana's face turned red, but she smiled, looking down at her food.

"What?" Steve looked around at everyone. "What did I say?"

Jill and Lana glanced at each other as the Warriors got up from the table. Steve followed, asking what was so funny. Jill just shook her head with a large smile, but her smile faded as she made eye contact with Slade, who turned and walked out of the kitchen.

"Have you ever been to Metropolis?" Jill asked, pushing her plate away.

Lana nodded. "Me and my sister have been a couple of times."

“What do you wear to this place?” Jill looked uncomfortable asking.

Without being too obvious, Lana looked Jill over. She wore sweats and a t-shirt. “Want to go shopping?”

“Not really,” Jill grimaced. “But I guess I don’t have a choice since I don’t have many clothes.”

“It will be fun,” Lana assured her. It would be nice to go out with another woman. She hadn’t done that in so long, and it was one thing she missed doing with her sister. “We can go get your hair and makeup done. You’ll feel like a new woman.”

“I don’t know about all that, but I’d appreciate the help.” Jill actually looked like she was in pain when the word ‘makeup’ was mentioned.

“You want to catch the doctor’s eye, don’t you?” Lana grinned, exposing the secret she knew Jill held.

“No.” Was the only response Jill could come up with.

“Liar.” Lana took the last few bites of food, lifted the corner of her empty plate for Jill to see and then stood. “Let me tell Sid we’ll meet them here later, and then we’ll go.”

Chapter 20

Sid dropped Lana and Jill off at the warehouse where Lana's car was parked. As soon as they were safely in the car and driving away, he grabbed his cell phone.

He dialed the number then waited. "Hey man, I got a favor to ask you. Can you meet me at University Hospital? Yeah, on my way there now. I'll meet you out front."

Tossing his phone in the passenger's seat, Sid pulled out of the driveway heading toward the hospital. Thoughts of last night and Lana filled his drive time. She was so different from the women he went after, or actually came after him. She was a mix for sure. She was a hard ass with a huge heart who made him laugh and definitely turned him on. Just thinking of last night had him hard. She didn't play games. She went for what she wanted in an honest way, and he was more than happy to give it to her however and whenever she wanted.

"Jesus." He was getting himself all worked up just thinking about it.

Pulling into a parking place, he got out and headed to the front where Slade stood waiting for him.

"What's up?" Slade asked, looking more like a biker in a motorcycle gang with his leather jacket than a doctor saving lives.

"I wanted to see if you could check over Lana's sister." Sid went into detail about what he knew. "She has been unreachable for a month. The last time I was here, I tried to read her and got very little."

"I would love to, but I don't know much about this sort of thing, and I can't do anything without release from her doctors."

"I got a hold of her father who is meeting us here." Sid led the way with Slade following. “Her grandmother is also coming. She has the same gift as Lana and her sister Caroline.”

Miles was waiting when the elevator doors opened. “Good to see you again, Sid.” Miles shook his hand and then looked up at Slade.

“How you doing, Miles?” Sid nodded. “This is Dr. Slade Buchanan. I really appreciate you coming.”

“Always happy to come see my little girl.” Miles shook Slade’s hand and then laughed. “I’m sorry, son, but you don’t look like any doctor I’ve ever seen.”

Slade smiled, not taking offense. “I get that a lot.”

“I bet you do.” Miles stopped them at the door of Caroline’s room. “What is this all about?”

“I want to see if Slade can help Caroline.” Sid glanced in, seeing an older woman sitting in a chair holding Caroline’s hand.

“Son, we have some of the best doctors taking care of her.” Miles frowned.

“I understand that, but none of them are as good as Slade or have the power of getting into a person’s mind. I will go through every VC Warrior we have to see if any of us can reach her. I already tried last night. I saw flashes, but not enough to reach her.” Sid replied, deliberately leaving out the possibility of feeling her move.

Miles bit his lip, nodding. “I appreciate that very much.” Miles cleared the emotion from his throat. “Where is Lana?”

“She already has so much guilt about this. I didn’t want to get her hopes up until I was sure one of us might be able to help.” Sid put his hand on Miles's shoulder. "I think it's worth a shot."

"Anything that can bring my girl back is worth a shot." Miles moved out of the way, leading them toward Caroline.

"I need a release from her current doctor before I can do anything," Slade informed them both.

"She has three doctors. Do you need all three?" Miles already had his phone out ready to dial.

"Just the main physician is enough. The one calling all the shots." Slade, already making assessments, stepped to the end of the bed Caroline was propped up in.

"This is my mother, Georgia Fitzpatrick," Miles introduced. "This is Sid Sinclair and Dr. Buchanan."

The old woman stood. Her face was wrinkled, but her eyes were bright with intelligence from years of living. She looked both men up and down with her wise gaze.

"You think you can help my granddaughter?" Her voice was strong.

"We are going to try, ma'am," Sid smiled down at the woman.

"So you're friends with Lana?" She asked; her eyes sparkled at Sid.

"We work together." Sid glanced over to see Miles still on the phone.

"That's not what I asked, young man." She snatched his attention back by grasping his arm in a strong grip. "Are you friends with my granddaughter?"

“Yes, I am,” he grinned, liking her spunk.

“Make sure you take care of her. Something wicked is at work here.” Her eyes then went to Caroline. “And it’s stronger than me and my granddaughters put together.”

Sid took her arm, walking her a few steps away from the bed. “Is it possible for you to get physically harmed through a vision?”

“It’s very rare, but yes,” she replied, a frown marring her wrinkled face. “Has something happened to Lana?”

“After a reading, she had marks on her neck and her necklace was broken.” Sid divulged small fragments of the facts.

“You can’t let her read anyone else.” She shook her head. “If she does, she could be lost like her sister. Please don’t let her.” Fear for her granddaughter lit her eyes.

“I promise to keep her safe,” he assured the worried woman as much as he assured himself. The fear in the old woman’s eyes sent his protective instincts into high gear. Nothing was going to happen to Lana; he would make damn sure of it.

Miles walked over, pocketing his phone. “It’s done,” he nodded to Slade. “The nurse will be bringing in all of her files.”

Slade walked around to the side of the bed, moving the chair out of his way. They all moved closer, but far enough away to stay out Slade’s space. Slade reached up, and grabbed the wall-mounted otoscope to use the small light on the end.

“Caroline, I’m Dr. Buchanan,” Slade’s deep voice soothed a warning to the woman on the bed. “I’m going to look into your eyes.”

Sid watched as Slade examined Lana's sister. The last thing he did was grab her small wrist in his large hand, standing still as his eyes stayed on hers. After a while, he finally let go.

Slade turned with a sigh.

"What did you see?" Miles asked, looking between the two men.

Sid warned Slade with his eyes to be careful what he said. "Not much, but she is fighting back."

"What do you mean fighting back?" Miles tone took a protective fatherly tone.

"Vampires can read people's minds, their thoughts," Slade explained. "Sid saw only flashes that he couldn't make out. This time I saw Caroline fighting against something. She was trying to tell me something."

"Does this make any sense to you, Mom?" Miles looked to his mother.

"Yes, it does." She glanced at Caroline. "It means she is strong, but whoever has her, has more power and is holding her back."

"So this has nothing to do with the officer who broke her away from the girl she was reading?" Miles asked, wanting answers.

"No, but it's something I've never seen before. Someone strong is holding her captive." she answered, shaking her gray head looking more tired than she had a second ago. "I don't know how to help her."

Miles grabbed his mother's hand offering comfort, but turned his attention to Sid. "Is there anything we can do?" Miles again looked between the two men. "Anything at all?"

"I've already texted Adam, but he hasn't responded," Sid told Slade before Slade could ask. "He may be able to break past whoever is blocking her. Adam is pretty powerful reading through blocks."

"Okay, great." Miles looked hopeful. "Where is he?"

"We don't know, but I will find him and get him here." Sid grabbed Miles' shoulder. "Whatever it takes, I will get him here."

"Thank you both," Miles nodded before gently clasping his mother's elbow. "You spend as much time as you need to here. I need to get Mother back. These trips are hard on her."

The nurse brought the files to Slade who got busy flipping through them.

Sid nodded, smiling down at the older woman. "It was nice meeting you."

"Take care of my Lana, young man," she ordered with a pat on his arm.

"Yes, ma'am," he replied, watching them leave.

As soon as they were gone, Slade looked up from the files, closing them. "She isn't reliving anyone's death," Slade frowned. "Someone has her trapped in her own mind."

"What?" Sid shook his head, not understanding any of this at all.

"Whoever has the block on her released it long enough for her to give a warning to Lana." Slade ran his hand through his hair. "Whoever it is wants Lana in return for Caroline's release. She wants to warn Lana not to read anyone else because he is waiting. Whoever it is tried to block that last part, but she's a fighter. We need Adam to break the block completely."

"Son of a bitch," Sid cursed, as he looked over at the unblinking stare of Lana's twin.

******

Lana stared at her reflection and grinned. "Hello, Linda Lovelace." Her long dark hair was covered with a short blonde wig. She had made her blue eyes up to look smoky and sensual. Instead of a dress, she wore blue jeans with black-heeled boots and a low-cut blouse under a leather jacket.

"Who?" Jill walked into Lana's bedroom, getting a good look at Lana. "Wow!" she laughed.

"It's my undercover persona," Lana laughed, glancing at Jill through the mirror. "And talk about wow…you look great."

Jill's hair had been colored, the blue tints washed away and cut into a stylish spikey cut. Her makeup was playful, but seductive. She drew the line at a dress because if it came down to it, she didn't want to fight with her ass hanging out. She also wore jeans with boots, but with a shorter heel than Lana's. Her red shirt was tight-fitting with long bat-winged sleeves. She looked ready for a night of dancing and fun.

"You really think so?" Jill looked down at herself with a frown.

"Definitely," Lana nodded.

"Hey, is anyone home?" A female voice came from the front door.

"We're in here, Susan," Lana yelled, grabbing her bag, and headed out with Jill following.

“Well, hello Linda,” Susan grinned.

“Hello to you, Amy,” Lana teased back.

Jill just looked at them like they were crazy.

“Jill, this is Susan in *her* undercover persona, aka Amy.” Lana laughed at Jill’s confused expression.

“Well, since you confused the shit out of me, hopefully I won’t have to remember all of this tonight. Why don’t we get going?” Jill headed for the door when the doorbell rang.

“That’s probably Sid and Slade.” Lana walked to the door. “They said they’d meet us here to go over everything.”

Opening the door, Lana smiled when Sid glanced at her, before he took a step back looking at the house, then back at her.

“It’s me, Sid.” Lana rolled her eyes.

He glanced behind her at Susan. “Now, her I know.” He looked Lana up and down. “But you I’ve never met.”

“Come in. We’re just about ready.” Lana stepped back so they could walk in the door. Both men had to duck so as not to hit their heads.

Jill walked out of the bathroom just as Slade entered. Their eyes met and held before his slowly went from her eyes down her body and back up.

“Did you wire her?” Susan asked, giving a wave to Sid and a smile to

Slade who was still staring at Jill.

“Damn, I forgot,” Lana frowned, going to the closet and pulling out a small suitcase. Grabbing what she needed out of it, she headed to Jill. “Pull up your shirt for a sec.”

Sid frowned. “Who’s running this show?”

“You, but we thought if she gets separated, at least we can still be in contact with her, plus we can hear the conversations,” she replied, pulling tape and running the wire up Jill’s flat stomach. “Reach down your shirt and grab the wire,” she instructed.

“We’re vampires, Lana.” Sid reminded her. “We can hear fine.”

“Well, Susan and I are human and can’t, and we will be closer to her than you guys.” Lana pulled Jill’s shirt down. “Go in the other room, Susan.” She tossed her a small earpiece.

“Why are you going to be closer to her?” Sid crossed his arms, his eyes on the way Lana’s ass filled out her jeans.

“How does that feel?” she asked Jill.

“Fine.” Jill nodded, her eyes staying on Lana and off Slade.

Susan walked out of the kitchen. “Heard her loud and clear.”

“Good.” Lana grabbed two more earpieces and handed them to Sid and Slade.

Slade looked at the earpiece before walking away without taking it. He walked up to Jill, putting his large hands around her waist and ran them around to her stomach and up under her breast.

"What are you doing?" Jill pushed his hands away.

"I can feel the wire." Slade's hands reached under her shirt, touching bare skin. Heat flared in his eyes. "I need to move this to the side where your arm can rest against the wire. If anyone touches you, they will know you've been wired."

Jill nodded, her eyes pleading with Lana to save her. Lana shrugged with a wink. "Better safe than sorry."

"Stop sucking in your stomach, Jill." Slade un-taped the wire, moving it over. It caught on her breast under her bra.

"Sorry." Jill reached inside her shirt, adjusting her boob, and wanted to die.

Once he was done, he stepped back, looking at her shirt. "Where's the blue?"

She looked down at her shirt confused. "It's red."

His lips curved in a crooked grin. "Your hair." His voice was low and deep. "Not your shirt."

"Oh." Her hand fluttered to her hair. "Thought I needed to look more…normal."

"That was your normal." Slade frowned, "Change it back after tonight."

Lana's eyes widened hearing their conversation. Glancing at Jill, she saw she was just as surprised as she watched Slade walk away.

"Can I talk to you for a minute?" Sid walked up to her. He didn't give her time to answer, but grabbed her hand, heading toward her bedroom and closing the door.

“What are you doing?” Sid leaned against the closed door.

“Getting ready.” Lana crossed her arms like him.

“That’s not what I meant,” Sid shook his head. “We don’t want any suspicion directed toward Jill. It could blow everything.”

“Give me some credit, Sid.” Lana glared at him. “This is my job and I’m good at it. You need someone close to her while this is going on. Susan and I are good at what we do.”

Sid was quiet for a minute just staring at her. “Just be careful, Lana.”

“It’s Linda,” Lana’s smile flashed wide. “Linda Lovelace, and if you’re nice, Linda will give you a special treat.”

Sid laughed, pulling her to him. “I’d rather have Lana Fitzpatrick give me anything she damn well pleases.”

“What? You don’t like the blonde wig?” Lana teased, shaking her head making her hair bob.

“Oh, you look beautiful, but if I wanted a Linda, I’d go find a Linda. Lana seems to be more to my liking.” Sid kissed her hard. “Watch your ass, Lana, and stay safe.”

“You do the same, Warrior.” Lana realized she liked being worried over by this Warrior.

Chapter 21

Metropolis was packed to the max. Everyone had driven separately to avoid suspicion. Jill followed Susan's car that carried both Lana and Susan. Slade followed on his bike and Sid brought up the rear. They went their separate ways as soon as they hit the parking lot, but Lana stayed close to Jill. One of the worries they had was Adam spotting and recognizing Lana, but the night he had seen Lana and Susan, he had been in a rage.

Sid and Slade parked and immediately split up. Duncan, Jared and Damon were already in place in different spots inside the dance club. Sid spotted Jill making her way in the door. She was to meet Adam inside. Lana and Susan were two people behind Jill. His trained eyes scanned the crowd just to make sure Adam wasn't running late and was already inside the club. They all had to keep their minds closed so Adam couldn't get a sense they were there. Pulling out his phone, he checked his texts. He had one from Jared saying they had Adam in their sights.

"Show time," Sid said to himself as he made his way up to the door to pay. Walking in, he turned to the right, heading up the steps to the upper level that overlooked the dance floor. Making his way through tons of people, he ignored the inviting looks from the women, which was new. Even in operations like this, his eyes took in the candy being offered to him. Tonight, he couldn't care less.

Finding a spot along the rail, Sid's eyes scanned the crowd, pin pointing where everyone was. He finally found Lana and Susan standing a few feet away from Jill and Adam, who were standing by the bar. Adam kept looking around, and so far, he hadn't detected any of them. Sid looked back to Lana, who was staring up at him. She looked away quickly doing the same thing he had done, locating where everyone was. He always had his eye out for his fellow Warriors, but this new worry over Lana was new to him and set him on edge. He had never feared anything before, but with Lana, he feared something happening to her, and that had his senses on high alert. Half an hour passed and still no one approached.

Adam put his phone to his ear, nodded as he talked then put his phone back in his pocket. He grabbed Jill's hand, leading her out onto the dance floor. A popular song was playing, so the crowd doubled. As they began to dance, Lana and Susan set their untouched drinks on the bar and headed out, making sure to keep a small distance from Jill.

Sid's eyes searched the crowd, but kept going back to Lana, who moved her body in perfect time with the music. Fuck, how the hell was he supposed to keep his mind on the job when she was down there moving that perfect body, making it jiggle and wiggle in all the right places? Glancing at Jared, who was stationed directly across from him, he narrowed his eyes at the bastard's knowing grin. After scratching his cheek with his middle finger, Sid ignored him.

A man came up behind Lana, moving behind her like he was humping her ass. Sid saw red. Watching her dance away, the guy kept grinding toward her. By just watching her facial expression, he knew she didn't want to make a scene, but the guy was pissing her off. Hell, pissing *her* off? His grip on the railing made indention marks. A couple standing next to him moved away after hearing him growl.

"Get a grip, Sinclair," he ordered himself. Susan was having a hard time keeping guys off her, also.

Finally, there was movement toward Adam and Jill. An unfamiliar man made his way to Adam. Something exchanged hands, but Adam grabbed the man's arm, holding on, and Sid knew he was reading him. The man pulled away, giving Adam a push before he turned to Jill with a friendly grin and began dancing with her. The music changed, as did the lighting. Strobe lights flashed making it hard to track Jill; she was on the move. Lana and Susan were slightly behind them, and that was when everything turned to shit. Sid leapt from the top level to the dance floor below.

******

Lana loved to dance, but hated dancing when she was undercover, since she couldn't make a damn scene and punch the guy in the nuts who was grinding into her ass. It was messing up her focus. She could barely hear Jill and Adam's conversation over the music and people, but what she did hear was Adam ordering her to follow through with whatever happened and he would make sure she was safe. Jill did great by not giving Adam any indication that there were seven others there watching her back.

Spotting a man making his way toward Adam, Lana watched closely, making sure it wasn't just someone heading to the bar. When he stopped and discretely passed an envelope to Adam, the man turned, smiling at Jill, who smiled back and began dancing. Lana watched as Adam made his way off the dance floor, disappearing into the crowd. Her eyes made contact with Sid, who was watching the scene.

The music changed as the lights went dark followed by strobe lights. Motion was broken up by the lights, making it hard to see anything in real time. The man had finished whispering something to Jill, who nodded, took his hand and then headed off the dance floor opposite to where Adam disappeared. Lana danced, turning away from them as they came toward her and Susan's way. As soon as they passed, she gave one nod at Susan. Before she could take one-step after Jill, a man stepped in her path, blocking her.

"Watch out!" Lana tried to get around him, but he stepped in her way again, grabbing her arm in a hard pinching grip.

"Come with me," the man demanded, dragging her through the crowd.

"Get the hell off me." Lana started to reach for her gun.

"Do you want to help your sister?" The man glared down at her.

That stopped Lana's struggles. "What do you know of my sister?" she shouted over the crowd and music. She stopped Susan, who finally pushed through the crowd.

He looked around before looking down at her. “Come with me.”

“Go after Jill,” Lana told Susan, staring at the guy. She had to take a chance if this man could tell her anything about her sister. She didn’t know who he was, but he obviously knew her. “Go!”

Susan hesitated for a second longer before taking off and pushing through the crowd.

Lana let the man lead her off the dance floor. Turning, she looked up to find Sid, but he was gone. Dammit, she hoped she wasn’t making a big mistake. They headed toward the back of the club, stopping in front of one of the men’s bathrooms. A man stood outside the door, pushing it open.

Something stopped Lana from going in. She dug her heels, refusing to move forward. “Who are you?”

The man who held her made eye contact with the guy at the door. They both grabbed her, pushing her into the bathroom. “Here she is, now where’s our money?”

Lana glanced around. There were three men in the bathroom: two very large vampires and a shorter man who was facing a mirror over the sink. The short one had a long jacket with the hood pulled up. She had a bad feeling she knew who he was, and when his voice echoed in the bathroom, she knew she was in deep shit.

“Lana, you’ve been keeping terrible company, but finally we find you alone.” The raspy voice was angry. “Your wig is hideous.”

“Shit. You’ve been following me?” Lana asked the obvious, while backing out of the bathroom, but was quickly stopped. “What do you want?"

"That's a long list," he replied, turning around and lifting the hood off his head. "But at the moment, this isn't about what I want. My boss wants you and I'm about to deliver."

"So this has nothing to do with my sister?" Lana wanted to kick her own ass so badly for deviating from the mission. She knew better, but her sister was her weakness.

"Oh, it has everything to do with your sister," his voice cracked as he reached out toward her. "A life for a life."

"Man, I just want my money." The man who brought her into the restroom looked nervous. "I don't want to be a part of this."

"You already are, asshole." Lana frowned at him, noticing for the first time he was human. Her eyes raked over him, then to her surroundings, wondering briefly where the hell Sid was. She had a feeling she was going to need him and soon.

"Shut up!" The man in the jacket screamed; his scarred face distorted in rage.

Everyone became deathly silent. The only sound was the noise from the music and crowd outside. "What do you know about my sister?" Lana hissed, her anger getting the best of her. She eyed the scarred man who Sid thought was Kenny. What Sid had told her about this man and what he did to Duncan's mate made her itch to put a bullet between his eyes.

"Everything. I know everything about you and your sister." His rage turned into a disfigured smile in the blink of an eye. "Come with me willingly and your sister will be released."

Lana had no idea what in the hell he was talking about, but she didn't trust him, that was for damn sure. She knew there was no way they would release her sister when her sister had the same gift as her. She may have made a stupid move, but she wasn't stupid.

"I don't think I'll be doing that." She went to go for her gun.

******

Sid pushed through the crowd, searching. After he had landed in the middle of dancing, drunk ass people, they all stared in amazement. This was followed by a surge of drunken revelers geeking out and asking how he did it. He had pushed them away; his eyes were on Lana until she was swallowed up by the crowd. He made it to the back of the club and stopped short. His eyes scanned for any possible lead on where she went. Spotting a man at the men's room looking like he was nervously standing guard, Sid knew he had found her, and he'd better find her without one scratch on her body or there would be hell to pay.

Sid walked up, going for the door, but the guy stopped him.

"Bathroom is out of order." The man's voice shook slightly as he sized Sid up and found that he himself lacked the real strength to stop Sid.

"Not anymore." Sid pulled his gun, and grabbed the human, using his face to open the door, while he used the guy's body to shield himself from possible silver bullets. "Freeze, motherfuckers!" The first thing he saw was the disfigured face of Kenny Lawrence.

Sid's eyes found Lana, who immediately pulled her gun out. A large vampire went for her, but Sid stopped him with a silver bullet between the eyes. His gun swung toward the other vampire, who had foolishly pulled a gun, aiming straight at him. Lana swung her gun up and fired, a hole appearing in the man's throat. He dropped to the floor instantly. The thing with silver bullets used on vampires was that they killed them slowly. The silver would inch its way through the vampire's body, attacking blood cells and organs along the way. It was a painful and grotesque way to die. Exactly the sort of death these motherfuckers deserved, Sid thought.

Throwing his human shield into the other one, he kept his gun aimed, looking around. "If either of you move from that spot, I will hunt you down. This is VC Warrior business."

Both men plastered themselves against the wall. The one who Sid used as a door opener shook his head. "We ain't going nowhere, man." His nose poured blood as a large red bump had formed on his forehead.

Sid ignored him, looking around. "Where the fuck did he go?" He aimed his gun around.

Lana had ended up on the floor, but her gun was up as she looked around. "He had to have gone in a stall." She leaned down, looking, her eyes not missing a stall. "I don't see him."

"Are you okay?" Sid finally focused more on her. It had scared the shit out of him when he couldn't find her and then seeing her cornered in the bathroom sent him into a rage. She was going to be the death of him.

"I'm fine." Lana kept her guard up as she looked at him. "And you?"

"Better now that I found you." Sid glared down at her. "Don't fucking disappear like that again, Lana."

The door burst opened, causing Sid and Lana to aim that way.

"Fuck!" Duncan growled, aiming his gun at them. "What the hell is going on?"

throat. "You don't want to push me, Adam. Your sister is the only reason you're still alive right now."

"We have to follow her," Adam croaked from the pressure on his throat. "I promised."

"Slade and Damon have her. Nothing will happen to her, and I'm not leaving until I find out where Sid, Duncan and Lana are."

"I'll go back in and search." Susan started to rush away, but Jared stopped her.

"No, we're not separating," he instructed before returning his attention back at Adam. "You need to get your head out of your ass right now. If you want to find Angelina, then you are going to have to trust us and work with us. I have no clue if Duncan and Sid are in trouble, and I need to find them. Now, can I trust you?"

"Yes," Adam finally said when Jared eased off his throat.

Jared gave him one last hard glare before letting him go. "Don't make me regret this, Adam."

Rubbing his throat, Adam spit more blood out of his mouth. "You won't."

"Good, now stay together." Jared headed around the building. They had to help Susan over the fence, but once over, they made their way inside.

Adam looked around, his eyes stopping on a bathroom door that had a big dent. He observed that no one was going in or out, a little too suspicious on a busy night at a dance club. He headed towards the bathroom when he noticed a guy heading inside the men's. The man only made it halfway in before he turned and walked right back out.

Adam immediately called out to Jared,

"Over here."

All three stood outside the door, and Susan and Jared pulled their guns. Jared walked up and kicked the door open. Adam glanced around to see if anyone noticed, but no one cared. They all seemed happily dancing and drinking to the music. Once inside, two men stood against the wall, looking scared to death.

"What the fuck happened in here?" Jared asked them, but his eyes scanned the bathroom.

"We were told not to move and to tell everyone the bathroom was out of order," the one with an obvious bloody broken nose answered.

"Who told you that?" Jared demanded.

"I don't know, but he said it was VC Warrior business," the other replied. "They disappeared through there." He pointed to the last stall.

Adam slid past them and headed toward the stall. Knocking the door open, his eyes widened in surprise. "Well damn." He turned to look at Jared. "There's a door."

Susan passed through the door. Jared started to follow, but stopped, turning back to the two men. "Stay right there. Don't move."

"Dude, they are going to have to pry my ass off this wall," the one with the bloody nose responded.

"Good." Jared gave them a glare for good measure. "Cause if we have to hunt you, it won't be pretty." He disappeared into the stall.

Both men stood still as stone. "I have to piss."

"Well, good luck with that, man, because I am not moving a fucking muscle. I don't think they're kidding when they say don't move." Bloody nose tried to snort, but got choked up.

"Yeah, think I'll hold it." He stayed against the wall, but crossed his legs.

******

"God damn, it stinks in here." Sid wrinkled his nose. The small hallway behind the walls of the dance club was dark and narrow as hell. He could feel Lana's hand on his back and knew she couldn't see anything.

"Where in the hell does this lead?" Duncan kept his voice low, and then cursed when his head hit something.

"Don't have a fucking clue, but this is the only way that bastard could have escaped." Sid kept his guard and gun up. "You okay, Lana?"

She didn't answer for a second, causing Sid to slow down. "I'm fine; it's just there's a lot of dead people talking to me at once." Sid did stop and she ran into him. "Keep going and turn left at the end of this."

"Are you really talking to dead people right now?" Duncan asked, not sounding especially thrilled about the idea.

"As much as this creeps you guys out, aren't you all dead?" Lana whispered over her shoulder.

"Kind of dead," Duncan replied, sounding offended. "We are kind of dead."

Sid chuckled, "Yeah, we're non-creepy dead."

Lana rolled her eyes, wondering if they went into all unknown danger jokingly. A warning screamed in her head. "Stop."

"What is it?" Sid's voice was no longer light; it was dark and dangerous.

"As soon as we turn, there is going to be a big room at the end of the hall, but there is something before that. It's a…" Lana frowned, tilting her head.

"A what, Lana?" Sid whispered over his shoulder.

"I don't know. I lost it." Lana gave him a small push. "Just go and be ready. I'm seeing danger signs so be careful."

They made it to the turn. "I see a door," Sid informed them, taking another step just as the floor disappeared under him.

All three of them clawed air as they fell. Sid and Duncan landed on their feet. Lana wasn't so lucky, landing on her side. The air whooshed out of her as her gun skidded across the floor.

Sid and Duncan scanned the area as Sid rushed over to Lana. "You okay?"

Pushing herself up, she took a raspy breath. "Yeah, I'm fine. Just knocked the air out of me."

"So you think maybe those danger signs had anything to do with the floor disappearing?" Sid helped her to her feet, handing her gun to her.

"That's a big possibility," Lana smirked. "Now, how we are getting out of here?"

"Same way we came down, but this time we're going up." Sid glanced at Duncan. "Once I'm up, toss her to me."

"Toss me where?" Lana frowned, and then stepped back in awe as Sid took two running steps, jumping straight up through the hole. "You can't be serious."

"You ready?" Duncan walked directly under the hole, crooking his finger at her.

"No." She frowned, but walked toward him. "What if you miss the hole when you throw me up there?"

Duncan pulled her in front of him, putting his large hands on her waist. "You'll be fine, maybe a little headache."

"Do you guys have comedy class during your training?" Lana glared at Duncan over her shoulder. Before she knew what was happening, she was flying straight up into the air, right into Sid's arms.

Duncan landed next to them. "Good catch," he nodded. "Now, let's find that son of a bitch so I can kill him again."

"One thing I can say is being on the job with you guys is a little more exciting than the police force." Lana limped along behind Sid. "So, what's the plan once we bust through that door?"

"Shoot anything that moves," Sid replied, stopping in front of the door. "You ready?"

"No, but go for it." Lana positioned herself. Light from underneath the door gave her some sight.

"I'm always ready." Duncan positioned himself beside Lana, giving her a wink. "You've definitely earned my respect, lady."

"Well, if I live through this, that will mean a lot to me," Lana nodded at him.

"Are you two finished?" Sid asked. "I mean, I can wait to kick the door in, while you two finish your fucking conversation."

"Is he always this touchy before kicking down a door when he doesn't know what's behind it?" Lana used her shoulder to wipe the sweat running down her face.

"Yeah, he gets a little moody," Duncan nodded.

"Aren't your dead people telling you anything, Lana? Like maybe, what the hell is behind this door?" Sid growled.

"Yeah, they're saying we're fucked." Lana looked at them both when they turned their heads to stare at her. "I'm kidding. They're silent. Can we please go before I decide to go back the way we came, minus falling through the floor?"

"Don't get killed," Sid warned her.

"Ah, okay." Lana rolled her eyes. "That's the plan, boss."

Sid's lips curved up at the corner before he turned his head back around, lifted his foot, and kicked the door so hard, it flew off its hinges, flying across the room. All three ran into the room. Guns ready as they went in different directions, their intent was to make themselves a harder target.

"Oh, my God." Lana looked around; the room was stacked with cages. Women were cram--packed inside each one. It was dark and smelled strongly of fear and urine. In the back of the room, stood the scarred man. The women cried out, reaching through the bars toward them in hopes of being rescued. In all her years on the police force, Lana had never seen anything close to this and prayed she never would again. Anger swirled in her stomach, making her want to throw up.

"Nowhere to run, huh, Kenny?" Sid held the gun on him, his eyes scanning around, making sure he was the only threat. "Brought an old friend of yours with me."

"Fuck you, Warrior," Kenny spat out.

Sid stopped Duncan from rushing toward Kenny. "Chill, bro," he whispered. "Soon."

Duncan pushed away. "I'm good."

"How's my kid, Duncan?" Kenny's laugh chilled the air. "You still with that bitch? My leftovers."

Duncan growled low in his throat, but stayed rooted where he stood. "This time you will die, motherfucker."

"You better hope so, because I'm planning on seeing my kid and paying back that backstabbing cunt," Kenny hissed, his face turning into a mass of rage.

Duncan was across the room before Sid could stop him. He grabbed Kenny by the throat, repeatedly punching him in the face. The women cried out in fear.

"Ah, you going to stop him before he kills him?" Lana walked up next to Sid, who stood watching. "We do need to ask him questions. We also need to get these girls out of here."

"He isn't going to answer anything no matter what we do to him," Sid replied as he walked up to Duncan. "Bro, hold on a second. Let's see what he has to say."

"I don't give a fuck what this son of a bitch has to say." Duncan gave him one last punch before dropping him to the ground.

Kenny dragged himself to lean up against the wall; his face a mass of scarred blood. "Fuck you!" He spat blood.

Jared, Adam and Susan ran into the room, guns drawn. Seeing things under control, they dropped their guns.

"What the fuck is that?" Jared looked at Kenny. "Is that Kenny?"

Sid nodded. "We need to get these women out of here. Susan, call 911. We need all the help they can send."

"On it." Susan glanced at Lana as she made the call.

Adam walked to the cages and looked at each girl, looking for Angelina.

"Keep an eye on Kenny and Duncan," Sid instructed Jared. "Once we get the women cleared, we'll question him, but I seriously doubt he'll tell us anything. We'll probably get more out of the women than him."

"Will do." Jared looked around at the women who quietly cried, too terrified to make noise.

Sid walked over to Lana. "I'm going to break the locks. You guys get them out of here. Tell whoever is in charge out there that we need names, addresses and where they are transported to on every woman here."

Lana looked around at the women who appeared so terrified; they weren't even screaming or crying out. They just stood with silent tears, watching with so much hope it broke her heart. "Done."

"We are going to set you free, but please follow directions so we can get you out safely." Sid looked at each cage. "If someone is injured and cannot walk, let us know and we will make sure you're taken care of."

"What about the floor?" Lana asked. "They can't make it over that."

"I'll take care of it." Adam walked over, looking defeated at not finding Angelina.

Sid nodded, broke the first lock and opened the door. Lana helped them out, pointing them toward Susan, who waited at the doorway. Almost all the women thanked them, crying in relief for their freedom.

Lana hadn't paid much attention to what was going on with Sid and the rest of the Warriors, but after the last woman was released and out of the room, she turned her heated glare, toward the bastard who did this. He was standing now with the Warriors surrounding him. She pushed her way past the Warriors to stand in front of Kenny, interrupting their interrogation.

His words still echoed in her head. "What did you mean when you said a life for a life?" Lana stood waiting, but when he simply stared at her without saying a word, she pushed him. "What did you mean?" she screamed her rage.

"I'm not telling you shit," he spat at her. "But there is someone in this room that knows."

Lana punched him as hard as she could in the face, and followed it up with a brutal kick to his balls. "You disgust me. You need to die, you bastard."

"I'm not telling any of you anything." His rage echoed in the room as he stared down each and every Warrior. "But if you don't kill me now, I will come after what you love most, starting with her." He pointed at Lana.

Lana spat at him before walking away. "If someone doesn't kill the bastard, I will."

"As much as it pains me, I know this is your right," Sid spoke directly to Duncan, whose lips quirked up in a smile that didn't quite reach his eyes.

"Just know one thing, Roark. Pam will always be a whore who will never forget me and—"

Lana turned at the sound of a sword leaving its sheath. Duncan had reached behind his head and down his jacket, pulling out a large sword with a wicked blade.

"Your *son* will be a bast—" Kenny never finished the sentence. Duncan had spun in a full circle, and with expert precision, brought the sword down and across, severing Kenny's head from his body.

Sid had grabbed Lana, putting her face to his chest, but she had seen enough. The sound of Kenny's head hitting the wooden floor was both relief that he would never harm another woman again and a sense of justice for the ones he had.

"That's actually an improvement," Jared glanced down at Kenny's headless body.

Duncan bent down, wiping his sword with Kenny's jacket. Standing straight, he slid the wicked sword back into its sheath underneath his long coat, turned and walked out without looking at anyone.

Chapter 23

Jill prayed they were being following. So far she felt things were going smoothly and she was playing her part nice and cool. They had made small talk, but now the car was quiet and she was getting nervous.

"I appreciate you going out with me." The man, who called himself Mark, smiled over at her. "I'm new in town and heard Metropolis was the place to be, but honestly, I would rather take you out for a bite to eat and talk."

"That sounds fine with me," Jill smiled, trying to keep herself from looking in the side mirror.

He clicked his blinker on, pulling down a dirt road. This time she did discreetly look in the mirror and felt a little panic set in when she saw no headlights.

"What restaurant are we going to?" she asked with a laugh. "I seriously doubt they get much business down a road like this."

He also laughed, playing it cool. "My house is down here. I was so nervous about meeting you, I forgot my wallet." He smiled over at her. "Hope you don't mind if I grab it real quick."

Jill wanted to smack him for thinking she was an idiot. He would have needed money to get into the club as well as his license. "No, not at all."

He pulled up to a large, beautiful two-story mansion at the end of the dirt driveway. There were at least ten cars. "My parents must be having a party."

This time Jill did look over at him, giving him a look. "You still live with your parents?"

The guy slammed the car in park before turning to give her a grin that didn't reach his eyes. "Yes, I do." He got out and opened her car door. "Why don't you come in? I'm sure they would love to meet you."

Jill hesitated for just a second before taking the hand he reached toward her. Once out of the car, she scanned the area and saw no hint of anyone. Knowing he was watching her closely, she smiled at him. "Do they own all of this property?"

"Yes." He took her arm in a tight grip rather than a gentle leading manner. Once inside the house, he clicked the lock, leading her through the entryway and into a large room filled with men. They became silent as they looked her over, not as a guest, but as a piece of meat they were ready to tear their teeth into.

From what Jill could tell, they were all human, ranging in ages, and dressed in business suits, but that wasn't the only common thing they shared. They were all there for her. Whoever had the fattest wallet would be taking her home, or more adequately, to her Hell. Reminding herself to play it cool, she stood her ground.

A tall man in a suit separated himself from the group. Walking up to her, she had to mask the recognition behind a fake smile. "You must be Mark's father?" She held her hand out, but dropped it when the room erupted in laughter. "I'm sorry. I guess I was mistaken."

"They get dumber and dumber," Mark snickered, shaking his head. "If you just pay me, I'll be on my way."

Okay, she knew it was the time for her acting to come in to play and she hoped she pulled it off, because it looked like she would be saving her own ass. She glanced from the man she had drawn from Lana's memory to the man who brought her here. "What's going on?" She didn't really have to make her voice shake; it pretty much did that on its own.

"Your friend sold you," Mark grinned at her. "Welcome to the wonderful world of trafficking."

"That's enough." The older man handed Mark cash. "Now, get out of here and wait for my call."

"Good luck." Mark smacked her cheek with his cash as he walked out the door.

Jill couldn't help the sneer that marred her face as she committed his face to her memory. If she lived through this, she would find the asshole and kick his ass.

"Oh, I see we have one with fire," The tall man called out with a huge smile. "That just brought up the price, gentlemen."

There were moans, but the men still watched her. Their eyes were all over her body, making her feel dirty. "I'm not for sale." Jill pulled her arm away when he grabbed it.

"Is there a problem, General?" one man asked, walking forward.

"No problem at all," he glared down at her in warning. "Just get settled and we will start the auction in a few minutes."

He grabbed her arm in a bruising grip, taking her into another room. Shutting the door, he pushed her on a sofa, throwing a robe at her. "We can do this one of two ways. You can either get out there and hopefully be bought by a man who may treat you with some respect, or I can call this off and send you in with the humans who are whored out to the lowest bidder."

Jill held the robe close to her.

"Because of your half-breed status, I can sell you to powerful men who have money. The men out there are the elite with invitation only. The rest of the women are sold to pieces-of-shit who want either a fuck-toy day and night, or a low-life who uses you for money with your blood or pussy. So, you get to pick, because either way, I am making money off you." His sneer was plastered across his face.

Now was the time to freak. Because her emotions were all over the place, she felt her fangs grow; she actually wanted to tear this bastard's throat out. But Jill had a job to do and just nodded. She didn't have much choice. There was no way she could fight her way out alone; she needed backup. *Where in the hell are Adam and the rest of the Warriors?* "Where do I change?"

He rubbed his crotch as an ugly smile split his face. "Right here so I can see the goods before anyone else."

A mixture of bile and hot anger filled her throat. "Can I take a piss first or do you want to see me do that, too?" Jill asked, anger like she never felt before consuming her.

He nodded toward a bathroom, giving her a look of disgust as he grabbed her face in a cruel grip. "You better curb that tongue, girl. Go ahead." He took his hand off his bulge pushing her away. "Be totally naked when you come out of that door with only that robe on. There is no escape out of this room, but if you did manage, I have guards stationed around the house. So don't even try to test my patience more than you already have."

Jill stood, grabbed the robe and walked to the bathroom with as much dignity as she could. Slamming the door closed, she locked it even knowing the man could bust in any time he wanted. Pulling off her shirt, she ripped the wire off, thanking God he let her go to the bathroom. If he had found this, she would have been dead. Looking around, she didn't know where to put it. Lifting the lid off the toilet, she wrapped it up, and shoved it down in the water and quietly replaced the lid. Once she was undressed, she pulled on the robe and looked at herself in the mirror.

"And who wanted to be a Warrior, idiot?" she told her reflection as she headed out into her first test of how she was going to handle this situation. She hoped she handled it with dignity and a kickass ending.

******

"Do you see her?" Damon asked, glancing in the window. "All I see are men."

They had already taken care of the guards stationed outside and the piece of shit who had bought her off Adam. He lay knocked out, tied up and gagged in the bushes.

"No, not yet," Slade cursed. "Did you get ahold of Sid?"

"They're on their way." Damon checked his guns. "This doesn't look good, brother."

"You're telling me," Slade replied. He froze as he spotted Jill. She wore a pale pink robe and she looked scared to death. Every protective instinct he possessed surged to the surface, making his frozen limbs shake with rage.

"Slade, cool it down," Damon warned. "Backup will be here in a minute. She's fine. She's a Warrior playing a part. We got her back."

Nodding, Slade tried his best to stay calm. "They better hurry the fuck up." His eyes never left her.

A man came into the room, which sent both Damon and Slade on to high alert. "It's him; the one Jill drew from Lana's vision," Damon observed.

Slade watched the man grab Jill's hand, leading her up on a large box. He took a step back.

"We are going to start the bidding at ten thousand, gentlemen," the man said loudly, making Slade grind his teeth. "Take off your robe."

Slade's eyes burned. "I can't let her do this." He started to get up, but Damon stopped him. "She's not being hurt, Slade. Give it a few more minutes."

Knocking Damon's hand off his shoulder, he glared at him. "If that were Nicole up there, would you sit back and wait?"

"If she were a Warrior, yes," Damon replied. "If we go in there right now, we are going to kill half the men in there. Right now, we need information. Let her do her job. Plus, you forgot one thing. Nicole is my wife. Jill is just a fellow Warrior to you." He raised his brow, looking as though he half-expected Slade to challenge him.

Slade cursed, pulling away. Looking back through the window, he watched as Jill dropped the robe. He was just as guilty as the men inside as his eyes looked upon her body. She was fucking perfect. Both her hands flew up in the air as she flipped the men off. The room erupted in shouts of laughter, hoots of sexual tension and high bidding. "Yeah, she is fucking perfect," Slade mumbled to himself as he watched her defiant stance, while she stood naked in front of twenty men.

******

Sid and Lana rode with Duncan, while Adam, Susan and Jared followed. "What did Kenny mean when he said someone in that room knew what he meant about a life for a life?" Lana had been quiet as they left the nightclub.

Sid, who was driving, glanced over at her. Shit, he really didn't want to go into this. "Can we talk about this after?"

"What do you know, Sid?" Lana wasn't going to back down.

"I took Slade up to the hospital to see Caroline, with your dad's permission." He sighed. He didn't want them focusing on this when they were ready to walk into something that could go bad. He wanted her focused on the job.

"When?" Lana frowned. "And why didn't you say anything to me?"

"Today, and I didn't want to get your hopes up." Sid wondered if not telling her was a good idea; at that moment, it didn't seem too bright.

"What happened?" Lana sat up, unbuckling her seatbelt. "And don't you lie to me."

"Slade was able to read her." Sid pulled onto the dirt road, turning off the headlights. He drove a few more feet before pulling off into the field. "She was warning you. We believe the man Jill drew is the one holding your sister. He wants you in exchange for her release."

Lana sat staring at him in shock. "Why didn't you tell me this?" Lana whispered, looking at him like she had never seen him before. "You knew how important that information is to me."

"We'll talk about this after." Sid got out of the car. "We have a job to do first."

"Fuck you!" Lana hissed. "I have all I need to know."

He grabbed her arm before she could walk away from the rest of them. "I said we'll talk about this later."

Lana snapped her arm away, shaking her head. "I have nothing to say to you."

"We'll see about that." Sid watched her take off at a run with Susan and the rest of them. "Fuck!"

Lana rushed with the rest of them knowing the quicker she could get this over, the quicker she could find the man who held her sister.

Jared grabbed her arm, slowing her down. “Wait.”

Damon came out of the darkness, giving them the information. As soon as the plan was agreed, they separated. Lana and Susan were to stand behind Jared and Duncan who were going in through the front door. Slade and Damon, along with the rest, would be entering through the windows.

Lana prayed she lived through this; her sister was the only thing on her mind.

“Ready?” Jared asked, glancing behind him.

“Ready,” she nodded with the rest of them.

As soon as Jared kicked the door, she heard glass breaking, shouts and screams. Even though she wanted to kill Sid herself, she hoped he stayed safe. Men started running out of the room, but were quickly stopped.

“Get on your knees with your hands behind your head!” Jared yelled. “Now!”

The men dropped to their knees as ordered; a few crying in fear. Lana moved around to see the same scene in the room. The Warriors had everything in order. The men, who were bidding in the auction, were not fighting men. Her eyes moved to see Slade covering Jill up with his jacket. Sid, along with the other Warriors, was patting the men down for weapons. Something caught her eye and she looked down the hall. A tall familiar man stopped; he turned, his eyes landing on her. Shock registered on his face before he turned back around, running out the back.

Lana didn't hesitate; she took off after him. Busting out the back door, she practically fell down the steps.

"General! Wait!" Lana called out, running toward the field. She stopped, turning in a circle. "I know you're out here, you son of a bitch. You want me? Here I am." She clicked the safety on her gun, throwing it behind her. Knowing the chance she was taking, Lana didn't care; this may be the only way to help Caroline. Her desperation far outweighed her fear and unease.

"Well, aren't you a brave one?" The man stepped out of the shadows. His slimy smile didn't reach his eyes. "And persistent."

"Release my sister," Lana demanded; her voice shook. Her thoughts went to Sid for a second, but she knew he would be fine. He would miss her for a minute, but would soon find someone to replace her. A cold knot formed in her throat at the thought, but she continued to fight for her sister's life. "You wanted me. A life for a life. Let her go."

"Do you know what two of you would bring me?" he sighed, grinning down at her. "Twins at that."

"You bastard." Lana took a step toward him. "You said you'd release her."

"Oh, I did. I did and I will," he smirked. "But I never said that I would let her go. Of course, I would release her. No one wants a woman in her state."

"You can't do this," Lana growled, but knew she would do anything to get her sister released out of the hell she was in. She would figure the rest out later.

"I can, Lana, and I will." His eyes went from gold to red in a second flat.

******

Sid walked up to Jill who was now dressed. “You did good, kid.” He gave her a hug. “Real good.”

“Thanks.” Jill gave him a half smile. “Wish you guys would have gotten here a little sooner.”

“Damn, Jill, I’m sorry.” Adam walked up, his eyes barely meeting hers. “I still can’t believe you sold me out though.”

“Are you kidding me?” Jill stabbed him in the chest with her finger, pushing him back. “If I wouldn’t have, I’d have been sold tonight. Where the hell were you?”

“I know,” Adam replied. His face was strained, his eyes weary. He didn’t look like the same Adam. “I fucked up and I’m sorry.”

“Well, you’re forgiven as soon as you clean the mats at the warehouse for the next month.” Jill hugged him before walking away. “Glad you’re back, asshole.”

Sid watched the exchange and grinned. “You back, or is your pussy-ass still quitting?”

“I’m back if Sloan will have me,” Adam shrugged. “I think I’ve removed my head from my ass enough to think straight.”

“Well, it’s about time.” Sid smacked him on the back of the head. Looking around, he did a mental head count and one was missing. His easy-going manner turned into full Warrior mode. “Where’s Lana?”

“I don’t know.” Adam looked around. “The last time I saw her, she was heading down that hall.”

"Shit!" Sid took off with Adam following. Sid flew out the back door and spotted Lana's silhouette against the darkness of the field; a tall shadow towered over her. He carefully made his way to her.

"Lana, get away from him." Sid's voice was harsh. He had never felt fear like he felt at that moment. It clawed at his insides. The click of his gun echoed in the stillness of the night.

"Sid, please, no." Lana turned her head and pleaded with her eyes. Even knowing that this bastard planned on keeping them after Caroline's release, she still pleaded because her sister would at least be free from the hell she had been living in and could possibly fight back. Her conflict and confusion was clear in her eyes. "He's going to release her."

"He's lying, Lana." Sid didn't take his eyes off the man. "Step away from him, now."

This time, Lana turned around totally. "You've done enough, Sid," Lana hissed at him. "I'm not moving."

"I don't care what you promised her. You're a dead man," Sid's tone was calm and cool, but his body was tense and ready to protect her at all costs. His eyes never wavered from his target.

"No!" Lana went to move toward Sid, but the man grabbed her by the hair, pulling her back.

"Let her go, you bastard." Sid's aim was strong and steady.

"Please, Sid." Lana begged. "My sister. Please don't kill him. Let him take me."

"I'm not going to watch you die, Lana." Sid's eyes gave her an apology as he looked back up at her threat. "Plus, if I put a bullet in this bastard's forehead, your sister may be released anyway."

"That's not a risk I'm willing to take, Sid," Lana hissed, confusion evident on her face.

"You cock that gun and I'll tear her throat out," the General growled, baring his growing fangs, his eyes beaming red in the night.

"It's already cocked, motherfucker," Sid smiled grimly. Before the General could make a move, a hole appeared in the center of his forehead as the echo of the shot flooded the field.

"No! No!" Lana stumbled with the dead man. She turned, grabbing his shirt and trying to shake him back to life. "Please, don't be dead."

Sid put the gun back in his waistband, walking toward Lana. He reached down to grab her.

Lana rolled off him and stood, avoiding his touch. "Why? Why did you do that?" Her eyes filled with angry, lost tears. When he went to touch her again, she smacked his hand away. "Oh God, what if she's lost forever?"

Slade, Jill, Susan, Adam and Jared stood behind Sid. Lana looked at them all for answers, but no answers came.

"Do you know?" She stumbled to Slade, her face frozen in fear. "Is she lost forever?"

"I don't know," Slade replied, looking down at her. "I'm sorry."

She turned to Susan. "I have to get to the hospital."

"I'll take you." Sid took her arm again. This time, she didn't smack it way, but turned her livid face up to his.

“I think it’s best you stay away from me, because if you just killed any chance to get my sister back, I will kill you myself.” Tears fell with each word spoken.

“I couldn’t watch you die, Lana,” Sid repeated, letting go of her arm. Dammit, he just wanted to take her into his arms and tell her that everything would be okay, but he didn’t know that for sure. He had no way of knowing if he had just doomed her sister to a life of living in a nightmare, but he absolutely could not watch Lana die in front of his eyes.

“If you killed the only chance my sister had, you are going to watch me die anyway.” Lana turned away. “So you being the hero was all for nothing.”

“I’m going with her,” Jill touched Sid on the arm. “I’ll let you know.”

He nodded, tossing her his keys. His eyes never left Lana, who ran toward their cars.

“You made the right choice, brother.” Jared patted him on the back.

Everyone walked away leaving, Sid alone in the field. “Did I?” He looked back at the man lying dead on the ground with a silver bullet in his head. “Did I?” He repeated before looking up at the sky.

Chapter 24

Lana ran into the hospital with Jill and Susan following behind her. Instead of waiting for the elevator, she flew through the stairway door, running up the eight flights of steps. Her heart beat hard in fear. She prayed each and every step she took.

Throwing open the door, she skidded to a stop at her sister's door. The room was crowded with people. She looked toward her dad who stood at the head of the bed, his eyes red with tears.

"Oh God." Lana felt her legs give, but Jill and Susan held her up. "No!" Lana wiped her tears away.

"I'm so sorry," Susan whispered, squeezing her tight.

"No!" Lana repeated pulling away. The sound of laughter had Lana rushing to the bed. Her sister sat against the head of the bed, her eyes shining with light, with life.

"Caroline?" Lana put her hand over her mouth in shock.

"Where have you been?" Caroline frowned at her as tears filled her eyes.

Lana couldn't say anything; she stood staring at her sister. "How?"

Shaking her head, Caroline looked around at everyone. "Can I have a few minutes with my shocked sister?"

Their overjoyed parents kissed them each before following everyone out. "How did this happen?" Lana still had tears flowing.

"I don't know." Caroline wiped a few tears away herself.

Lana reached out, grabbing her sister in a tight embrace. “I’m so sorry. I should have never asked you to do that.” Lana squeezed her tightly. “It should have been me.”

“No, it happened the way it was meant to happen.” Caroline pulled away. “I saw and heard everything that was going on around me. I just couldn’t communicate. I tried to warn you so many times about the man. He was after us both, but he wanted you, and you were always too strong for him to break. You have to be careful, Lana. Even though I’ve been let go, he’s going to keep coming.”

“No, he’s not,” Lana frowned, her eyes widening. “Sid killed him. That has to be why you were released. When did you come out of it?”

“About an hour ago,” Caroline grinned. “Scared the crap out of the nurse who ran screaming to call the doctor.”

Lana laughed, wiping tears off her cheeks. “Wish I could have seen that.”

“Is he really dead?” Caroline asked, her eyes still haunted with fear.

Nodding, Lana felt sick. Sid had actually saved her sister.

“What’s wrong?” Caroline grabbed her hand.

“Nothing.” Lana plastered a fake smile on her face. “I’m just still in a state of shock, I think. I was so afraid when Sid killed him that you would be lost forever.”

“Well, I need to thank him,” Caroline laughed. “Is he one of the cuties that was here? The one that came on our birthday or the doctor?”

“I can’t believe you saw and heard everything,” Lana rolled her eyes. “I bet you wanted to smack me a few times and tell me to shut up.”

"No, I didn't, but I'm sorry about the way Rod treated you, Lana," Caroline frowned. "He's not the man I thought he was."

"It's okay," Lana shrugged. "He was just worried about you."

Caroline eyed her. "Is that how you really feel, Lana?"

"No, it's not." Lana knew better than to lie to her sister. "He's an asshole and you can do way better."

Miles walked in, breaking up their laughter. "You have a few people who would like to meet you, Caroline."

Lana leaned down, kissing Caroline on the cheek. "I'll talk to you in a minute." Lana smiled, turning to leave. Sid and Slade stood in the doorway. Sid's eyes searched her for a split second before going to her sister.

"You must be Sid and Dr. Buchanan." Caroline smiled, reaching out to take their hands. "Thank you so much for everything."

"Call me Slade, and we didn't do much." He smiled down at her.

"Oh, but you did." She looked at Sid. "You killed the man holding me which released me. I can never thank you enough."

Sid looked really uncomfortable and that bothered Lana. She had done that to him and she hated herself for it. He had done the right thing. It was she who had let her emotions for her sister get in the way. Looking away from him, her eyes searched the ground, not able to meet his gaze.

"But it could have gone the other way. I took a chance that may not have been a chance I should have taken," Sid replied, glancing only once more at Lana, who was staring at the ground.

“But you did, son.” Miles held on to Lana when she tried to break free to leave the room. “And by doing that you saved both my girls. Susan explained everything to me. I can never repay you for what you have given me tonight.”

Sid nodded and then looked at Caroline. “I’m glad Lana has her sister back. She’s missed you very much.” Without a glance to anyone, he turned and walked out of the room.

Slade also bid farewell and followed, his disappointed gaze landing on Lana for a brief second.

“What was that about?” Caroline frowned, looking at Lana.

“I think I made a big mistake.” Lana glanced out the door. “No, I know I made a big mistake.” A terrified look shadowed her eyes.

“Then make it right.” Her father gave her a squeeze.

“Make it right, Lana,” Caroline grinned. “Especially if making it right is with that handsome man who looked like he could gobble you up in one bite.”

“Okay, let’s not get carried away,” Miles frowned at his daughters. “You’re still my little girls and I don’t want to hear about handsome men gobbling you up. I still have my guns, you know.”

Lana reached up, kissing her dad on the cheek. She then rushed to Caroline, giving her another tight hug. “I will talk to you soon.”

“Just go get that man,” Caroline laughed.

Lana raced out of the room, searching. Slade smiled. “He went down,” he nodded toward the elevator.

"Thanks." Lana pushed the button, but didn't wait. She headed for the steps. Going down was by far easier than going up, especially when you fell down most of them.

Slamming the door open, she ran out searching.

"Why the hell didn't you call me right away?" Rod stepped in front of her, blocking her path.

"I don't have time, Rod." Lana tried to step around him, but he blocked her again.

"Just because she's awake, don't think you're going to be running your mouth about everything," Rod hissed. "She will believe me over you."

Lana grinned at that. "Whatever you say." This time, Lana pushed him out of the way. "Why don't you go on up? She's real anxious to see you."

"Soon you're going to be out of the picture, Lana." Rod called after her. "She was already turning away from you, but since this happened, I'm going to make sure she wants nothing to do with you."

That stopped her cold. Lana turned and walked right up to his face. When his brother took a step forward, Lana pointed at him. "I will shoot you," Lana warned his brother before she reached back and punched Rod square in the face. "Don't ever try to come between me and my sister again."

"You bitch." Rod held his nose as blood ran freely down his hand.

"When it comes to my sister, you better believe your ugly ass I'm a bitch." Lana took a step forward, making him back up a step. "I have a gun and a badge, you bastard. Don't try me. I'm done with your threats," she whispered for only him to hear.

Lana turned away, ran outside, and searched the parking lot. A sick feeling hit the pit of her stomach. She was too late. He was gone. "Dammit!" Lana felt defeated. Tears welled up in her eyes as she turned around. Looking up, Sid stood behind her.

"I knew you had it in you." Sid gave her a lopsided grin. "I saw him in the lobby and didn't want to leave if he started trouble."

"Even after everything I said to you, you still wanted to make sure I was okay? Still watching out for me?" Lana wiped a tear away.

"You were right. I took a chance with your sister's life, and I shouldn't have done that, but I couldn't watch you die." Sid frowned at her tears. "I will always watch out for you, Lana."

Lana squeezed her eyes shut at his words; more tears flowed down her cheeks. "I don't get emotional much, Sid." Lana opened her eyes. She reached out, touching his arm. "But when it comes to those I love, I get overly emotional. If I would have really thought about it, her chances of coming back were greater with you killing the bastard. I should have thanked you instead of blaming you for something I didn't know even happened."

Sid looked down at her. "Lana, it's fine." He pulled his arm away. "I'm just glad she's okay and you have her back. That's all that matters." He stepped around her and started to walk away.

"No, that's not all that matters, you asshole. Didn't you hear me? I get overly emotional when it comes to people I love. I get mad. I cry and call people names like asshole, you asshole!" Lana cried and yelled all at the same time.

Sid stopped without turning around. "Are you saying you love me?"

"If you want me to go totally berserk, I will, dammit." Lana was sobbing now in front of the hospital with people looking at her like she had lost her mind. "Yes, I love you. I have fallen so in love with you that I'm an emotional mess, and it's your fault. How can you leave me like this, you asshole?"

Sid was in front of her in a flash. "Will you stop calling me an asshole?" he glared down at her before his lips smashed down on hers. "And I wasn't leaving you. I was going to my car to wait for you to come out so I could kidnap you, take you back to my place, and have my way with you, so you never wanted to leave."

"No, you were not." Lana pinched his stomach. "You were leaving and I don't blame you. I treated you terribly. I'm so sorry, Sid."

"You said it yourself; you did it out of love for your sister." Sid leaned down and kissed her softly. "I have never known a love like that. It was pretty awesome."

His lips were soft and tender. He was so beautiful as he looked down at her with a mixture of pride and respect. She could never tire of looking at him. Lana reached both arms around his neck, holding him tightly. "Well, stick with me, because that's the way I love."

"I love you, Lana." Sid pulled her back so he could look at her as he said it. "I've never spoken those words to anyone in my life."

She felt her womb constrict at his declaration. Since meeting this vampire, she had been nothing but a soggy hormonal mess. What this man did to her was nothing short of amazing. He'd managed to turn her into a whimpering girl. Lana's lip quivered. "Never?"

"No, and I do love you very much." Sid searched her eyes. "And I don't say that lightly."

"I will cherish those words, Sid." Lana cried some more. Okay, seriously, as soon as this night was over, she swore she would never cry again. Okay, maybe not ever again, but at least not in public with a whole lot of onlookers witnessing her melt down and their declarations of love. But for the time being, she was more than happy to be in his arms. "I will cherish that I'm the only person you've ever said those words to."

Sid leaned down to kiss her, but a commotion nearby had him pulling her behind him.

Slade, Jill and Adam were escorting Rod and his brother out of the hospital. "Don't ever let us hear of you coming within a few feet of this family again. Do you hear me?" Slade pushed Rod out the door with his brother following close by.

Miles came storming out the door pulling out a gun from his jacket. "I warned you I'd stick my 45 up your ass."

"Dad!" Lana raced toward her dad, grabbing his arm. "Put that away."

"You're all crazy." Rod shouted and then turned, running into Sid.

"Kicked you to the curb, did she?" Sid laughed, and then glared when Rod took a step forward. "Go on. Get the fuck out of here."

Lana looked on with lust and love as she observed Sid's fierce protection of her family. When Rod looked like he wanted to say something, Sid made a move toward him, which sent Rod and his brother busting ass into the parking lot.

"Isn't that his car?" Lana asked, watching them running directly past it.

"Sure is," Miles grinned, all of them laughing. "I like this new family we got here. You all need a new VC Warrior? I might just come out of retirement."

Lana rolled her eyes at her dad. "And Mom will kick your ass." She led him inside while holding tightly onto Sid's hand. "Come on, badass. Let's not tell Mom about the gun. I have plans and don't need you camping out at the house again because you made Mom mad."

Chapter 25

It was four o'clock in the morning by the time Sid pulled into Lana's driveway. He walked her to her door, but before she could pull her key out, he cupped her face in his large hands and just stared into her eyes. Slowly leaning toward her, his intense eyes pinned her to the spot as he slowly kissed first the corner of her mouth, his tongue lightly running the seam of her full lips until she opened for him. One hand slipped behind her head as the other stayed on her face. The kiss was slow, but deep and mind-blowing, and sure as hell didn't last long enough. He separated from her, again staring into her eyes. "I'll see you tomorrow," he whispered.

"What?" Lana tried to focus after that kiss and wasn't sure she heard what she thought she heard.

"I'll see you tomorrow. I'll pick you up about ten. We have a lot of interviews to finish up with the women that we released and the men we arrested." Sid nodded toward her house. "You need to get some rest."

"Are you serious?" Lana frowned, still reeling from his kiss, a kiss that made every kiss she had ever had in her life seem like a peck on the forehead.

"Yes, I am." Sid then actually gave her a kiss on the forehead.

Lana's eyes heated in anger. Well, two could play at that game. "Well, okay, if you're sure you don't want to come in." Lana reached up, wrapped her arms around his neck and seductively rubbed herself against his growing hardness. She made sure her breasts were plastered against him as she placed a kiss against his neck. She then tiptoed so she could nip at his earlobe. She moaned for good measure, and as she pulled her lips away from his neck, she nipped at him. "Goodnight."

She opened the door and squealed when she was pushed the rest of the way in. Plastered up against her wall, Sid's hands were all over her. "You woke the beast." He bit her neck with playful nips. "Now, you will get no rest."

"I never said I wanted rest," Lana shot back, doing her own kissing and biting.

"Since we said we love each other, do we just make love now?" Sid's hand went under her shirt, pinching her nipple hard.

"Fuck me, now." Lana grabbed his hardness through his jeans, working him over. "We can make love later."

"I was hoping you'd say that." Sid ripped off his shirt, watching as she did the same. When she bared her tits, he growled, especially when they bounced and swayed with her efforts of taking off her jeans. He leaned down, taking a nipple in his mouth as he finished getting out of his own jeans kicking them to the side. Lana's legs gave out, and he swiftly caught her, pulling her flush against his naked body. His hand cupped her as his fingers rubbed the small nub, making her arch her back in pure ecstasy. Lana's head fell backwards banging against the wall.

Sid chuckled as he relentlessly rubbed and pulled on her nub. "You're absolutely killing me." Lana sighed, which quickly turned into a moan when a large finger slipped inside her.

"Does this feel good, Lana?" Sid breathed into her ear. "Do you like to be fucked this way?"

When he talked like this to her, it made her so damn hot she felt like she was going to explode. "Yes, but I'd rather have you inside me."

Sid removed his finger, putting it to his mouth tasting her. He smiled seductively as she watched, moaning. "You taste so damn good."

"I'm going to pay you back for this," Lana breathed heavily.

"Can't wait." Sid lifted her leg, and in one swift push was deep inside her.

Lana had to remind herself to breathe before she passed out from the pleasure. She stood on tiptoes until he picked her up. He moved inside her like a man possessed.

"Too much?" Sid asked, his voice harsh.

"No." Lana slammed down on him, meeting his thrusts. "Please, don't stop."

Sid growled, walking her to the couch, still deep inside her. When she wiggled, he grasped her hips, picking her up and slamming her down on him a few more times before sliding out of her. When she started to protest, he kissed her, turned her around and bent her over the arm of the couch. He lifted her hips up, slamming into her. Lana screamed her pleasure, making a proud all-male smile spread across his face.

"I'm just trying to find ways to please you," Sid gritted out between clenched teeth. "And by that scream, I think I succeeded." She had her hands braced on the couch. He looked around, watching her heavy tits bounce with his thrusts. He felt his build-up coming and reached around, finding her clit. With expert fingers, he brought her to orgasm, letting her ride it out on his hard cock.

"I want to bite you." Sid leaned over her pressing into her back. "I'm addicted to you, Lana."

She moaned as she turned her neck for him.

That was all the go ahead he needed. His fangs sunk into her soft skin as he pumped into her tight warmth. It was only seconds before he came, harder than he ever had before.

Lana went limp on the couch. Sid slowly pulled out of her, licked the two small wounds closed, turned her around and picked her up. She curled into him as he made his way to her bedroom. Laying her on the bed, he found the bathroom and a washcloth. Going over to her, he cleaned her off and then himself. Pulling the covers back, he laid her down and crawled in next to her. She automatically curled into him.

“I love you, Sid,” her voice was sleepy and soft.

“And I love you, lovely Lana.” He smiled down at her; soon she was asleep, a small satisfied smile tipping her lips. . He knew then and there, at that very moment he would live the rest of his long life making this woman happy.

******

Jill cursed, wrinkling her nose. “Well, that was a total fail.”

“What the hell are you doing to my kitchen?” Sid walked over, looking into the trashcan. “Was that pancakes?”

Jill also looked at her poor attempt. “Yeah,” Jill laughed. “Pretty sad, huh?”

“Have a seat and I’ll fix some up real quick.” Sid grabbed what he needed.

Jill pulled up a stool so she could watch him. “Where’s Lana?”

“At her place. I let her sleep in,” Sid grinned, thinking of the sex marathon. He seriously thought he’d met his match. “She requires a little more sleep than I do.”

"I'm glad things worked out for you two," Jill sighed. "I really like her."

"She thinks a lot of you also." Sid glanced at Jill as he whipped up the batter. "How you doing, Jill? I know last night was pretty traumatic for you."

"Why is that? 'Cause everyone saw me naked?" Jill snorted. "I'm fine. I'm just glad we caught the bad guy."

"Well, I'm proud of you. I know that was hard, but you handled it like a true Warrior." Sid poured out perfect pancakes onto a hot skillet. "But there will be someone else replacing the asshole we got last night. There always is."

"Job security," Jill nodded, rubbing her stomach.

Sid saw her action and laughed, "You hungry, Jill?"

"Starved, so hurry up." Jill hopped down, getting a plate ready.

"That's not what I'm talking about." Sid frowned. "You need to feed."

"I know."

Sid set the pancakes aside, turning toward her. "You're like a little sister to me." He lifted his wrist to her mouth. "You can feed from my wrist."

"The hell she can." Slade walked in.

"She needs to feed," Sid glared at Slade. He had known Slade was about to walk into the kitchen and was trying to make a point, but the damn doc was so fucking hardheaded.

“I’ve got this,” Slade nodded. “Sloan wants to see you.”

“I’m heading back to Lana’s if you guys need me.” Sid walked past Jill, tugging at her hair. “Stay out of trouble, brat.”

“You do the same, old man,” Jill grinned, but grabbed her stomach with a groan.

“Come on, Jill.” Slade stepped to the side. “You need to feed.”

“Did you talk to Alice about me after you…had sex with her?” Jill asked before moving a muscle.

“What the hell are you talking about?” Slade frowned down at her.

“Did you ask Alice to feed me so you wouldn’t have to again?” Jill’s eyes didn’t waver from his.

He walked straight up to her and leaned forward. He had bent so close they were almost nose-to-nose. “I have never touched Alice in a sexual way, ever. And I definitely would not talk about you to that nasty bitch.”

Relief surged through Jill at his words; she believed him instantly. She licked her lips, her eyes leaving his to his neck. “Are you sure you don’t care if I feed? I promise to behave myself.” Her eyes popped back to his. “I can take it from your wrist. I’m sorry, but I’m so hungry.”

“Take it from the same place you took it before.” Slade’s voice was deep; it rumbled throughout the room. “And don’t apologize.”

Jill nodded, putting her hand on his shoulder to steady herself. Her mouth opened as she gently sunk her fangs into his neck. She took long deep pulls and couldn’t help the moans as his delicious blood slipped down her throat. He tasted so damn good. His blood made her feel alive and her nipples hardened almost painfully. She was shocked when Slade's hand landed on her thigh, his fingers tightening and moving up her leg. She tingled in all the right places and wanted more than anything in the world for his hand to go between her legs. It seemed like her wish was going to be granted as his hand traveled so close, but stopped when someone cleared their throat.

Pulling away quickly, she was surprised when Slade turned toward the intruder with a growl. Steve stood in the doorway. "What the hell do you want?"

Steve looked surprised, but hid it quickly. "We found Angelina."

"Does Adam know yet?" Jill asked, peeking around Slade.

"No, not yet," Steve shook his head. "But Jared wants some of us to go with Adam."

"Okay, I'll be there in a minute," Jill assured him. Once Steve had left, she glanced up at Slade. His neck was oozing blood from her feeding. Slowly, she leaned in, licking the wounds closed. She enjoyed the moment of closeness and the chance to have her skin next to his.

"You get enough?" Slade stare was intense.

Not even close, she wanted to say, but nodded instead. "Thank you."

"You're welcome." Slade helped her off the stool.

"I guess I better go." She turned away walking out.

Slade leaned against the wall, closing his eyes. Looking down at the huge bulge in his pants, he adjusted himself. "You are so fucked, Buchanan." He glanced at the door Jill had just walked through. All his good intentions were about to go out the damn window.

******

Sid walked into Lana's house, finding her on the phone. He had left to run back to the compound to clean up giving her time to do the same. He also needed to clear his head a little. He had broken his number one rule, never to spend the night with a woman, but Lana was not just any woman. He knew that, but it still floored him how quickly she had become the most important thing in his life. And he was ready.

He could watch her every minute of the day. She was not only a beautiful woman, she had a spirit that matched his. She made him whole. He had woke Lana doing wicked things to her body. Then spent the early part of the morning in bed, not only learning each other's bodies in ways that even blew his mind, but learning about each other. Sid had never talked to a woman in such depth, but Lana intrigued him. He wanted to know everything there was to know about her.

He grinned when she spotted him. She came straight to him, placing a soft kiss against his lips.

"He just got here," Lana said into the phone. "Hold on. Let me ask." She placed her hand over the phone.

"Hello," Sid smiled, nuzzling her neck.

"Hi yourself." She leaned her head back with a sigh.

"Someone on the phone?" Sid grinned.

"Huh, oh yeah," Lana rolled her eyes. "My sister would like to know if we could take the day off and head to the hospital today. They are letting her go home and she wants the whole family there."

"Sure, I can drop you off and pick you up later." Sid tried to hide his disappointment.

"She wants you there, Sid," Lana frowned. "And so do I, and the rest of the family."

Sid felt a knot in his throat, and didn't that make him feel like a big pussy. He gave her a half-grin before he nodded. She touched his cheek, putting the phone back to her ear, informing her sister they would be there.

"What's wrong?" Lana asked after hanging up.

"Nothing," Sid smiled. "You ready?"

"No, I want to know what's wrong," Lana pushed. "If you don't want to go, I'll understand."

Sid sighed, "It's not that. I'm just not used to being a part of a family, Lana. I've never had one, so when I hear family, I don't consider myself."

Lana kissed him. "Well, get used to it because you've been adopted into a crazy-ass family."

"I love you, Lana." Sid hugged her tight, realizing he couldn't stop saying the words; plus, he discovered, he didn't care. He didn't care what his brothers had to say to him. He dished the shit out to them and he was going to have to take what they dished back. Looking at Lana, he knew whatever it was, it would be worth it. If it meant him being a pussy, then he was a pussy; he didn't give a fuck.

"And I love you, my Sidilicious," Lana said seriously before letting loose a snort.

"No." Sid shook his head. "Hell no. If you call me that again, I'll spank that sweet ass."

"Promise?" Lana gave him a sultry smile over her shoulder.

"Think we're going to be late to the hospital," Sid growled, tackling her into the bedroom and slamming the door closed.

******

Adam stood outside a large two-story home. She was inside; he could feel her. Glancing behind him, Jill and Jared stood at his back. He and Jared had made their peace that night at the warehouse. This was after Jared pounded his face.

After the interviews of the women they released at the club, and the men, who had been arrested, a girl fitting the description of Angelina had been traced to this address. They had been told she had been sold to a businessman.

Taking the steps two at a time, he stopped at the door. Lifting his hand, he knocked and then waited for answers he had sought for months. He heard light footsteps coming toward the door.

The door slowly opened and there she stood, more beautiful than he remembered.

"Adam?" Her voice shook, her eyes widened in surprise. "What are you doing here?"

That set him back. "What do you mean 'what am I doing here'? I'm looking for you. I've been looking for you since the night you disappeared."

"Honey, who is it?" A man's voice echoed out the door.

Adam looked behind her as a man appeared. He was older than Angelina by at least five or six years, dressed in a business suit and was holding a coffee cup.

"An old friend." Angelina's eyes never left Adam.

"Oh, I'm an old friend?" Adam hissed before finding it within him to tamp his anger down.

The man opened the door wider, sticking his hand out in a friendly gesture. "I'm Angelina's husband, Robert. It's nice to meet you."

Adam had to hold his growl back. He took the man's hand in a shake, but his eyes stayed on Angelina. "Adam."

"Adam," the man smiled. "It's nice to finally meet you. Angelina has told me a lot about you."

Adam felt like he was caught in a nightmare or the fucking Twilight Zone. What he wanted to do was beat the fuck out of this dude, but the son of a bitch was being nice, inviting him inside his home.

"Are you okay?" Adam asked the only question he had to ask before he turned around and left. He had to make sure he wasn't leaving her in a situation she was being forced to stay in.

"Of course she's okay," Robert laughed, putting his hand on her shoulder.

"I asked her." Adam did growl this time. "Are you?"

"Why wouldn't she be okay?" Robert looked confused and a little worried.

"Because she was sold." Adam finally took his eyes off Angelina. "I've been looking for her since the night she disappeared, and I'm not leaving this fucking porch until I hear it from her that she is okay."

"It wasn't like that." Angelina's voice was as soft as he remembered. "Robert was there with his brother trying to stop him from getting in trouble. He didn't really even know what was going on until they started auctioning women off. He was getting ready to leave when they put me up. He saved me, Adam."

And wasn't that a punch in the gut. This man had done something Adam wasn't able to accomplish. "Do you love him?"

"Yes, I do," Angelina didn't hesitate with her answer.

With the man standing so close, Adam had to make sure. If he didn't, it would haunt him forever. Reaching out, he grasped her arm, touching her for the first time to read her. Getting his answer, he let her go.

"I should have called you." Angelina was looking down at the ground. "I'm sorry."

"Yeah, you should have." Adam glanced up at the man who was watching him closely. "Take care of her or deal with me."

The man actually smiled. "I will and thank you for caring about her that much. I know if anything happens to me, she'll be taken care of."

Adam nodded and then turned heading down the steps.

"Adam, wait." Angelina flew down the steps throwing her arms around his neck. "I never meant to hurt you, Adam. I'm sorry. It just happened."

Hugging her back and then letting her go was the hardest thing Adam had ever done. "I'm glad you found your happiness, Angelina. Call me if you ever need me."

Adam turned, walking the rest of the way down the steps. Jared and Jill had made their way to the car, but stayed outside just in case.

"You good?" Jared stared at him, watching him closely.

"Yeah, I am," Adam nodded. "I'm going to walk back. I need a minute."

Jill walked toward him and gave him a gentle knuckle bump. "Hurry back. I have an itch to kick your ass. Haven't trained with you in a while."

A genuine smile lifted his lips as he looked at Jill. "You got it." He play-punched her in the chin. "You better warm up and get some extra practice in before I get there. You've been looking weak."

Seeing the worried look in Jared's eyes, Adam gave him a cocky grin. "I'm not going to kill anything. I'll be fine, Mom."

"Asshole," Jared shook his head with a grin.

"Dickhead," Adam smiled, walking away.

Once they passed, he gave them a wave as he watched them disappear. He knew they were worried and he guessed he would be too because of the way he had acted, but seeing Angelina was okay and happy was enough. He loved her enough to know she was better off where she was. He was a half-breed with no future and nothing to offer her. The weight was off his shoulders feeling he was responsible for her disappearance. He had walked up those steps a boy and had walked back down a man. The thought took him unaware. He was a VC

Warrior and had a new mission. He would be the best Warrior the Council had ever seen. He continued down the street without looking back. Forward was now the only way for him to travel.

16689752R00157

Printed in Poland
by Amazon Fulfillment
Poland Sp. z o.o., Wrocław